MALICE

MALICE

ROBERT WANGARD

AMP&RSAND, INC.

Chicago • New Orleans

ISBN 978-1-4507-9593-7

Design
David Robson, Robson Design

Published by
AMPERSAND, INC.
1050 North State Street
Chicago, Illinois 60610

203 Finland Place
New Orleans, Louisiana 70131

www.ampersandworks.com

———

www.rwangard.com

Printed in U.S.A.

For Barbara and Dwight Reed.

ONE

Pete Thorsen and his fly-fishing companion, Harry McTigue, were motoring south on the scenic highway and singing along with the Eagles when Cap called about the body.

Harry pulled over on the shoulder, turned down the volume, and clamped the cell phone to his ear. Pete could see a peculiar intensity cloud Harry's eyes as he listened. Then Harry dropped the phone on the seat and abruptly declared, "We've got to go back." He cranked the Ford Explorer around in a tight U-turn and headed back north like a heat-seeking missile. A reported murder on the mean streets of Chicago or Detroit might not cause much of a stir, but in a small community where the annual crowning of Miss Coho made the front page, it attracted the local newspaperman like a magnet drew iron.

Harry ignored the posted speed limit signs and gripped the steering wheel with white knuckles as they careened around curves on the twisting highway. They retraced their route of a few minutes earlier through wooded areas and fruit orchards and along bluffs overlooking Lake Michigan. This time, Pete wasn't admiring the scenery. The call had brought back painful memories of shotgun blasts and blood-splattered walls he'd been trying to suppress.

Pete was roused from his dark reverie when Harry hung a hard left that threw him against the passenger-side door. Harry gunned the Explorer through the gate to the Mystic Bluffs Golf Club and accelerated up the access road. He swerved left again when he saw a cluster of vehicles parked randomly at the far end of the parking lot. As they got closer, Pete could see that many of the vehicles were police cruisers bearing the seal of the county sheriff's department.

Harry skidded to a stop next to the vehicles and bounced out of the Explorer. Pete got out on his side and couldn't help but admire the agility his friend suddenly displayed. In the distance, through the mist that still shrouded the course, Pete could see a throng of blue-clad figures moving slowly about. Harry saw them, too, and headed in their direction at what for him was a trot. He cut across a fairway and through waist-high gorse that concealed rocks and uneven terrain. As Pete followed, he could hear Harry curse when he stepped in a hole and stumbled.

When they reached the area where the uniforms were milling around, they scrambled up one of the mounds for a better look. They were greeted by a jarring sight. A man, naked except for red-patterned boxer shorts, was sprawled on the turf. His arms and legs were splayed out in spread-eagle fashion, like the figure in the famous old drawing by Leonardo da Vinci. Vitruvian Man, without the extra set of arms and legs superimposed.

But this was not art. The man was obviously dead. His wrists and ankles were lashed to stakes driven into the green, and the left side of his head had been hacked so badly that his features on that side were unrecognizable. A golf club — an iron and presumably the murder weapon — lay a few feet away. Dark stains saturated the turf under the man's head.

"Jesus," Harry muttered. He stared at the body as though mesmerized, still breathing hard from their trot across the course.

Pete heard him, but couldn't tear his eyes away from the grisly scene either. Everything looked surreal in the early morning light. The man's skin was gray as a result of his heart no longer pumping blood through his body. Yellow crime-scene tape that had been strung around the green hung limply in the still air. The three officers inside the tape left ghostly footprints on the dewy turf as they moved cautiously about the area. Pete recognized one of them; it was acting Sheriff Franklin Richter. The officers outside the tape milled about the area and tried not to be obvious when they stole glances at the victim. Only the occasional murmur of hushed voices disturbed the eerie silence.

"Can you tell who it is?" Harry whispered.

Pete shook his head slowly as he stared at the golf club. The club's face was caked with dry blood. He shuddered as he visualized the killer repeatedly striking the victim's head with the iron. There was something primitive and savage about it.

Harry looked at the crowd around the green, then cupped a hand to his mouth and whispered to Pete, "I see Cap. I'm going to see if he'll talk to me."

Pete watched Harry maneuver his egg-shaped body down the mound and through the crowd toward Deputy Ernie Capwell. Harry looked more squat than ever in his floppy hat and worn tan fishing vest. He had a lot of idiosyncrasies, but none more fascinating than his habits on a day when he was going fishing. As soon as he got dressed, he donned all of his fishing gear except his waders and ate breakfast with it on. Then he would sit in the car on the way to the trout stream looking like an overstuffed manikin. Pete once asked why he didn't wait to don his gear when they reached their destination like everyone else. Harry had shot him a sly look, like he was about to reveal a secret to one of the universe's great mysteries, and said that wearing the vest and hat got him ready to do battle with the brookies and rainbows and other species that populated Michigan's prime trout streams. Pete smiled at the memory and rolled his eyes.

He watched Harry catch Cap's eye and jerk his head away from the crowd. Cap looked nervously at his boss, the acting sheriff, who was in a whispered conversation with one of his other deputies. Then he slowly backed out of the crowd toward where Harry was waiting by a gnarled old tree.

As Pete waited for Harry to return, he surveyed the seventeenth hole. It had no true fairway, only rough terrain dotted with patches of sand and brush and a few scrub pines. Several deep bunkers were strategically placed around the green to catch errant shots. High above it all loomed a rocky knob that served as the tee box. He'd played other courses with similar holes only this one was all carry. A golfer would peer down at the green a hundred feet below and not much farther out, and if he had the right club and hit a good shot, his ball would float through the air as though suspended by a parachute and slowly descend to the undulating green. If he erred in any way, well, it was scramble time. With Lake Michigan in full view on one side and rolling forests on the other, seventeen was the signature hole on a tract that was said to have a lot of them.

A photographer with police credentials dangling from a chain around her neck had just arrived. Pete recognized her from that day on the beach the previous summer when they found Cara Lane's body. After conferring with Richter, she began to take photographs, slowly working her way around the perimeter of the green. She finished the long-distance shots and ducked under the police tape to begin work closer in.

She photographed the ground around the body first, then zoomed in on the victim's hands and feet. Finally she got to his battered head, and in the hushed silence, he could hear the sound of her camera. *Click, click. Click, click. Click, click.* Pete was impressed with her thoroughness and the professionalism she brought to her duties.

Harry struggled back up the mound and, when he reached where Pete was standing, needed a few moments to catch his breath.

"Well?" Pete asked, impatient for a report.

Harry gulped air again and said, "It's Les Brimley."

4

Pete frowned. "The guy who's building this place? You're kidding."

"Nope, it's Brimley. Cap told me they've made the ID. He didn't want to talk much because he was afraid Richter would notice us, but he said there's no question it's Brimley."

Pete looked back at the figure on the green. Brimley's Mystic Bluffs project had dominated the local news for years. He knew it was controversial, but this? "Who said it's Brimley?" he asked.

"The head pro and another employee," Harry said. "I guess Brimley's wife is on her way over, too."

"That doesn't make sense," Pete said. "If they've already identified the body, why do they want to subject the widow to this spectacle?"

Harry shrugged. "Cap said she became hysterical when they talked to her on the phone. I guess she insisted on coming. I'm with you, though. This is not something you'd want the spouse to see."

"Where did they reach her? She was at the show in Glen Arbor last night, remember?"

"Sure I remember. From what Cap tells me, they reached her at her friend's house. I guess she stayed there overnight."

Pete turned and stared at the body again. The sun was rising in the sky and had started to burn off the dew and dissolve the footprints left by the sheriff's department personnel who were permitted inside the tape. Brimley's body — assuming that's who it was — was still staked to the turf. The photographer had finished with the body and was working her way down the path from the green to the golf cart parking area. The path had also been taped off. She was meticulously photographing the ground in the area.

"This could tear the community apart," Harry said, looking thoughtful.

Pete looked at him again and asked, "Why do you say that?"

"You haven't been around here full-time until recently," Harry said. "I have, and things have only settled down in the last year or so as the opponents of the development accepted the inevitable. Now people will start picking at the scabs again and there'll be all sorts of recriminations as supporters of the project worry about whether someone will step into Brimley's shoes. They'll point fingers at the opponents of the project and tensions will rise. Rumors will fly."

Pete studied Harry for a minute. "Do you think one of them might have killed him?"

"Someone opposed to the development? Who knows? As I said, things got pretty ugly for a while and Brimley made a lot of enemies. The environmentalists, people who didn't like expansion of the local airport, Jim Underhill's heirs who felt Brimley had bought the property for a song in the first place. All of them were riled up. Then there was the Native American group."

"That's a long list," Pete observed.

"And I probably missed some," Harry said. "But the murder has to be connected to this golf course."

"Brimley had a lot of supporters, too, didn't he?" Pete asked.

"He did. Most of the town people were behind him. They smelled jobs and economic development. The county fathers were salivating over the higher property tax base that would come with the development, too. This is a damn poor area, you know. But all of that just makes my point. There were people lined up on both sides."

Pete watched the photographer some more. She was still taking photographs of the path area. After a few minutes, he turned to Harry again and said, "The course was supposed to open in a week or two, if I remember."

"Four days from now to be precise. I understand that only fourteen lots have been sold, though. The economy and everything. Brimley had to open the course to the public, at least temporarily, and offer special deals on greens fees to attract people. There've been a lot of rumors that the project was in trouble financially."

Pete nodded and continued to watch the photographer.

After a few more minutes, Harry continued. "I wonder why the killer dragged Brimley way out here to beat his brains in? He risked someone seeing him, didn't he?"

Pete shrugged. "You'd think so."

"Any theories?" Harry asked, studying Pete and prodding him to get more involved in his speculation.

Pete just shrugged again. He thought about the last time he'd become obsessed with what he was convinced had been a murder and how it had slowly taken over his life. There wasn't any question that this was a homicide, but he was determined not to get involved in another murder case. He had responsibilities to his stepdaughter, Julie, and the experience last summer had already caused him to re-evaluate his life and step aside as managing partner of his law firm.

"You have no theories about why the killer took the body out here," Harry asked, "or you have none you're willing to talk about?"

"Neither."

Harry wasn't one to give up easily. "For a guy to kill another man by bashing his head in with a golf club, there had to be a lot of passion behind it, wouldn't you think? And like I said, to drag him way out here … It's almost like the killer was sending a message."

Pete had thought of the same thing. But this wasn't his fight. He was perfectly content to let acting Sheriff Richter handle it. That was his job, regardless of what he thought of him personally.

As the morning wore on, the crowd grew and two men in plain clothes arrived. Obviously, they had some official positions, because after they conferred with Richter, they began to scour the murder scene. Just like on the CSI television shows, Pete thought.

Pete watched as Richter walked over to the technicians, taking care to stay close to the tape. He stood there for a minute with his thumbs hooked in his belt. Then he squatted down and surveyed the area where the technicians pointed. They all moved forward a few paces and did the same thing. Richter spoke to the technicians in a low voice. Pete couldn't hear what they were saying, but it obviously had to do with whatever they'd found on the ground. Possibly marks where the killer had dragged Brimley's body to the green.

Richter stood and hitched up his pants. He glanced up at the onlookers on the mounds surrounding the green, and when he saw Pete, he locked eyes with him and stared.

TWO

Pete stared back. He thought of waving to Richter, but decided that would be unnecessarily provocative. Instead, he just maintained eye contact with his old nemesis. As he stood there, thumbs hooked in his belt, Richter's powerful torso looked out of proportion to his lower body and his muscles strained his uniform shirt. His baby face looked as shiny as ever and his hair was immaculate. It was as though he kept a supply of styling gel in his cruiser and had applied a fresh dab before he came to the crime scene. Richter finally turned away and went about his business.

Pete couldn't help but grin, and felt satisfaction that his very presence seemed to bug Richter. He was sure Richter was wondering what he was doing there. Maybe he was even worried that Pete would get involved in the case and show him up again. He grinned once more at the thought.

Harry nudged Pete and asked in a low voice, "What were you grinning at?"

"I wasn't grinning," Pete said.

"Bull, you were grinning. What was it?"

"You're imagining things."

"I wasn't imagining anything. I saw the looks you two gave each other."

Pete just shrugged.

Harry studied him for a moment and said. "I guess time doesn't heal all wounds, huh?"

"I doubt whether there'll ever be enough time," Pete replied. It had been almost a year, but Richter had never apologized for hounding him as a suspect in his investigation into Cara Lane's death. Feelings had been rubbed raw and weren't likely to heal soon.

"Now that he's acting sheriff," Harry said, "I hear he's worse than ever."

"Is that possible?"

"All I know is that Cap is nervous as hell. Thinks Richter is trying to find a way to get rid of him."

Pete looked at Harry and said, "Cap keeps talking to you and he will be gone. Knowing Richter, he's probably already trying to figure out how we just happened to come to the golf course when there was a murder. I'm sure he thinks Cap is the one who tips you off to everything that goes on in the department."

"Cap can't stand the guy, you know."

"Well, I'm sure that seeing the two of us here is going to trigger a new inquisition. Tell Cap to be careful."

"Cap's thinking of running against Richter in the next election," Harry volunteered.

Pete looked at Harry with raised eyebrows. "Do you think he'd stand a chance against Richter?"

Harry took a while to answer. "Probably not," he finally replied, looking thoughtful again. Then he added wistfully, "We didn't know how good we had it with Bill Haskins."

"Yeah, well, it's just unfortunate Bill wasn't more engaged in his job instead of out politicking all the time," Pete said. "If he had been, the Cara Lane case might have been handled more professionally."

"Bill's not a bad guy," Harry noted. "If you overlook his political ambitions, that is."

"No," Pete agreed, "not a bad guy. How's his campaign for the state senate going?"

"He's leading in the polls, I understand," Harry said. "Thanks to you, I guess he's had to scramble for new sources of campaign funds."

Pete didn't smile or comment.

Harry watched the activity on the green for a while, then glanced at Pete again and asked hesitantly, "Why don't you run for sheriff?"

The suggestion came like a bolt from the blue, and Pete looked at Harry with his mouth open. "Have you completely lost your mind?" he asked.

"No, I haven't. You're up here basically full-time now and seem to be looking for a new challenge. You showed some pretty damn good instincts on law enforcement matters in the past."

"That's not what you said at the time," Pete replied dryly.

"I know I was skeptical at first when you felt that woman's death was murder and not an accident, but in the end, you were like a laser and zeroed right in on the bad guys."

"Hardly like a laser," Pete said. "We both know I stumbled onto the truth. I was completely off base with my suspicion of that scumbag Romer, remember?"

"Yeah, but you still did a helluva job. A lot better than the folks in the sheriff's department."

"Harry, the answer is N – O."

"Even if it means another four years of Frank Richter?"

"Even if it means another *eight* years of Frank Richter," Pete said. "Case closed."

"Okay, just a thought."

Pete shot him a look and shook his head disgustedly. He was watching the activity on the green again when a murmur rippled through the crowd. Pete turned and saw a woman wearing large sunglasses and a headscarf climb out of a golf cart. Deputies on either side escorted her toward the green. She walked with them a few steps and then broke away into a run. Richter saw her, and jumped into her path. She sagged against him momentarily, sobbing audibly, then pushed him aside and started running again. Richter hurried to catch up.

When she got to the police tape and saw the figure on the green, she put her hands to her face and just stared for what seemed like a long time, but in reality was only a few moments. The crowd was so quiet that a leaf falling from the old tree by the green would have sounded like a thunderclap. Then Susan Brimley began to shriek wildly. She burst through the tape in spite of the efforts of Richter and his deputies to restrain her and fell to her knees by the body. She touched the dead figure's arm and then the side of his face that wasn't covered with blood, quickly pulling her hand away, only to reach out and touch it again. Then she flung herself on top of the body and stroked his hair and shrieked some more. Her body convulsed as the crowd watched.

Richter and the deputies stood behind her, seemingly frozen in place, as though uncertain of what to do. Finally they regained their composure and pried the woman off her dead husband. She sagged against Richter again, like she needed support, and allowed him to guide her off the green and to the golf cart that had transported her to the scene. Two deputies finally got her into the cart. One held her steady while the other drove. They moved slowly down the adjacent fairway toward the parking lot. As they faded in the distance, Pete saw Susan Brimley lying back in the seat, her face turned to the sky.

"Damn," Harry said, taking a couple of deep breaths, "I don't have to see anything like that again for a while."

Pete nodded. "I agree."

"They should have kept her in the parking lot and not let her see Brimley's body that way," Harry continued, obviously perturbed. "If they needed confirming identification, at least they could have waited until they got him to the morgue and cleaned him up."

Pete nodded again. "Just one more example of Richter's fine police work."

They resumed watching the forensics team. Pete thought about Susan Brimley's histrionics and the integrity of the crime scene. The only saving grace was that she'd made a beeline for the body and hadn't disturbed much of anything else. It would be interesting to see how the prosecution handled the case if it ever went to trial. He was sure that a skilled defense lawyer would try to make a big deal out of the way the crime scene had been violated.

"I bet Richter's going to be under pressure to make an arrest fast," Harry said. "I wonder what he'll do. I just hope someone like John Hicks doesn't get railroaded because he was so vocal in opposing Brimley's project."

"You think Hicks will be a suspect?" Pete asked.

"Unfortunately I do. I know how people think. Someone opens his mouth, something bad happens, and the vocal one gets blamed. Especially if the vocal one is a guy with Hicks' reputation."

When the forensics team was finished, the deputies untied Brimley's hands and feet and, with some effort, slipped his body into a heavy blue bag. Then they loaded the bag into one of the EMS vehicles parked behind the mounds. Pete knew from past experience that they would take the body to the morgue at Munson Health Center in Traverse City for further examination by the Medical Examiner. The deputies placed the ties and stakes in evidence bags, labeled them, and prepared to wrap things up. Before they left, they patched together the crime scene tape where Susan Brimley had busted through it. Then they all headed for the parking lot.

Suddenly, Pete felt drained. He looked at his watch; it was noon. "Well," he said, looking at Harry, "what do you think? Should we still try to do the Manistee?"

Harry shook his head. "I've got to get my arms around this story and work on a draft. Let's just have dinner at Rona's. Regular time?"

"See you there," Pete said, knowing that their "regular time" of 6:30 p.m. meant 7:00 p.m. in Harry's world.

◆ ◆ ◆

Pete sat on his screened-in porch looking east down the eight-mile stretch of Crystal Lake. It was serene with no hint of the horror he'd just witnessed at Mystic Bluffs. The water sparkled and a few sailboats with spinnakers billowing in the breeze added a touch of color to the lake. A pair of windsurfers glided across the surface. It was peaceful now, but he knew the bedlam of summer was just around the corner.

The incident at Mystic Bluffs had played havoc with his plans for the day. With trout fishing out, he had nothing on his agenda until dinner. Harry was lucky; there was always something to do at *The Northern Sentinel*, especially on a day when the biggest news of the year occupied center stage. But for Pete, an interruption in his plans left him feeling disoriented.

After a short run along the lake, he called his former partner and friend, Angie DeMarco, and caught up on the gossip at his old law firm. Then he called Bud Stephanopoulis for some one-on-one basketball, thinking the competition would take his mind off things. He gave away five inches to the six-seven former collegiate star, but the games always got him fired up. Bud wasn't home, adding to his feelings of emptiness.

He sat with tight lips, looking out over the water. What he'd witnessed that morning slowly took over his thoughts again. While he lacked Harry's detailed knowledge of the community, he knew Les Brimley had bought the Mystic Bluffs property seven or eight years earlier from Jim Underhill. Underhill was a revered figure in the area. He treated his property as a private nature preserve and welcomed all comers as long as they observed two simple rules: no boom boxes and no littering. He spent a lot of his own money to create a network of walking trails and rustic benches and a couple of shelters.

Pete remembered how he used to take his late wife Doris and stepdaughter Julie for outings on the Underhill property. The walking paths ran along the bluffs overlooking Lake Michigan and, to the east, through rolling heavily-forested terrain. He recalled how Julie, then a young girl, would hide behind trees and jump out to scare them as they passed.

Pete also remembered standing with his small family on the rocky knob that was to become the tee box for the seventeenth hole of Brimley's dream course. The Rock, as everyone called the knob, held special significance for Native Americans because an Ojibwa chief had his vision there as a young boy. Later on, The Rock and the adjacent area also became the site of annual powwows of the so-called "Three Fires" of the area tribes. The powwows were only occasionally held there after Jim Underhill purchased the property, but everyone knew the legend and local Native Americans clung to their heritage.

A Native American group led by a descendant of the Ojibwa chief, Leonard Wolf, who years earlier had taken his ancestor's name of Talks with Wolves, was part of the opposition to Brimley's project. Wolf and his followers tried to get The Rock excluded from the Mystic Bluffs development, making a host of cultural arguments. However, they couldn't claim that the development would disturb ancient burial grounds, a fact that regulatory authorities ultimately found dispositive. One by one, the arguments against Brimley's project by other opposition groups failed, too, and Brimley was given permission to move forward with the development.

Pete thought about Susan Brimley and what a coincidence it was that he'd seen her at the one-woman show in Glen Arbor the previous night. He was invited because he owned two of Susan's paintings. The show was packed, and before he could approach her and strike up a conversation, Harry McTigue had hauled him out to make their dinner reservation at a local restaurant. With him, food always trumped art.

He glanced at his watch; it was just after 4:00 p.m. Oh well, he thought, somewhere on the planet, it was the cocktail hour. He mixed a vodka and tonic, using his usual Thor's Hammer vodka, and then inspected his music collection. There were oldies and oldies and oldies. God, he loved that stuff. He looked at a double Little Richard set with "Good Golly, Miss Molly" and other classics. Much as he liked the iconic musician with the driving piano and boogie-woogie sax accompaniment, he wasn't in a mood for his music. He selected a Gordon Lightfoot CD and slipped it into the player.

As he listened to the lyrics, he wondered how the killer had disabled Brimley long enough to get his body to the golf course. He also wondered, as Harry had, why the killer had selected the seventeenth green as the site of his crime. He mixed another vodka and tonic, took a healthy swallow, and closed his eyes and let Les Brimley compete with the music for his thoughts.

THREE

When Pete forced himself out of bed the next morning, his mouth felt like flannel and his head throbbed like a Chinese gong was at work inside. After popping a couple of aspirin, he climbed into a pair of shorts, donned an old tee-shirt, and laced up his Nikes. He felt like crap, but needed to go for a run to get his system into equilibrium. It was kind of penance for his sins of the night before.

The first thing he noticed when he walked down his back steps was that his Range Rover wasn't in its usual place. He thought for a moment and then remembered. Harry had insisted on driving him home after dinner; his car was still in town, parked in front of Rona's Bay Grille. He grimaced at the recollection and headed for the road at a trot.

When he returned from his run, he took a long shower with the dial turned as far to red as he could stand, then shaved. He wouldn't exactly say he felt good after he finished, but he was convinced he would survive. He screwed up his courage, dialed Harry's number and sheepishly asked his friend if he would come get him so he could retrieve his vehicle. Harry said he was in the middle of something, but as though they'd been expecting his call, said that Rona would be right over.

She arrived within a half-hour, and on their way to town, he had to endure her pointed looks and not-so-subtle references to his drinking. He suffered her comments in silence, thankful that they were traveling less than two miles. Rona Martin was a good friend, but she was being a little gratuitous with some of her comments. It really wasn't anyone's business if he had a couple of drinks. Besides, the whole exercise was unnecessary because he was sure he could have driven home the night before.

He was relieved when Rona dropped him off in front of her restaurant. He said his thanks, kissed her on the cheek, and took his leave before she could make any more snide remarks, or worse, launch into the sermon that seemed to be on the tip of her tongue. Then he moved his car a couple of blocks up the street and parked across from Ebba's Bakery.

For the first time he could remember, Ebba's didn't have a line when he walked in. That had its downside, too, because on a day when he didn't care to talk to anyone, Ebba Holm had a captive audience of one. After studying the network of red in his eyes, she told him every scrap of gossip that was floating around town. The topic *du jour*, of course, was Les Brimley's murder. Ebba passed on in a hushed voice everything she'd heard. And if she hadn't heard it, it probably wasn't worth hearing. Her green eyes gleamed under flaming red tresses that looked as though they'd been subjected to a healthy dose of Clairol that morning.

He finally escaped from Ebba's clutches and took his breakfast sandwich down to the dock and found a bench where he could sit and eat. The speculation Ebba had passed on was remarkably similar to Harry's musings at the golf course. Virtually all of the whispers centered on the opponents of Brimley's golf course project. No one mentioned possible suspects by name, Ebba said, but it was obvious to whom they were referring. Pete thought that was a little unfair because, as far as he knew, no evidence had yet come to light implicating anyone.

At the same time, he remembered only too well his own experience in the Cara Lane case. Richter treated him as a suspect merely because he'd had dinner with the dead woman and taken a walk along the lake the night she drowned. Maybe people in the community who were buzzing about suspects knew acting Sheriff Richter and how he was inclined jump to early conclusions.

He checked his watch; it was shortly before noon. The crowd in the town library usually thinned out about that time as people left for lunch. It would be a good time to do some research for the article he was writing on Viking longboats. He'd gotten interested in the subject as a result of his work with the group whose mission it was to raise money to refurbish the replica of a longboat that was built in Norway and sailed to Chicago for the 1893 Columbian Exhibition.

The old craft had bounced around the Chicago area for as long as he could remember. At present, it was housed in Good Templar Park in Geneva, a far-western suburb of Chicago. He smiled when he thought about some members of his group who harbored dreams of building a lakefront museum to house the boat and serve as a center of Norse culture. He liked the idea, but was realistic enough to know that it probably was not going to happen in a period of tight resources. Still, it gave people of Scandinavian descent something to shoot for.

Pete suspected something was up when he got close to the library. The small parking lot was jammed and cars lined the street for a half-block in both directions. When he walked into the library, he was greeted by a tangle of people and a cacophony of sound that set his head thumping again. The tables had been moved to one side and young children sat cross-legged in a circle five deep. He asked an adult what was going on and was told it was a program for preschoolers.

He suppressed a groan; his penance for the day obviously was not yet over. Inside the circle of children, a man and a woman were leaping about and acting out a production that had to be *Cats*. Both performers wore grease paint to accent their eyes and simulate whiskers. They had long tails pinned to the back of their jeans. The female half of the entertainment tag team had a stout figure and short page-boy hair. The man was tall, maybe Pete's height, with close-cropped hair and a manicured salt-and-pepper beard.

Neither performer would make the finals of American Idol, but what they lacked in musical polish, they made up for in enthusiasm. They took turns singing and bounding around in the circle. The children seemed to enjoy it the most when the oversized feline pair came out among them and let them pull their tails. Whenever that happened, the performers would stop singing and shout, "Who pulled my tail?" That sent the children into a frenzy and they all grabbed for one of the tails and laughed even more uncontrollably. The finale came when the man scooped up the woman, and with some effort, held her over his head and turned her in the air. As soon as he put her down, both of them dashed around the room twirling their tails. By the time they were finished, the kids were in a frenzy that no sugar-high could match.

It was all great fun and Pete felt bad about resenting the fact that the program had intruded on his own quiet time. The din in the library grew louder and the cupcakes and other goodies on a table indicated the fun wasn't over. He headed for the counter to get the books the research librarian had found for him. He'd take them back to the small suite of offices he'd rented where he could work in peace as long as the real estate lady next door didn't have too many raucous clients waiting to see her. When he approached the counter, the library staff chided him for not joining the kids and grabbing for a tail. He grinned and let them have their fun while he waited for his books.

He walked back up Main Street toward his office. It felt good to be outside again. When he passed *The Northern Sentinel's* offices, he glanced in the plate glass window and saw Harry on the phone. The newspaperman saw him, too, and waved animatedly for him to come in.

Harry hung up the phone as Pete entered the office. He studied Pete's face for a moment or two, then said, "You've got pretty good powers of recuperation. You were flying pretty high last night." He pointed to the books under Pete's arm. "What are you doing, going back to school?"

"Research for my article," Pete said, ignoring Harry's jibe about dinner. "I planned to hide out in the library for a few hours, but ran into a program for preschoolers. A little noisier than I wanted today."

Harry shook his head. "That program is new this year. Not long on literature, I understand, but a lot more fun. What were they doing today?"

"*Cats.*"

"Umm," Harry said. "If they had the same team, they probably really got the kids stirred up, huh?"

"They did. Who are the performers?"

"I covered the program for my paper a couple of weeks ago so I've met them. The woman's one of the librarians. You'd never believe she's almost fifty by watching her prance around. The guy works at Birchwood Press. He's good, too."

"And strong. At the end, he picked up the woman, held her over his head, and twirled around. I was impressed."

Harry grabbed one of the books Pete had laid on his desk and thumbed through it. "Maybe you could do another article for the *Sentinel.* That series you did on the old logging days in Michigan was a real hit."

"I thought you didn't like my stuff," Pete said sarcastically. "As I recall, you called it 'amateurish.'"

Harry scoffed at his comment. "I was just trying to get you going, which you knew, but you did create a problem for me. I had so many favorable comments on those stories that now it's hard for me to run the drivel my other freelancers crank out."

"Maybe you should put me on your payroll." He gave him a sly look.

Harry sighed. "I would if I could. The problem is that the margins in this business have gotten so thin, there just isn't any room to hire good staff."

Pete looked at the legal pad on Harry's desk. He wasn't good at reading upside down, but it looked like Harry was playing with headline options for his next edition. "What's your headline going to be? '*Cats* Performers Wow Library Audience?'"

Harry ignored Pete's comment. "You know, the Brimley murder is the biggest news to hit the area this year." He shoved the pad across the desk to Pete. "Which one do you prefer? I have to make this special."

Pete studied Harry's headline alternatives and slid the pad back to him. "They're all good," he said, meaning it.

Harry was now a small town newspaperman, but he brought the same high standards to his weekly that you'd find at any national paper. He refused to compromise quality. That was one of the things Pete liked most about him. He'd be embarrassed for weeks if an issue went out with a typo or some factual inaccuracy. That set him apart from many small-town editors who just wanted to get their rags out the door. It was the town's good fortune to attract him after he took the fall, wrongly, in a scandal that rocked the big Chicago daily where he was in line to become the next managing editor.

Harry stared at the headline alternatives. He grabbed a pen and changed a word in one of them. Pete watched him for a moment and then said, "Ebba bent my ear for a half-hour this morning, but has the number one newspaperman in Frankfort heard anything new?"

His friend looked at him with a devilish grin. "For a guy who's so intent on staying out of the case, you seem awfully interested."

"Harry, interest is one thing. Involvement is another."

"I understand that," Harry said, looking serious now. "I've never seen the rumor mill crank the way it has been since they found Brimley's body. Of course, as I predicted, most of the rumors center on the environmentalists and the Native American groups."

"Ebba said the same thing." He paused for a moment. "I don't know all the facts, but I'm surprised there isn't speculation about Jim Underhill's heirs, too. That was a bitter fight as I understand it."

"Bitter isn't the word," Harry replied, "but it played out in probate court in Chicago so people up here aren't familiar with all of the details. But there's no question it was a nasty fight."

"Do you know any of the heirs?"

"I met Underhill's twin sons once. They were up here right after the old man died. The apples fell a long way from the tree in their case. They didn't have many tears in their eyes over the old man passing, but the money lust sure showed through. I don't know anything about the other heirs, but I heard they aren't much better." He sat quietly for a few moments, then added, "It makes you wonder how a courtly, community-spirited guy like Jim Underhill failed to pass on any of his good genes to his kids."

They sat without speaking again. Then Harry winked at Pete and said, "I know what a conspiracy guy you are, so I think you'll enjoy this. A man came in this morning and did everything but pull the blinds and search the place to make sure no one was lurking around to listen. Even then, he spoke in a whisper so I could hardly hear him. My take on what he was saying was that a lot of folks think Brimley's death was a cult killing. You know the way his body was spread-eagle like the man in that old drawing? Well, this guy said he'd read in one of the tabloids that the da Vinci figure has become a symbol for a cult that engages in ritual killings. He was convinced that's who's behind Brimley's death."

Pete chuckled and said, "You're right, I am a conspiracy guy. And here's one for you. Some suspicious characters have been seen around town lately. The story is that they arrived on a UFO and their mission is to see if they can buy Brimley's golf course for use as a landing area."

Harry laughed. "That's a good one. UFOs."

Pete rose to his feet. "Well, I've got to run," he said. "I'm driving down to see Julie tonight."

Harry looked disappointed. "I guess that leaves out dinner, huh?"

Pete grinned. "Unless you want to sit around with a bunch of teenagers and have the school elders hit you up for cash."

FOUR

Pete was struck again by how Julie's prep school campus looked more like an elite college than most elite colleges. Classic buildings surrounded by spacious lawns shaded by old trees. He remembered his own college days. He'd attended the University of Wisconsin-Madison with its mixture of old and new buildings set on rolling hills overlooking Lake Mendota. That was hard to beat, but Julie's school came close.

Julie was just finishing her sophomore year at the school. After his late wife Doris died, Julie's biological father, Wayne Sable, regained legal custody. It was a body blow followed by a right cross to Pete's life. Pete finally regrouped and convinced Sable to enroll Julie in prep school. Sable initially resisted, probably for show, but then relented when Pete told him that her expenses would be paid from the trust fund established under Doris' will. The trust wasn't substantial enough to cover all the expense of a private school, but Pete didn't tell Sable that. He quietly paid the balance out of his own pocket. The arrangement kept Pete's stepdaughter close and gave him the opportunity to have regular contact with her without constant squabbles with Sable. For his part, Sable found the arrangement convenient, too. It let him drink to his heart's content, something he had represented to the court he no longer did, and cavort with his many bimbos while engaging in the fiction he was caring for his child.

Pete found a parking spot in back of Julie's dorm, and climbed the stairs to her second floor room. Julie's door was open and she was seated at her desk tapping away at her computer. He hadn't seen her since Christmas, and was struck by how mature she looked. She'd lightened her hair a little and added highlights.

He stood in the door for a moment, just looking at her, and then said, "My, haven't we grown up."

Julie looked up from her work. "Dad!" she squealed and jumped to her feet and rushed to give him a big hug.

She stepped back, hands on his shoulders, and replied to his comment. "Well, I *am* almost a *junior*, Dad. Only a couple more weeks. The school year ends right after my birthday."

Pete feigned surprise and said, "Birthday. Gosh, I'm glad you reminded me. I would have forgotten all about it." Then he grinned at her.

"Oh, Dad! You're such a tease! Say, what's this I hear about another murder at the lake? What's going on up there?"

"I thought you young people didn't pay attention to the news. Where did you hear about the murder?"

"You couldn't help but hear it, Dad. It's been all over television and everything. First that woman last year, then this guy. It sounds awful. What's happening to that place?"

"The police are on the case," Pete said. "I understand they already have suspects. They'll catch the killer."

"Jeez, I hope so. I'm almost afraid to come up there anymore. You're not involved in this case, too, are you?"

"Heavens, no. The police are on it, like I said."

Julie looked thoughtful. "Do you think it will be safe for me to come in August again? The parents of a boy I know have a vacation place near the lake and told him there are rumors that a cult was involved." She crossed her arms and gave a little shudder.

Pete remembered what Harry had told him. Obviously, the cult story had spread beyond Frankfort's borders. He said, "There's no cult. It's just the usual kooks spreading unfounded rumors. They see furtive groups and dark rituals behind everything that happens. They're the same people who report seeing UFOs over town every year on the eve of the autumnal equinox."

"My friend's parents aren't kooks."

"I didn't mean to imply they are. But they probably were just repeating the story a small group of conspiracy theorists have been spreading."

She looked at him skeptically. "Are you sure?"

"Positive. Now, do you have dates for your August visit yet?"

Her face brightened. "Not the exact dates," she said, "but let me tell you about my schedule for the summer. When school's out, Mikki has invited me to spend ten days with her in California. I'm so excited. I've never been to California. Wayne said I could go."

Pete frowned at the idea of Sable exercising parental prerogatives even though he now had legal custody. He hoped his pique didn't show. Two more years, he told himself, and he wouldn't have to put up with Sable anymore. Instead of commenting on Sable's decision, he said, "Didn't you just spend the entire school year with Mikki?"

"Well, sure, Dad, but that was *school*. I'm talking about *vacation*. It'll be so much fun."

"Don't you think you should have checked with me, too, before you told Mikki you could come?"

"Dad, this all just happened. Anyway," she said with an impish smile, "I knew you'd say 'yes.'"

He looked at her. Maybe he was too much of an easy touch. But it was hard to be a disciplinarian when he was locked in perpetual combat with someone whose sole connection to his daughter was biological.

"You know me too well," he forced himself to say. "Speaking of Wayne, did you tell him about Spring Parents' Day?"

She wrinkled her nose. "I didn't mention it. Not all parents come in the spring anyway. Besides, you're my Dad, not him."

Pete wanted to laugh. The latter comment was more along the lines of what he wanted to hear. It also impressed upon him how much Julie was capable of picking and choosing and changing direction depending on the situation and what she sensed the reaction would be.

"Just asking," Pete said in response to her flip comment. "Peace in the family and all of that."

She let out a deep sigh. "We both know it wouldn't be peace in the family. You two would be at each other's throats the whole time. Anyway, I wanted to see you, not Wayne." She snuggled close and gave him a peck on the cheek.

"He's going to be hacked off, you know."

"So? How will he even hear about it?"

"Okay," he said. "So what do you have planned for the rest of the summer?"

"After I get back from California, it's summer school and training for cross-country in the fall. Then up to the lake. If they've caught the killer by then."

"That doesn't leave much down time. How about the agenda for this one-father affair?"

"There's a Parent-Student Dinner tonight. I've already made reservations for us. Tomorrow there's a soccer game and some other stuff. And before dinner tonight, it's at leisure and we're going to do your favorite thing — go shopping. I have no summer clothes that fit me, and I can only imagine how all those California girls will be dressed."

Pete laughed. "Plastic Daddy. That's me. Ready to go?"

◆ ◆ ◆

The Gap was jammed. He waited patiently while Julie tried on tees with every imaginable design, skirts made with so little fabric they should be illegal, and shorts in an array of garish colors. She had him wait upfront while she perused the lingerie section. He wanted to peek to see if he approved of what she was buying, but restrained himself and instead leafed through a stack of magazines that catered to teens. They walked out of the store with several shopping bags bulging with her purchases.

"Let's stop in here, Dad," Julie said as they passed a music store.

The sounds blaring from the store made him want to wretch and quicken his step rather than go in. He never patronized those places and in fact, avoided them like the purveyors of some dread disease. He had well over a hundred CDs and virtually all of them came from infomercials on late-night cable television. Hassle-free shopping, no running from store to store and enduring music he detested. And cheap. For $19.95, often less, he could get a CD with the greatest hits by one of the leading artists of all time. And he got to hear some of the songs on the CD to boot, although it irritated him that they usually didn't play his favorites all the way through.

Julie wedged her way through a flock of teens gathered around the section with the latest releases. "Look," she said, holding up a CD, "Lady Gaga. She's *hot*!"

"Uh huh," he replied, feeling nauseous. Lady Gags would be more like it.

"Do you want a copy?" Julie asked.

"You're sweet, but no thanks."

She looked at him quizzically. The disdainful look on his face must have shown, because she said, "You're just not open to new things, are you? How did you get so into oldies, anyway?"

"I told you. A guy I was in the Army with used to play classic rock tunes all the time. He's a DJ now, specializing in the same genre. I liked the stuff he played. It's my brand of music."

"You're behind the times, you know."

Pete shrugged. "I like what I like."

She gave him a look and said, "You're hopeless, Dad." She checked her watch. "Yikes, we've got to get going. Dinner starts at six. Can I get this?" She held up the Lady Gaga CD.

Pete feigned holding his nose and handed her his credit card.

The next morning, Pete was standing with some of the other parents watching the soccer game and thinking about dinner the previous night. It was good to see the parents he knew, but he was still miffed that they didn't serve liquor. He should have taken a flask with him so at least he could have enjoyed a drink at the motel.

The score of the game was tied in the last period. Julie, playing sweeper, came down the right side of the field with the ball. She faked, then heel-passed to a teammate behind her. Julie paused for a moment, like she was out of the play, then accelerated toward the goal. Her teammate hit her in full stride while she was going to the net. The ball came off her foot with sidespin — bend it like Beckham, as they say — and it curved just out of reach of the goalie and caught the inside of the net. The home team and fans went wild. Julie trotted back toward midfield, high-fiving her teammates as she went. Like she'd been there before.

"Did you see my goal, Dad?"

"See it? I was jumping around on the sidelines like a madman. You were great!"

"Practice, practice, practice."

"And having an instinct for rising to the occasion when the game is on the line."

"I got that from a guy I know," she said, grinning at him. "Go for the jugular."

Pete laughed. There was no question whose girl she was.

They sat quietly for a moment, then Pete said, "Let me know when you have the dates for your lake visit. I don't want to be in Chicago or somewhere when you come."

"I will. And you tell me when they catch that killer." She paused and then added, "I hope you're right about it not being a cult."

"For the last time, it wasn't a cult."

"That's what I like about you, Dad. You're always so in control. Some of you must be rubbing on me. I've started to plan ahead, just like you do. Want to hear what I'm planning for next summer?"

Pete put his hands to his face in mock horror. "I'm almost afraid to ask," he said. "What are you planning for next summer?"

"Drum roll, please. Paris. I want to attend art school."

"Paris. You're kidding."

"Nope. You know where I got that idea? Your friend, Lynn. That's what she did. Said it was the best experience of her life."

"I knew I shouldn't have left you two alone," Pete said, laughing. He looked at her quizzically. "Is your French good enough to take art classes over there?"

"Not now, but it will be. I'm taking French both semesters next year, and I plan to work with a tutor. Besides, when you're in a foreign country, that's when you really learn the language. It's called total immersion."

"You have an answer for everything, don't you?"

She smiled brightly. "I've thought it all through. It's what I really want to do. Is it okay?"

"Probably, but we should talk about it some more. You know me. I like to noodle things through."

Julie folded her placemat to conceal a food stain. "Why did you stop seeing Lynn?" she asked, still looking at the placemat.

"I didn't *stop* seeing her," Pete said, feeling a little defensive. "She went to Seattle to be with her daughter. Her daughter was having psychological problems, I understand. Lynn hasn't come back yet."

Julie assumed the role of wise counselor. "Long-distance relation-ships are hard," she said. "But they can work if both partners want them to." She paused and then said, "Did you ever tell her you loved her?"

Pete was growing uncomfortable with the conversation. He hadn't told Lynn he loved her, but suspected she knew. She hadn't told him, either. They were alike that way; they didn't wear their emotions on their sleeves. And the separation had been so sudden. Lynn was already on her way to the Traverse City Airport when she called to say she had to go to Seattle. She'd just talked to her son who'd told her he feared his sister was suicidal. Pete offered to come out to support her, but she discouraged him. He didn't know how to interpret that. Maybe she didn't feel the same about him as he felt about her.

"Don't you think you're getting a little personal, young lady?" he said.

Julie shook her head. "Typical man. Afraid to share his feelings."

Pete let that comment pass. Their server brought their check and he was looking at it when Julie suddenly switched gears and asked, "Do you know what I'd like for my birthday?"

Pete looked up and after thinking for a moment, said, "Money for California?"

"That, too, but this is my *sixteenth* birthday, you know. Cassie McDougald is taking me down to get my driver's license as soon as I'm eligible. She got hers last month."

"Taking you down? She has access to a car?"

Julie held a finger to her mouth. "She's got this beautiful yellow Beetle, but she's not allowed to drive on campus. She parks the car at her parents' house — she's from Bloomfield Hills, you know — and uses it only on weekends or for special errands. Next year she'll be legal because she just got a parking permit."

"Juniors are eligible for permits? I thought only seniors could get those."

"Juniors, too, but you have to have your parents' consent *and* win a place in the lottery. For seniors, you only need your parents' consent."

31

Pete just nodded, having an inkling of where their conversation was headed.

Julie sat quietly on the edge of her chair as if she were hesitant to raise the issue that was really on her mind. "I entered the lottery, too," she finally said quietly, "and won a permit. In fact, I got a lower number than Cassie."

"But you don't have a car," Pete said.

She bit her lip and said, "Not yet. But I was just looking at my bank balance. I think I can afford a good used car."

"How much money do you have?"

"Almost $17,000. It's money I've gotten for Christmas and my birthday over the years."

"Hmm. I didn't realize you had that much."

"Cassie took me to some car places last weekend. I think I can get a very good used car for less than what I have in the bank." She looked at him shyly. "If you would contribute a little, I wouldn't have to drain my account down to zero."

"Don't you think it would be wise to wait a while until you get a car? You could drive my car while you're at the lake, things like that."

A look of frustration clouded Julie's face. "I just knew you'd say that. All my friends will have cars, and I'll be grounded here on this crummy campus."

"Crummy campus? This place is beautiful."

"Oh, sure. Dad. You don't have to be here every day."

"I can't believe all of your friends will have cars."

"Oh yeah? How about Cassie, she already has one. Mikki is going to raise the issue with her dad when she gets home; she thinks he'll say yes. Same with Joanne. Everyone but Julie, a straight-A student. She'll just be sitting around her dorm room, twiddling her thumbs."

"I'll tell you what," Pete said, "let's talk about it some more when you're at the lake in August. I'm sure we can work something out."

"What's the use? I know what you'll say."

"You never know," Pete said, doing his best to lighten the mood.

Julie sat with her arms crossed. "I'm always bragging about what a modern, up-to-date person you are. I guess I'll have to change my story."

"That's not fair, Julie."

"No? You're not even my father and you're telling me I can't buy a car with my own money. What does *that* tell you?"

From her demeanor, Pete sensed the conversation was over. He'd seen those crossed arms and that petulant scowl before.

FIVE

Pete sat in the pew, still brooding over his conversation with Julie and wondering how he'd let himself get talked into attending Les Brimley's memorial service. For Harry, the service was part of a continuing news story and it was unthinkable that he would not attend. He didn't have the same interest and, besides, it likely would remind him of things he wanted to forget.

But after Harry's third call, Pete relented and said he'd be there. Harry told him he wouldn't be sorry because it was going to be a spectacle. His parting advice was to get to the church early because the crowd was expected to be huge. Pete heeded his advice, and when he arrived, the pews were already half full. But predictably, no Harry.

Pete scanned the crowd and recognized a few people from the lake community. There weren't many, though. To most of them, Brimley was the arch-devil and a threat to their way of life. They wanted to keep the area the way it was, and even an upscale project like Mystic Bluffs was viewed with distaste if it was situated within driving distance. The proposed expansion of the nearby airport, still bottled up in regulatory red tape and citizen opposition, only exacerbated matters.

The pews could have served as the meeting site of the local Chamber of Commerce or the Rotary Club. Every merchant in town seemed to be there. They sat tight-lipped and grim-faced and conversed in hushed voices. According to Harry, many of them had already expressed fears that a buyer for Mystic Bluffs might not be found for years. They saw their meal tickets jeopardized by Brimley's death.

Harry came puffing in, saw Pete, and squeezed into the pew between him and a buxom woman he apparently didn't know. She gave Harry a dirty look when he sat down and moved closer to her emaciated companion who looked like he'd stepped out of an American Gothic painting. Harry mopped his brow with a handkerchief and wriggled his shoulders to create more room for himself.

"I would have been here earlier," Harry whispered, "except for that damn phone."

Pete glanced at him and smiled. Since he arrived, the church had filled up and two men in back were dragging in folding chairs and setting them up to accommodate the overflow crowd. People standing in the aisles jockeyed for one of the new seats.

Harry leaned against Pete and said in a low voice, "What did I tell you about the crowd? Everybody in town is here."

Pete shook his head and said, "I hope the crowd at my funeral is ten percent as large."

Harry looked at him and a sly smile crept over his face. "You're not thinking about checking out anytime soon, are you?"

"Not soon," Pete whispered back. He leaned close to Harry and added, "I plan to outlast that jerk, Richter."

Harry couldn't completely stifle his laugh and uttered some comment in response. Pete realized that their conversation must have gotten louder than they intended because the woman seated next to Harry shot them a disapproving look and just about squeezed her feeble husband off the end of the pew to gain more separation from them. Pete waited until she looked the other way, then nudged Harry and raised his right hand to belt-level with one finger extended in her direction. Harry convulsed again and winked at Pete.

At the front of the church, Susan Brimley was escorted to her seat. She was dressed in a high-necked black dress with stylish lines and wore a pair of simple earrings. Pearl, probably. She wore no other jewelry except a watch. With her dark hair pulled back from her face, she looked serene, stoic even, more like the artist Pete remembered than the woman, seized by hysteria, who flopped on her husband's dead body that day at Mystic Bluffs.

Harry had his small spiral notebook out and was busy taking notes. Probably recording details of the atmosphere in the church to add color to his next story about the murder. Pete watched the minister as he walked over to Mrs. Brimley, clasped her hands in his, and spoke to her in an inaudible voice. When they were finished, the minister took his accustomed place at the pulpit and began.

"We are gathered here today on a very sad occasion to celebrate the life and premature passing of our friend and neighbor, Lester Brimley." After listening to the minister for a few minutes, it was obvious to Pete that he'd been well-briefed, but didn't know Brimley personally. He sounded scripted when he spoke of how Brimley had come to town years earlier, and from the very beginning, had made enormous philanthropic and civic contributions to his adopted community. He glossed over the fact that Brimley also maintained a home in the Chicago area and split his time between there and Michigan.

He spoke at length about Brimley's acumen as an entrepreneur and the foresight he'd shown for the economic development of the area. And while Brimley and his wife had no children of their own, he spoke glowingly of the way the deceased had been an inspiration to the area's youth. "Few men have contributed more to the City of Frankfort than Lester Brimley," the minister intoned, "and he will be sorely missed." He closed with a prayer for the souls of Brimley and the person who had committed the heinous act against God and man.

When the service moved to the eulogies, the minister introduced Clarence Russell, the town's mayor and one of the leading supporters of the Mystic Bluffs development. Russell was a tall man of about sixty with thinning silver hair and a paunch that hung over his low-slung belt. When he reached the pulpit, he sucked in his gut and buttoned his checked sport coat over it, then took his glasses from a breast pocket. They were the same half-glasses that Harry wore. He put them on and looked over the lenses at the overflow crowd, not saying a word for a full minute. Then he began to speak.

"Last week our town lost one of its leading citizens. Not a native son, mind you, but a man as dedicated to this area as any person could be. Since the day he set foot on our blessed soil, Les Brimley worked tirelessly on behalf of our community and its citizens. You can't pass the managed-care senior housing on the outskirts of town without thinking of him. You can't pass the new youth center without thinking of him. You can't visit our fine library with its impressive new wing without thinking of him and his contribution. I was born here and except for a few years when I served in the Army, I've lived here all my life. I can tell you today that I cannot think of a single man — not a single man, mind you — who's done more for our community than Les Brimley, whether he's been here five years or fifty."

The mayor paused again for effect and looked around the church once more. A few women dabbed at their eyes, and the merchants looked even more stern and grim-faced. They seemed to be thinking, who among them would pick up the torch from Les Brimley? Who had the talent and drive and dedication to fill his shoes? Pete could see the wheels grinding in their minds as the mayor's words sank in.

Then Russell commenced speaking again and he continued to extol the virtues of Lester Brimley for the next twenty minutes. He concluded by saying, "No one can replace Les Brimley, that much is clear. No one can match his vision and energy and unbridled passion for improving our community, his desire to elevate it to the next level, to make it a better place for our children and their children and generations of children to come. He's gone, but we must carry on and shoulder the burden and try. As the old poet once said, 'We must strive, we must seek, we must find, and we must not yield.'"

There wasn't a dry eye in the church when Russell sat down. Not bad, Pete thought, with apologies to Alfred Lord Tennyson for improving on his language. Russell was a tough act to follow, but Bill Haskins, the long-time sheriff and now a candidate for higher office, gave it his best shot. He praised Brimley's courage and told in great detail about the time when he, Brimley and five or six others were fishing on Lake Michigan and Brimley jumped into the freezing water to save a comrade who'd fallen overboard. Pete was familiar with that incident and noted that Haskins had omitted some of the details, notably that the man in the water was drunk as a skunk and Brimley had only stood near the stern and thrown the man a life preserver. But it wasn't a day for picky details or truth squads, and Haskins was just getting rolling, repeating many of the points Russell had made but repackaging them in language that was even more flowery.

It was downhill after Russell and Haskins. Several merchants were next to speak, including the owner of the local building supply company, but while they expressed themselves from the heart, none quoted Tennyson nor had stories to tell about the time Brimley single-handedly saved the full complement of passengers and crew when a sunset cruise boat capsized on Lake Michigan.

As they were filing out of the church, Pete was struck by how different the memorial service had been from many he'd attended. There were lots of flowery kudos and lofty words, but nothing tender or personal to evoke the inner man. No funny stories or cute anecdotes. Just scripted, impersonal rhetoric.

"Boy, that was something," Harry said. "I bet you're happy you came, huh?"

"Very interesting," Pete replied. "I didn't see many lake people, though."

"I'm not surprised. Brimley wasn't the most popular guy with that crowd. I was a little surprised not to see John Hicks there after his call."

"Hicks called you?"

"Yeah, he called yesterday. Wanted to know the time of the memorial service and some other details. But I got the feeling he was really calling to pump me."

"Pump you? About what?"

"Well, it was kind of an awkward conversation. He pitter-pattered around the issue, but it seemed to me he'd heard the rumors that he or some of his supporters were involved in Brimley's murder. He seemed to be looking for corroboration that I'd heard the same thing."

"Did he sound nervous?"

"Yeah, he did."

"But you told me before that you don't believe he did it."

"No, I really don't. I've gotten to know the man, as I said, and while he's passionate as hell about environmental issues, I don't think he's a killer. He just gives people the wrong impression because of his strong views and the intemperate way he expresses them. His reputation from out West doesn't help, either."

"Hey Harry, Pete!"

Pete heard the familiar voice and turned to see Bill Haskins making his way through the crowd. He slapped them both on the back, then put his funeral expression on again. "Sad day, huh?"

"Very sad," Harry replied. "By the way, I liked your remarks." He lowered his voice and added, "I thought you were better than Russell."

"Really?" Haskins said.

"Don't you agree, Pete?" Harry asked.

"No contest," Pete said. "More genuine and personal."

Haskins looked pleased, then said to Pete, "I don't think I've seen you since right after that incident last summer."

"I think that's right. September."

"Yeah, right. Your life back to normal?"

"More or less."

"Pete's up here full-time now," Harry volunteered.

"Is that right. You retire or something?"

"I've segued," Pete said.

Haskins looked at him quizzically and finally laughed. "Segued. That's a good term. I've done the same. You've heard I'm running for the state senate, right?"

"I have. Congratulations."

Harry jumped in again and said, "Pete and your old deputy are still going at it."

Haskins looked at Pete with arched eyebrows. "Richter? What's the problem? I thought that was over."

Pete waved a hand dismissively. "It's nothing. Harry just likes to stir things up."

"I'm not stirring things up," Harry said in his defense. "Richter tried to stare him down when he saw us at the murder scene."

"What were you guys doing at the murder scene?" Haskins asked, now really looking puzzled.

"I'll explain," Harry interjected before Pete could respond. He told Haskins how they were on their way to the Little Manistee River that morning when he got a call saying there seemed to be a problem at the new golf course. He said they doubled back to check it out.

"Who called you?" Haskins asked.

Harry apparently noticed the look on Haskins' face and quickly said, "Some guy I know. He heard the sirens and called me to say he thought there might be a problem." Pete could tell from the way Haskins looked at Harry that he was wondering if someone from the sheriff's office had called him.

"I see," Haskins said, not looking convinced. He turned back to Pete. "I wish I'd known about your problem with Frank sooner. He just left. I would have gotten the two of you together and patched things up. I'll say something to him the next time I see him if you like. Any bad feelings between the two of you should have been buried months ago. Shucks, the way the Lane case ended helped us, too."

"Has Richter talked to you about the Brimley murder?" Harry asked, trying to change the direction of the discussion after he realized what he'd opened up.

"Once or twice," Haskins replied. "Why do you ask?"

"Just wondering," Harry said. "I heard Richter is in a pissing contest with the state boys over who should take the lead in the investigation."

"They'll work it out," Haskins said, waving a hand. "Say, I see one of my campaign contributors over there. I've got to run. I'll say something to Frank," he said to Pete. "We can't have our new sheriff and one of our leading professionals squabbling." He flicked Pete with the back of his hand, grinned, and was off to see his moneyman.

SIX

Pete was in the zone. As he tapped on his keyboard, he visualized a fleet of Viking longboats skimming across the water, easily outrunning the slower craft of the day. As they approached shore, their shallow drafts allowed them to pull up on the beach rather than anchor in deeper water and leave their warriors vulnerable to attack as they waded or swam to land. And if forces on shore proved stronger than anticipated, the double-ended boats let them retreat quickly, without turning their craft around. Superior seafarers supported by the most innovative ship builders of their time.

The words flowed and one page followed the next. Pete periodically glanced out the window at the bay. It was as if he were in the North Atlantic in the tenth century, bearing witness to the Viking Era. He knew "zone" was an over-used expression, but it fit and reminded him of a writers' conference he'd once attended. An attendee — a pre-published author, as he called himself — asked the featured speaker how many drafts he normally went through when writing one of his books. The speaker, an internationally-acclaimed author of suspenseful thrillers, gazed at the man for a moment and then asked, "Do you mean the beginning of the book or the end?"

The pre-published author seemed perplexed at first, but then a look of triumph appeared on his face and he said, "The end, of course," apparently thinking that the speaker would name some ridiculous number of drafts for those crucial final scenes.

"Ah," the speaker said, "the end. I sometimes run through ten or even fifteen drafts of the opening chapters, but by the time I reach the climatic action scenes, my first draft is often my last. I'm completely in the zone by then and the words just flow."

That's the way Pete felt now as he moved on to page four. He was so engrossed in his writing that he barely heard the knock on the inner door of his office. Vaguely aware of someone's presence, and irritated at the disturbance, he looked up and saw a woman standing in the doorway.

"Am I disturbing you?" she asked softly.

He stared at his visitor. He hadn't been expecting anyone, least of all Susan Brimley, the murder victim's widow. Before he could reply to her question, she added, "You looked so into what you were doing, I almost didn't want to disturb you."

He felt awkward and smiled. "Just concentrating," he said. "Please come in."

Now it was her turn to smile. "I know what you mean about concentrating. I sometimes get that way when I'm painting. Are you sure I'm not disturbing you?"

He shook his head. "No, no," he said, "it's okay." He realized both of his side chairs were stacked with files and books, and quickly cleared one off. "Please sit," he said.

Susan Brimley took the chair and pushed her sunglasses up on her head so they held back her long dark hair. She wore a lime-green top with white slacks and flip-flops.

"Do you know who I am?" she asked.

"Yes, of course," he said. "I have two of your paintings." He didn't want to mention that he'd also been on the golf course that day and witnessed her hysteria when she saw her dead husband stretched out on the green.

She looked at him with wide-set hazel eyes and appeared to think for a few moments. She said, "The pastel of the old railroad bridge over the Betsie River before it widens into the bay, right?"

"Yes," he said, surprised that she'd know which of her paintings he had.

"I make it a point to know who buys my work. That pastel is one of my favorite pieces. I've thought several times that I shouldn't have sold it. I'm afraid I've drawn a blank on the other painting."

"Wild flowers at Point Betsie."

"With the lighthouse in the background."

"Yes," he said.

"I didn't get a chance to talk to you at the Glen Arbor show," she said.

"There were a lot of people. I also had to leave early because of a dinner engagement with a friend."

An awkward moment passed when neither of them seemed quite sure of what to say. She broke the silence. "I'd like to talk to you about my husband."

A red flag snapped up in his mind. He fumbled for words to express his sympathy, but all he could think of to say was, "I'm very sorry about what happened."

Susan looked away for a moment. "I'm beginning to come to grips with it. When you see your husband stretched out like a dead animal …" Her voice trailed off and she brushed a tear from her cheek.

Pete just shook his head sadly.

Susan reached into her purse and found a tissue and wiped her eyes. There was another awkward moment of silence. He was used to corporate deals. They could get heated, but the stakes usually came down to dollars. That was his thing. In fact, he was damn good at it. But the raw emotion of death and personal tragedy, that was different.

He thought of one of his former partners, Dave Stratton, and how good he was at dealing with situations like that. Attending a wake or a funeral or meeting with the widow afterward, that was his thing. On those occasions, a look of compassion would be stamped all over his face and he would speak in soothing tones. Dave was made for that line of work. Pete, on the other hand, felt uncomfortable with it and was always afraid it showed. That's how he felt now. And he continued to wonder what exactly Susan Brimley wanted. He didn't have to wait long to find out.

"I'd like to hire you to advise me on my rights as the heir to my husband's estate," Susan continued.

Ah, now it made sense. Everyone in the area knew of his involvement in the Cara Lane case, and Susan Brimley obviously did too. However, only Harry McTigue and a few others knew of his determination to avoid involvement in anything like that in the future. He had to nip this in the bud.

"I don't know if you're aware of this," Pete said easily, "but I'm a corporate lawyer. Deals, mainly. Estate work is something outside my area of expertise." And investigating another murder, he thought, was both outside his area of expertise and beyond what he wanted to get involved in.

"I'm aware of the difference between corporate and estate work," she said, sounding slightly miffed at his point. "I need someone with good financial sense, not a nuts-and-bolts estate lawyer. Rona Martin suggested I speak to you. She told me about your desire not to get mixed up in another murder investigation and I respect that. But that's not why I want to hire you."

Pete glanced at the telephone. He'd noticed the blinking light on his phone when he came in, but wanted to get to work on his article while he was still inspired and not get bogged down in conversation. Anyway, he assumed it was Harry wanting to get together for dinner.

But maybe he was wrong. In retrospect, maybe it was Rona calling to warn him that Susan Brimley might be stopping by to see him.

"I see," Pete said. "I haven't talked to Rona. I have to warn you about something else, though. I spend more time these days pursuing personal interests than I do actually practicing law."

A small smile creased her face again. "Must be nice," she said. She gazed at him for a few moments and asked, "Is that a no?"

He saw the out, but something inside caused him to say, "Depends. What specifically do you want me to do?"

"How much do you know about my husband's affairs?"

"Very little, I'm afraid. I know that he was the developer of the Mystic Bluffs project and not much more. That and his philanthropic activities around town, of course."

"Are you aware that Mystic Bluffs was in trouble financially?"

"I've heard rumors to that effect."

"They're more than rumors. Les didn't share much with me and I wasn't involved in the business directly, but I know he was stretched very thin and was limping toward opening day. He felt that if he got the golf course open, he'd get all kinds of publicity and that would spur sale of the lots. He needed revenue from the lots to service his debt."

"He sold fewer than twenty lots, I understand."

"Fourteen, to be exact. Out of eighty-six. The bad economy, delays caused by all of the litigation, cost overruns in building the course. Creditors were screaming for their money."

"You seem to know a lot about it for someone who wasn't involved in the business."

"I have good hearing, Mr. Thorsen. You couldn't help but overhear some of the phone conversations with lenders, particularly when they got heated. I began to piece things together."

"Call me Pete," he said. "Did Les leave a will?"

"Yes," she answered, somewhat hesitantly. "If I have the latest one, he left everything to me except for some bequests to charity."

"Then he had a personal lawyer who handled his affairs while he was living?"

"Yes."

"Is that lawyer, or his law firm, handling the probate of his estate?" Pete asked.

Susan Brimley nodded.

Pete looked at her, trying to figure out where there might be some hidden purpose behind her desire to hire him. "Why don't you just speak to the estate lawyer?" he asked. "Based on what you told me, it should be cut and dried from an inheritance standpoint."

"I tried to talk to the lawyer. He was evasive and wouldn't tell me anything."

Pete frowned. "I don't understand. What reason would he have to be evasive if you're the sole heir?"

"He said he has nothing to tell me at this point. They had to get a handle on things was the way he put it."

Pete drew on what little knowledge he had of decedent's estates. "Do you have resources to tide you over while the estate goes through probate?" he asked.

"Yes," she answered. "Probably not as much as I'd like, but I do have resources of my own."

"Then it seems to me that you should probably let things play out in the probate process. After they marshal the assets and know who the creditors are, they're going to have to file a report with the court. You should know how things stand at that time. Who's the executor of your husband's estate?" He took a stab. "The lawyer?"

She nodded. "His name is Theo Radke."

"Who's he with?"

"The law firm that handled all of my husband's business affairs. Thompson, Barrett & Radke. Les switched his business to them a couple of years ago."

Pete thought back to his practice days. "Don't know the firm," he said after a few moments. "Are they in Chicago?"

"Yes, on LaSalle Street."

"Is Radke the one you spoke to?"

"Yes."

"I'm trying to understand. If you have sufficient resources to draw on in the interim, why don't you want to wait until they marshal the assets?"

"Because I don't trust Theo Radke. I know Les had assets separate and apart from the Mystic Bluffs development. He had several developments in the Chicago area. I don't want Radke to use assets from other projects to pay debts that relate to Mystic Bluffs, just as an example."

"In the first place, that would be unethical. Also, what makes you think he'd do that?"

"I had a bad feeling about Mr. Radke from the beginning," she said. "I'm concerned that cross-guarantees might magically appear, things like that."

"But again, Susan, apart from the ethics, what motive would he have to do that?"

"I only met him twice, but Radke seemed to have some control over my husband. I can't explain my feeling beyond that."

Pete processed what she'd just said. "So you'd like me to look at things independently, is that right?"

"Yes," she said.

Then another obstacle occurred to him. "I'm not sure I'd be able to do what you want even if I were to agree to represent you. Radke's law firm probably has the records, and I'm sure they wouldn't be receptive to me crawling all over them until they've sorted things out."

"Les kept the Mystic Bluffs records in his office up here."

"Okay, but that's not everything."

"It's a start, isn't it?"

"Susan, look, I'd like to help you, but even the records up here may be evidence in the murder case. I can't break into Les' office and start pawing all over things. The sheriff probably has his office sealed off, anyway."

"He doesn't. I drove past the office yesterday. There's no crime scene tape or anything."

"Did you go in?"

"No," she replied, choking slightly. "I couldn't. Not yet anyway."

"I understand," Pete said. "But I still can't just break in …"

"You don't have to break in. I'm an officer of LB Development LLC and have a key to the office. You'd be going there as my lawyer."

Pete thought about that, and then said, "I'll tell you what I'll do. I'll go to the office, and if there are no signs or police tape up, I'll look around. I have to go to Chicago in the next few days. When I'm there, I'll try to see Theo Radke as well. Then we'll talk after I get back. Please understand, though — I won't get involved beyond that."

"That's very fair."

"Do you want to go with me to the office?"

She hesitated a few seconds, then said, "I'd prefer not to. Maybe later."

"I understand. Can you at least give me an engagement letter authorizing me to enter the office and look through the records on your behalf?"

Susan nodded and dabbed at her eyes again.

Pete got out of the program for his article and began to work on a letter from Susan engaging him as her lawyer, specifically describing what he'd agreed to do, and authorizing him to enter LB Development's offices. When he was finished, he handed a copy to her. She read the document and signed it.

As Susan rose to her feet and prepared to leave, Pete decided he had to re-emphasize a point he'd already made. "I'm sorry for beating a dead horse, Susan, but I want to be absolutely clear about something. I feel bad about what happened to your husband, but there's no way I'll let myself get involved in helping to investigate his murder. I'm out of the private investigation business. What I've agreed to do is limited to the financial side as described in the letter you just signed. It can't be a backdoor way to get me involved in the investigation itself. Is that clear?"

Susan Brimley looked him in the eyes and said, "I understand completely, Pete. I know what you went through last year. I'd never ask you to do anything like that. All I need is your financial advice."

Pete watched her leave. He tried to get back to his article, but had lost his focus and was out of the zone. As he sat there thinking about Les Brimley, he felt a rush sweep over him. That worried him.

SEVEN

Les Brimley's office was on a side street just off the highway. A large sign with navy blue letters on a white background read, "LB Development LLC." As Susan had told him, there was no crime-scene tape or police signs warning people to stay out.

Pete got out of his Range Rover and walked to the entrance and tried the front door. It was locked. He used the key Susan had given him to gain entrance and stepped inside. He was in the reception area with a large teak desk and a desktop computer on a sideboard. To the left, in an area separated by several potted plants, was a seating area with four guest chairs clustered around a glass coffee table. On the other side of the reception area were two large wooden easels holding color photographs. One was an aerial shot of the Mystic Bluffs golf course complex; the other showed the clubhouse and ancillary buildings. He studied the pictures. It was clear Brimley had spared no expense with the development. But he knew from his visit to the course the morning Brimley's body was found that the clubhouse was unfinished. According to Harry, there hadn't been any construction activity for the past several weeks. In fact, a large trailer had been moved onto the premises to serve as the temporary pro shop.

He walked through a wide arch doorway into a showroom with artists' renditions on easels. Most were sketches of model homes nestled along the fairways of the scenic course. Some were on lots with spectacular views of Lake Michigan; others were on wooded lots that were merely impressive. No prices were shown for the lots or model homes. It was one of those places where if you had to ask the price, you probably couldn't afford it.

He retraced his steps and walked down the short hallway to the door marked "private." The door was cracked open slightly and he opened it further and walked in. It obviously was Brimley's office. A spacious mahogany desk with a matching credenza was centered on the back wall. The top of the desk was free of clutter except for a brass letter opener and papers arranged in three neat piles. Two more stacks of papers were on the credenza. A large color photograph of Susan Brimley in her "work" clothes, painting, hung on the wall along with several framed photographs of Brimley in golf attire. In one photograph, he posed with Arnold Palmer. Pete didn't recognize the celebrities in the other photographs. A small conference table and chairs occupied one corner. Across the room, a bank of file cabinets filled the wall.

Pete had gotten used to the hushed silence of the building and sat in Brimley's desk chair and began to flip through the papers. The first stack consisted of schematics prepared by the golf course architect. The other two included marketing materials prominently featuring the seventeenth hole, materials relating to the lots, and blank form contracts. The papers on the credenza consisted of a hodgepodge of correspondence from Brimley's lawyers, copies of completed contracts for the sales of three lots, and other material.

He began to look through the desk drawers. On top of the center drawer was a sheet of paper with a column of handwritten numbers and notes in the margin. He studied the numbers; they meant nothing to him. Other materials in the drawer consisted of pens, paper clips and sundry small office supplies. He put the sheet back and tried the other drawers. They were as messy as the top of Brimley's desk was neat. Papers were crammed in the drawers with little regard for organization; the primary objective seemed to be to get them out of sight. There were more schematics from the architect and copies of bills. There were copies of letters to three golf magazines and one page of a contract for rental of a trailer — presumably the one to be used as the temporary pro shop — and stacks of photographs of the course during various stages of construction. Again, nothing of relevance to Susan's interests.

Pete moved to the bank of file cabinets and tried the top drawer on the left. It was unlocked and he surveyed the contents. The first file jacket was labeled "Organization of LLC." He looked through the file. "LB Development LLC" was a single member limited liability company organized in Illinois and qualified to do business in Michigan. All of the member interests were owned by Lester Brimley. There was nothing particularly novel about the organizational structure. It obviously had been formed for the purpose of acquiring the Underhill property and developing it into the Mystic Bluffs golf complex. Correspondence in the file indicated it had been organized by some law firm in Chicago that he'd never heard of. It was not Thompson, Barrett & Radke.

In other file jackets, he found photocopies of older limited liability company documents, including articles of organization for a company named "Gemini Real Estate LLC." As best he could determine, Gemini had been formed about a dozen years earlier by the same law firm. It was unclear what the company was used for, but if Pete had to guess, it had been formed to hold one or more of Brimley's Illinois real estate projects.

He put the documents back and went on to the next file drawer. It was more interesting. All of the file jackets were labeled "Acquisition of Property." The documents showed that LB Development LLC had contracted with James Underhill to acquire the property on which Mystic Bluffs was constructed for $4.75 million. Underhill had died before the closing, and his heirs had contested the deal in probate court claiming, among other things, that Underhill was incompetent to enter into a contract at the time and that the price was grossly inadequate. There were numerous file jackets with documents relating to the litigation. It lasted more than three years, with the executor defending the estate against attacks by the heirs. It was a bitterly fought battle. The documents evidenced vitriolic personal attacks by both sides. The heirs tried, without success, to have the executor removed. In the end, the court held that the estate was bound by the contract.

One of the file jackets showed two other things of interest. MB Financial in Chicago provided $4 million to enable LB Development to complete the purchase of the land and took a first mortgage to secure its loan. And according to a letter in the file, at the time of the closing, the property, without improvements, was appraised at $8.175 million. That was considerably more than what Brimley paid for the property. Pete looked through the files for a copy of the actual appraisal, but didn't find it. The original appraisal was based on sales of comparable property in the area. He assumed the later appraisal was based on the same standard.

Pete made notes of what he had found and went on to the next bank of file drawers. They contained voluminous files relating to development of the project. There were contracts with various parties relative to construction of the golf course and contracts for construction of the clubhouse and other improvements. The files included stacks of photographs of the golf course during construction and the same for the clubhouse and other improvements.

He moved on to the files containing documents relating to construction financing. He spent two hours pouring over the contents of those files. Construction loans totaling $19.25 million had been obtained from four Chicago-based financial institutions. There was no telling how much of his own capital Brimley had committed to the project. Not much if he was the typical real estate developer. Regardless, Brimley had over $23 million of debt on the project counting the mortgage on the land.

The last file he looked at contained applications and supporting documents with regard to Brimley's efforts to obtain permanent financing for the project. As best he could tell, none of the applications had yet been approved or rejected by any of the lenders. Two of the lenders had requested guarantees from other Brimley enterprises. Brimley had always responded that it was his policy to keep various projects separate and projections showed that Mystic Bluffs could stand on its own. Pete went back through the individual loan files and found no guarantees from any of Brimley's other entities.

Pete sat in a side chair and mulled over what he'd just discovered. Then he thought back to the handwritten sheet of paper he'd found in Brimley's desk. He pulled it out again and studied the figures. On second reading, the sheet made more sense; it was a summary of the debt numbers. He matched the numbers on the sheet with his notes. Only two numbers didn't match — the last two for $2 million and $1 million. Like the other numbers, they had cryptic notes in the margin. They read only "Nautical" and "Z." The other notations on the sheets were clear enough for him to match the numbers with the names of the lending banks.

What were the last two numbers? Equity investments? Loans from Brimley's related entities?

He copied the numbers and marginal notes from the sheet and returned it to Brimley's desk drawer. It was almost 4:00 p.m. He'd learned a lot about the debt burdening the Mystic Bluffs development, with a couple of holes in his knowledge, but nothing about the net worth of the project. The latter, presumably, was what Susan Brimley was most interested in since it would determine her inheritance. All he had on the asset side was two out-of-date appraisals of the land. He had no feel for the value of golf course properties and any number he'd throw out would be speculative.

He also knew nothing about Brimley's non-Mystic Bluffs assets or liabilities. Susan told him that Les had projects in the Chicago area, but didn't know what those projects were worth or how much debt burdened them.

He wondered what he would learn when he paid a visit to Theo Radke. And he wondered what the guy's motive was in stonewalling the widow and sole heir of one of his firm's clients.

◆ ◆ ◆

When he got back to his cottage, Pete settled down on his porch with a Thor's Hammer and tonic and studied his notes. The last two numbers on the handwritten sheet continued to puzzle him. They could mean something or they could mean nothing, he wasn't sure. He decided to call Susan and report on his initial findings and see if she could fill in any of the gaps in his knowledge.

After giving her a summary of the numbers, he said, "I found a handwritten sheet in Les' desk. It seemed to be a recap of the debt on the Mystic Bluffs project. It had a column of numbers and marginal notes on the left. I matched most of the numbers with what I found in the financing files, but there were two numbers — $2 million and $1 million — that I couldn't match up. One had 'Nautical' in the margin and the other had 'Z.' There was nothing in the files to shed light on either of them. Do those references mean anything to you?"

Susan was quiet for a moment. "No," she finally said, "I don't know what those notes refer to."

"Well, anyway, the construction loans for the project total a little over $19 million plus an additional $4 million borrowed to buy the real estate. That comes to $23 million and change, or $26 million if you count those last two numbers as debt. It seems as though Les got a real bargain on the land, but I have no idea what the project is presently worth as a going concern."

"Hopefully more than $23 million. Or $26 million or whatever the number is."

"Hopefully, but I can't tell you."

"What happens if there's more debt than the property is worth?"

"That would be a problem as far as the Mystic Bluffs project is concerned."

Susan was quiet again for a few moments. "What about the other Brimley properties?"

"There was nothing in the files about his Chicago-area projects, so I can't say. But I understand Les had a reputation as a successful real estate developer and tried to keep his projects separate. I have to believe the other projects are worth something. I did find some old documents for a company called 'Gemini Real Estate.' Does that name mean anything to you?"

"I think Gemini is the name of one of Les' Chicago companies. Maybe the one that holds the Naperville property."

"I assumed it was something like that."

Susan was quiet for a third time, then, "Could companies like Gemini be liable for LB Development's debts?"

"Not if they were set up right. And assuming, of course, they didn't guarantee LB Development's obligations. I looked, but couldn't find anything to indicate that the other entities gave any guarantees."

"How about me?" Her voice sounded hesitant, like she was uneasy asking the question. "Let's say I got $5 million net from the Chicago properties. Could I be liable for, say, the $2 million and $1 million on Mystic Bluffs if they turn out to be debt?"

"I don't see how," he said, "assuming, obviously, you didn't sign anything. But, of course, if Les' estate were deemed liable, it would impact what you would receive as sole heir."

"Umm," she murmured.

"But let's wait until I meet with Radke. Then we can talk about this again."

"Pete, I don't want to be responsible for any of Les' debts."

"Don't worry. You won't be."

EIGHT

The blood!

It was everywhere. Great red gobs that splattered the walls and created macabre patterns. Like a garish cave filled with dripping blood. The pools of blood kept widening and seeping toward him. He stepped back and closed his eyes. When he opened them, the blood was closer. More of it. He stepped back again.

And the deafening sounds. They wouldn't stop. Kaboom! Kaboom! Kaboom! He put his hands over his ears to shut out the explosions, but they continued to pierce his brain like a fiery rod. Kaboom! Kaboom!

Through the sea of red he saw the old man's lips curl in hate as he again aimed the shotgun at the slumping figure in the chair. He reached for the gun's barrel but his feet were mired in sticky blood and he couldn't move. He cried out for the man to stop but he kept firing. Kaboom! Kaboom!

Pete jerked upright in his bed, his hands still clamped over his ears. His tee shirt was damp with sweat. He sat there, breathing hard, thinking back to that night. When would it stop? He tried to visualize the lake with its water like a million crystals or dinner with Harry or Julie's innocent face. It was no use. The horrible scene kept coming back, filling his consciousness, crowding out everything else.

He rolled out of bed and staggered to the bathroom. He turned on the faucet and filled a glass with water and chugged it greedily, like a man parched from days in the scorching desert sand. He looked at his reflection in the mirror. His eyes were red and his tee shirt hung on his frame like he'd just come in from a pounding rain. His watch read 1:16 a.m.

Pete stripped off his sleepwear and stepped into the shower. The hot water felt good as it cascaded over his body. After twenty minutes, he got out, his skin pink from the scalding water, and toweled himself off. He put on a clean tee shirt and shorts. The nightmarish scene that had wrenched him from his sleep was gone, but he feared it would return if he got back in bed.

He walked to his porch and looked out. The night was dark and quiet. The sliver of moon faintly illuminated the water. He sat there for a long time, just gazing at the lake, thinking about his life. The darkness reminded him of his youth when he would lie on his back outside his childhood home, feeling lonely, and look up at the stars and wonder and dream about what he'd do when he got out of there.

Pete went inside and broke open a fresh bottle of Thor's Hammer and looked for some tonic water. All he could find was a half-empty bottle that generated no fizz when he shook it. He grimaced and poured a splash into his glass and searched for a lime. After a few minutes of looking, he gave up and carried his drink to the porch and settled into his chair again and thought some more. As he sat there with closed eyes, he began to see that horrible scene again. Maybe some music would help take his mind off that experience.

He mixed a fresh drink and then looked through his music collection. He selected a compilation CD by Johnny Cash, one of his favorites. He slipped the disc into his player and settled back again. He took another sip of his drink and hummed along. After a few minutes, he decided the flat tonic water tasted like crap. He finished his drink, then went inside again and poured a full glass of Thor's Hammer vodka over fresh ice cubes and returned to the porch.

He listened to The Man in Black sing his early songs and tried to lose himself in the music. "I Walk the Line" came on and he hummed along some more. His mind drifted back to his youth again and he remembered how one of his best friends at the time started wearing black and taking guitar lessons by mail so he could become a star like Johnny Cash. He smiled at the memory and played the song again. He had to use the head, and on his way back to the porch, freshened his drink. By now, he was accustomed to the taste of straight vodka.

As he sat there staring at the lake shimmering in the faint light, he wondered why he liked Johnny Cash so much. He was a conventional, straight-arrow guy himself, whereas Johnny had built his reputation on songs that explored the darker side of human experience. But then Cash had contradictions, too. He sang songs about a convict's experience, but also sang of redemption and spiritual matters. Maybe it was possible for a man to have two sides.

As he listened to the icon with the distinctive voice, he thought about the Cara Lane case and how it had seized control of his life. He thought of his mother, too, and how much she was like Marian Janicek. What possessed him to help Marian and jeopardize a career that had taken him twenty-five years to prepare for and develop? Or was Marian the real reason he got involved? Maybe he was looking for something else in his life. But he wasn't prepared for that last night, of that he was certain. That fatal confrontation when the whole world exploded around him.

Harry had sensed that the experience had changed him, too. For months afterward, he would subtly suggest that Pete seek help to deal with it. He was a strong person, though, and had always relied on inner resources to get through rough times. Why should this be any different?

He glanced at his watch; it was well past 2:00 a.m. Maybe he'd have one more drink and then see if he could sleep. He returned with a full glass of vodka in time for Cash to launch into one of his signature numbers, "Folsom Prison Blues." He turned up the sound, closed his eyes, and sang along. He knew the words by heart. The part about hearing the train from inside the prison walls. And the part about shooting a man in Reno just to watch him die. And the part about rich people eating caviar and smoking big cigars.

After "Folsom Prison Blues," Johnny moved on to "Jackson" and sang about going to the southern city to mess around. Pete thought about Lynn Hawke and how he hadn't heard from her in two months. Maybe he should go to Seattle and mess around with her. The thought titillated him and he remembered the first time they'd made love. "Ring of Fire" was the next song and he sang along with it, too.

He went inside to make another drink and then looked through his music collection again. A Bobby Fuller Four CD caught his eye and he pulled it out. A lot of artists had recorded "I Fought the Law" over the years, but the Bobby Fuller version was always his favorite. He slipped the disc into his player, turned up the sound some more, and returned to his chair.

Pete sang along as the familiar lyrics filled the air with thundering sound. He sang at full voice this time, not merely humming or self-consciously mouthing the words. All out. He sang about breaking rocks in the hot sun and about the best girl he ever had. When Fuller came to the part about robbing people with a six-gun, Pete jumped to his feet, still singing loudly, and simulated a double-holster draw. He worked his thumbs to emulate pistols firing. He whirled around the porch and repeated his quick draw routine. "I fought the law" he sang at the top of his voice. After the song ended, he played it again and went through the same routine. He grinned as he pranced around the porch.

Damn, what a song! He looked at his watch again. Maybe he'd play one more CD and have another drink and then try to go back to sleep. He remembered how much Julie had liked Buddy Holly the previous summer, and when he came to those CDs, his fingers lingered over the plastic cases as he made a selection. Julie had referred to Buddy as a "super geek" until she heard his music. He smiled, then poured a fresh drink and returned to the porch and slipped the Buddy Holly disc into the player. He stood there, continuing to smile as he remembered how Julie had grabbed him and coaxed him into a wild jitterbug as Buddy's distinctive rock and roll tunes blared from the speakers.

He turned up the volume another notch, and when he heard "That'll Be the Day," he jitterbugged by himself and sang along at the top of his voice, recalling the moment with Julie. He turned the volume up to the max when Buddy moved on to "Oh Boy" and resumed dancing. He moved faster, feeling the beat, remembering Julie's moves when centrifugal force threatened to send her flying across the porch, gyrating his hips and jabbing upward with his index fingers. He continued to sing loudly.

As he swirled around the porch, playing air guitar, he knocked over a chair and kicked it out of the way. He danced wildly, pelvis thrusting, fingers jabbing, feeling the beat, remembering, not thinking of anything but the music and his stepdaughter. His voice drowned out the CD. "Oh boy!" he screamed, "Oh boy!"

"Hey Pete!" The voice faintly registered, but he paid it no heed and continued to sing and dance, still feeling the music, lost in his own world.

"Pete!!"

This time the voice came through to him. He stumbled to the screen, almost knocking over the burning candle on one of the tables, and pressed his face against the mesh to look out.

"Pete, it's after 3:00 a.m., for crissakes! Turn that damned music down, will you?"

Pete began to focus on the figure below him. It was his neighbor, Charlie Cox.

"Hey, Charlie!" he called. "Good to see that I'm not the only one who's up late. Want to come up and have a drink and listen to some music?"

"No, I don't want a drink or to listen to music! I want to sleep! Could you turn down that music?"

Pete stood there for a moment, looking down at his neighbor. He'd known Charlie for over ten years, ever since he'd bought the cottage. He'd never known him to be so unfriendly before. He went to the player and turned down the volume. Then he returned to the screen and said, "Are you sure you don't want to come up and have a drink?"

"For the last time, no, I don't want a damn drink! And keep that music down!" With that, he turned and walked back toward his cottage. As Pete peered through the screen, he could see that Charlie was clad in his pajamas.

Pete stood on his porch, dumbfounded at Charlie's reaction. Sure, he'd been playing a little music, but that was nothing to get worked up about. He strained to hear the rest of the Buddy Holly CD. Jeez, he could barely hear the music, but he didn't want to set Charlie off again so he left the volume down.

He sat down again and his thoughts wandered off to his last visit with Julie. A car! A car! For crissakes, she wasn't even sixteen yet! He missed Doris constantly, but never more than at times like this. She would know how to handle a teenage girl who seemed to feel she was twenty-five. "No," he was sure she'd say, after pretending to think about Julie's request for a while.

He wanted to do the same, but unfortunately knew he had Wayne Sable to worry about. He knew Sable would seize the opportunity to drive a wedge between Julie and him. He should call the jerk right now and tell him he wasn't doing anyone a favor by pandering to Julie's every whim. Of course, Pete thought, Julie wasn't even his daughter, much as he liked to pretend she was. She'd reminded him of that at Parents Day, and of all the things she'd said that day, that one hurt the most. He thought back to the custody proceedings. He wasn't sure what that hack of a judge was thinking when he granted Sable custody.

He'd come to hate that long drive to Chicago, and he had to do that again the following day. Or *today*, he thought grimly. Maybe he shouldn't have resigned as managing partner of his law firm. Even good friends like Angie DeMarco seemed happy to jump into his spot. She had waited what — two weeks? — before moving into his old office? Now when he went back, he had to use a horse turd office reserved for people who had been put out to pasture. This would be his first trip back since his resignation. He wondered whether his relationship with Angie would be the same.

He turned off his CD player and blew out the candles. He steadied himself by holding on the backs of the couch and chairs as he stumbled to his bedroom.

NINE

Pete was packing his business clothes when he heard a hammer pounding next door. He looked out the window and saw Charlie Cox working on some project. *Crap!* Charlie was the last guy he wanted to see or talk to after last night. Especially with the way he felt after less than five hours sleep and far too much Thor's Hammer. Well, he had to face him sometime. He went into the bathroom and finished cleaning himself up and put on a clean shirt. Then he headed down his back steps. If Charlie heard him approach, he didn't show it. Pete screwed up his courage and said, "Morning, Charlie."

At the sound of Pete's voice, Charlie stopped hammering and turned and looked at him coldly. No smile or other sign of friendship from a long-time neighbor. "Morning," he muttered.

"Say, I'm sorry if I kept you awake last night."

"You were a little loud," Charlie replied. He still didn't crack a smile or pass off the incident with a display of humor, however contrived.

"I didn't realize I had the volume up that high," Pete said. "When my daughter was here last summer, she played music loud, louder and ear-splitting. I guess her ways must have rubbed off on me."

"Happens," Charlie said, still not smiling.

Pete was beginning to feel uncomfortable with the conversation. Or the lack of conversation. "Well, I'll let you get back to your work," he said. "Again, sorry for the noise." He returned to his cottage, feeling relieved that the embarrassing encounter was over. Charlie could have been more gracious, but he wasn't sure how he would have acted in similar circumstances.

Pete pulled into the familiar parking garage next door to his law firm and walked to the building. He took the elevator to the floor where his new office was located, and when he stepped out, the glass door was closed and he didn't see a receptionist. Then he remembered. Angie had told him the firm had eliminated receptionists on all but the main floor as part of its cost-cutting program.

He used his key card to gain entry and walked down the hall to his new office. He clicked on the light and was pleasantly surprised to see that the office had a window. He looked out and saw the mechanical system on the roof of the old building next door. Well, it couldn't compete with his former view of Millennium Park and the harbor beyond, but at least he could see daylight. The walls were bare since he'd taken all of his art and certificates with him when he moved north. He rifled through the in-box on one corner of the small desk. All he saw were routine memoranda that firm lawyers who weren't equity partners were permitted to see. He screwed up his face. This was his thanks for leaving the firm with millions of dollars of prime legal business?

He was in Chicago for a day to satisfy the terms of his change in status agreement with the firm. That agreement required him to meet with current management once a quarter during the first year. He'd been tardy in meeting that obligation and in fact had rescheduled his visit twice. He reached for the phone to dial Angie's number to tell her that he'd arrived, but then thought better of it. In the old days, when he was the managing partner, Angie would pop into his office unannounced all the time. He'd do the same with her. He wasn't going to start making appointments just because he'd resigned his position.

Angie's door was cracked open. He rapped on it a couple of times and pushed it open and walked in. Angie was on the phone, but when she saw him, motioned for him to come in. She put the phone down a few seconds later, and came over and gave him a hug. She was dressed in her trademark navy blue suit that fit her body like Lycra on a cyclist. Dark curls framed a face that had mesmerized many a man. Pete had watched her use her looks as a weapon when it suited her purpose. He had to admit that on occasion, it had worked with him, too.

"Madam managing partner," Pete said, bowing from the waist.

"Oh, you don't have to call me that. Ms. DeMarco will do."

They both laughed.

"How are you?" Angie asked. She patted his waist area. "You're looking good. You lose a few pounds?"

He'd worn a charcoal gray suit for the occasion and noticed it felt a little roomier than usual. "I'm the 'Stud of the North' now," he said. "I've got to stay in shape."

Angie feigned a disgusted expression. "Some stud. I've been making passes at you for years and the only rise I've gotten in return is color in your cheeks."

They laughed again.

"C'mon," Angie said, "we're late. I reserved a table for us at Gibsons."

Before he followed Angie down the hall, he glanced around his old office. Familiar haunts, he thought. And a lot of memories. It looked different than when he occupied the office, though. It had a feminine touch now. Well, times change, he thought ruefully.

Gibsons was packed as usual. They pushed through the crowd that overflowed from the bar area and were shown to their table.

"I've got news," Angie said, "but I don't think you're going to like it. Marty Kral just hit us with a demand letter. He claims he was pushed out of the firm in violation of the partnership agreement."

"Knowing him, I can't say I'm surprised," Pete said. "What's he want?"

"Three million dollars."

"Three million! That's a bunch of crap!"

"I know, I know. He's got all kinds of theories to support his case. Claims you, in particular, had it in for him."

Pete had been responsible for bringing Kral into the firm a half-dozen years earlier, and one of his last acts as managing partner was to cut a deal whereby Kral and several of his cronies would leave by mutual agreement. Kral had made himself *persona non grata* to a majority of the partners. After a year of relatively good behavior, he began to attack firm management with increasing vitriol and constantly whined about how under-compensated he was.

The proverbial straw that broke the camel's back came when he tried to oust Pete as the firm's managing partner because of an anonymous tip he claimed he'd received that Pete was a suspect in the Cara Lane murder case. When it was all over, and the allegations against Pete proved untrue, Pete negotiated an exit plan that let Kral leave the firm while saving face.

"What a jerk," Pete said. "We could have dumped his butt out on the street without paying him a dime."

"I know," Angie said again. "Some of the partners who aren't in management and don't know the full story are criticizing us for not getting a release from him."

"We talked about a release, remember? He wouldn't have signed it. Besides, requesting a release would have telegraphed that we were worried about something."

"I think we did the right thing, but you should attend the equity partners meeting tomorrow morning. We're going to give a full report."

"I'm not an equity partner any more, remember?"

"Consider yourself officially invited to the meeting," Angie said, "So, what's new in the north country?"

"Lots of things, really. I picked up a new client the other day. You know, Frankfort, Michigan, isn't exactly like Chicago or New York when it comes to legal business, but every now and then an interesting matter comes along." He told her about Les Brimley's murder and the controversy it had engendered in the community and Susan Brimley's request that he represent her interests relative to her late husband's estate.

"I thought you weren't going to get mixed up in things like that again."

Pete looked at her and said, "If you're referring to the murder investigation, I'm not getting mixed up in things, as you say. I have an engagement letter with a bright line — financial affairs and nothing else. We even have specifics describing my duties on the financial side. I'm supposed to review records and liaise with the lawyer for the estate and nothing else."

"Is she a looker?" Angie asked with an impish smile.

Pete went right back at her. "Actually she is, but I have the same high ethical standards I followed at Sears & Whitney. No involvement with women who are clients."

Angie gave him a skeptical look and said, "I gather from what you said that you're not representing the estate itself."

"No," he said, "the estate has a separate law firm."

"If she's the sole heir and the estate already has a lawyer, why does she need you?"

"Angie, you can be remarkably naive. It's not uncommon for heirs to have their own legal counsel in these cases. Watch over the executor and things like that."

"Is it a big estate?"

"Don't know. It's got a lot of debt, that's for sure." He told her about what he'd discovered the day he visited Brimley's office.

"Did you have the sheriff's permission to go in there? Everything in Brimley's office is potential evidence in the murder case, you know."

"I don't see why I needed the sheriff's permission. No crime was committed in the offices, and they weren't taped off or anything. Plus I had permission to be on the premises."

"Permission. From whom? You said the sheriff didn't authorize you to go in."

"Angie, have I suddenly gotten dumb just because I moved north? Susan Brimley authorized me to enter the offices. She's a company officer and has her own set of keys. She gave them to me, and our engagement letter specifically authorizes me to act on her behalf."

"What's her position?"

"Secretary and Assistant Treasurer."

Angie waved a hand. "Those aren't real positions," she said. "They're titles."

"I wouldn't expect a litigator like you to know this, but they're more than titles. There are real duties attached to them. So, to sum up your honor, I'm Susan Brimley's lawyer, she has a right to be on the premises, she gave me her keys, and she signed an engagement letter authorizing me to act for her."

"When are you meeting with the lawyer for the estate?" Angie asked.

"Late morning tomorrow."

"What's the firm?"

Pete opened his wallet and pulled out a slip of paper. "Thompson, Barrett & Radke. Ever hear of them?"

Angie paused for a moment as if she were thinking. "That name sounds vaguely familiar," she said, "but I can't place it."

"Maybe you had a case against them or something."

"I don't think so. I'd remember that. But that name rings a bell."

Pete nodded. "Well anyway, I'm scheduled to meet with a lawyer from the firm named Radke — he's one of the name partners — at 11:00 a.m. tomorrow."

"Radke. What's his first name?"

"Theo."

"Theo Radke. Theo Radke. Don't know him. But the firm name does sound familiar."

"Well, if you remember by the morning, let me know, okay?"

"Let me see if my old boss at the State's Attorney's office remembers the name," Angie said. She reached for her cell phone and punched in a number. After the usual social banter, she asked her former boss if he remembered Thompson, Barrett & Radke. She listened intently. When she ended the call, she just looked at Pete without saying anything.

Pete had seen that mother hen look often enough to sigh and ask, "Okay, what is it?"

"Silas remembers Thompson, Barrett & Radke very well. The matter I was trying to remember was a case involving money laundering and some other offenses. Radke wasn't involved in the case and Silas doesn't know him. But get this — the firm's client in that matter was a reputed mob figure."

"Mob figure?"

Angie just stared at him some more.

"He couldn't be thinking of some other firm, could he?"

"He sounded pretty definite."

"But he doesn't know Radke?"

"No,"

"Mob figure," he repeated. "Of course, the fact that some lawyers in Radke's firm do criminal defense work doesn't mean the firm doesn't have other clients, right?"

"Right, but it makes you think, doesn't it?"

Pete just sat quietly, pondering what Angie had just told him.

Angie said, "Think about it. A man is murdered and his law firm represents the mob. Is it just a coincidence or was there more to this guy Brimley's business than you know about?"

Pete resisted the temptation to rib her about conspiracy theories and just said, "I don't know the answer to that. Let's see what I learn when I meet with Radke tomorrow."

"Isn't this how you got sucked into the Cara Lane case?"

He poured the remaining wine into their glasses and took a sip. "You worry too much. I told you what I agreed to do for Susan Brimley. I'm meeting with Radke because Susan says he stonewalled her when she tried to get information from him. Our feeling was that he'd be less likely to do that with me. Even if Radke's firm does work for the mob, I doubt if he's going to have me rubbed out just because I ask him a few questions."

Angie just looked at him again.

"Oh, one other thing," Pete said. "When I looked through LB Development's files, I found a sheet of paper with all of the bank debt listed and two other numbers. I couldn't match those numbers with anything else I found in the files. The notes in the margin next to the unmatched numbers were 'Nautical' and 'Z.' Nothing else. Could you have an associate or maybe even the librarian take a look and see if there's a bank or finance company with 'Nautical' in the name?"

"Do you have anything else to go on?"

"No."

She smiled. "Typical Pete Thorsen request. Okay, I'll see what we can come up with."

"You're a gem, you know that?"

Angie gave him a look. Just then the waiter dropped the bill on their table equal distance between them. She snatched it as though fearful Pete would insist on paying. He suppressed a smile. She'd invited him to dinner and also made a lot of money; why shouldn't she pay?

"Want to stop at the bar for a drink?" Pete asked after Angie had settled the bill and they were walking out.

"Only if you pay this time. I'm a girl, remember?"

Pete grinned at her and they joined the throngs of people milling around the bar. They were lucky to be standing behind a couple who had just been called for dinner and commandeered their stools. Pete ordered a Thor's Hammer and tonic with extra lime, and Angie had another glass of wine. He'd paced himself at dinner for two reasons:

he still felt like death warmed over from the night before, and he didn't want Angie to be the latest one to lecture him about his drinking habits.

"Well," he asked, "how do you like being managing partner?"

She looked at him with an earnest expression. "You know what, I love it. I wouldn't admit that to anyone else, but I think you know how I feel. It's just a shame that you felt you had to resign. It bothered me to step into your position like that."

"Yeah, well, other challenges and everything. Any problems other than the Kral thing? I mean, you are the first woman managing partner of Sears & Whitney."

"And only the second among all the major Chicago firms. No, no problems I didn't anticipate." She looked thoughtful for a moment, then shook her head and smiled. "You know what Steve Johnson did the day I was elected? We were walking down the street to the University Club for a celebratory lunch and all of a sudden he started pointing to me and saying in a loud voice, 'This is the new managing partner of Sears & Whitney! This is the new managing partner of Sears & Whitney!' I was so embarrassed because everyone on the sidewalk was staring at us."

"That's funny," Pete said, thinking of the reserved Steve Johnson stepping out of character and doing something like that. Steve had allied with Angie from the moment she joined the firm and the two had been close ever since. Now they were the senior management team of one of the oldest law firms in Chicago.

"Thanks again for all your support," Angie said. His hand was on the bar and she put hers over it.

"No problem," Pete replied. "You were the best man for the job. None of those other ladies could hold a candle to you."

She let go of his hand and slapped him playfully in the shoulder. "Oh, you're such a sexist pig."

They both laughed.

It was good to see Angie again. For all of her dedication to the law and to the firm, he always sensed she had a wild side beyond her flirtatious manner. After Doris died, he'd been tempted several times, but managed to hold back. He'd seen what could happen when the boss dipped his quill in the troops' ink. The fact that they were no longer partners didn't change anything. It could make it awkward around the firm, to say the least. Plus, she was married.

As they sat there, he could feel the warmth of her leg close to his. "How are things at home?" he asked innocently.

Angie shrugged. "The same," she replied with a note of resignation in her voice. "Why did you have to spoil a nice evening by bringing that up?"

"Just asking."

They talked a while. Angie filled him in on the latest scuttlebutt around the firm and the business end of things. Revenue was fairly good considering the recession, but expenses had gotten out of hand and some additional cut-backs were planned to maintain profits. Sears & Whitney had fifty-eight equity partners and they all acted like major shareholders of a publicly-traded corporation. Take the long-term view, the mantra went, but make sure the money we take home increases each year, too.

Angie suddenly looked at her watch and said, "Pete, I've got to go. I told the Grinch I was going out with a client and would be home by 9:00 p.m. It's already past that."

"Jeez, just when I was going to suggest that you tour the Fairmont Hotel with me." He shifted his position to bump her shoulder.

"Ha, ha," she said sarcastically. "The Stud of the North was about to swing into action, huh?"

"Hey, I'm slow, but relentless."

TEN

Pete took a seat at the side of the conference table and shook hands with the partners next to him. It felt strange; he was used to occupying a seat at the head of the table and running the show.

Angie DeMarco walked in and looked all business. Not at all like the woman he'd had dinner with the night before who was filled with innuendoes and one-liners. She whispered something to Steve Johnson and then sat down and shuffled through her papers and made a few notes. When all of the partners were seated, she called the meeting to order and made a few opening remarks. Then she turned the proceedings over to Johnson for a report on the Marty Kral demand letter.

Steve circulated copies of the letter and summarized it for the partners. Pete had already heard it all from Angie and was thinking ahead to his meeting with Radke. When Johnson finished his presentation, he said that management intended to interview lawyers to represent the firm in case the matter couldn't be resolved out of court. He promised to keep the partners up to date on developments, and opened the floor to discussion.

Questions from the partners followed. Could a settlement be reached with Kral? Would partners have to report the lawsuit, if one were filed, on credit and other applications? Did the firm have counterclaims it could assert if the matter went to litigation? Would any judgment against the partners be covered by the firm's insurance?

The discussion dragged on and Pete looked at his watch. He was due at Thompson, Barrett & Radke in a half-hour. He said goodbye to the partners alongside him, waved to Angie and Steve, and slipped out behind two partners who also had to leave.

◆ ◆ ◆

The reception area at Thompson, Barrett & Radke was like the reception areas at dozens of other law firms. Elegant wall coverings, original paintings of scenes from around Chicago, comfortable chairs, and a curved mahogany reception desk. Pete checked in a few minutes early and took a seat and waited.

And waited. His watch read 11:30 a.m. and there was no sign of Radke. He thought about the conversation with Angie the previous night, and the information her former boss had provided about the firm's work for the mob. And he thought about the brutal manner in which Les Brimley had been murdered. He glanced at his watch again, and then approached the desk and asked the receptionist if she knew when Radke would be available. She said she'd check. It was exactly noon when a sixtyish woman in conservative dress came out, and after conferring with the receptionist, approached Pete.

"Mr. Thorsen?"

"Yes."

"I'm terribly sorry, Mr. Radke had to go out right before you arrived. He just called and said something urgent had come up that would keep him out of the office for the rest of the day. He said to tell you he was sorry."

"I had an appointment with him."

"I know," the woman said, "I'm sorry. Could you call to reschedule? I'm afraid I can't do it now because Mr. Radke has some things that make his schedule a bit uncertain at the moment."

"Do I have a choice?"

The woman just smiled sadly.

◆ ◆ ◆

As Pete drove north to Crystal Lake, he reflected on being stood up by Radke and, again, his law firm's alleged connection to the mob. There were several firms in Chicago that represented mob figures, but he wasn't aware that Thompson, Barrett & Radke was one of them. Usually those firms were very small shops built around one criminal lawyer who was known for his courtroom prowess. Thompson, Barrett & Radke had about twenty lawyers according to Martindale Hubbell, the law firm directory, small by current standards in an era of mega-firms, but considerably larger than the average firm that did criminal work. Plus, Radke's firm seemed to have a general practice. The specialties listed for individual lawyers ranged from corporate and environmental to probate and tax. A few of the lawyers did list white collar criminal work, but they were in the minority.

Susan Brimley said that the firm had represented Les for the past couple of years. He knew the legal business, and that raised several questions. Why did Les switch firms? Who represented him before? Why Thompson, Barrett & Radke? The firm listed one lawyer who did real estate work, but it was hardly a firm with a big practice in the field. Did Brimley have some relationship with Radke or another lawyer in the firm who caused him to switch? And how did the firm's practice on behalf of the Chicago mob fit in? Or was it just a coincidence?

He pulled off the highway to use the facilities at a rest stop, and as he walked back to his car, that aggravating tune programmed into his new cell phone jangled. He reminded himself to figure out how to change it. Maybe substitute one of his favorite oldie tunes. He could see from the screen that the caller was Susan Brimley. She probably was eager for a report on his meeting with Radke.

"Hello, Susan," he said.

"I'm sorry to call you while you're driving, but I need to talk to you." Her voice sounded anxious.

"No problem. I'm at a rest stop. Is something wrong?"

"That man Richter — you know, the acting sheriff? — called me a couple of hours ago. He wants me to come to his office and talk to them about Les' death."

"What exactly did he say?"

"He said I might want to bring my lawyer. He said something like I should consider the interview as part of the official police investigation into Les' murder."

"It sounds routine," he said. "They're probably just 'dotting all the i's' and 'crossing all the t's.' You have an alibi, right?"

"Yes, but I'm worried. I'm afraid Richter will start grilling me. You know how the police are. They treat everyone as a suspect."

The Cara Lane experience flashed before his eyes. Susan was right about the way the police looked at spouses, particularly if the person doing the questioning was Richter. But he also sensed where she was heading and felt himself sliding in a direction he didn't want to go.

"Susan," he said, "I told you when I agreed to look into the financial side of things for you that I'm not a criminal lawyer. I just don't want to be drawn into the case. Besides, as I said, I don't see how you have anything to worry about. If it will make you feel better, though, I'll call Richter in the morning and get your interview postponed. Then I'll arrange a criminal lawyer to accompany you when it's rescheduled."

There was silence and he heard a sniffle. Finally she said, "I already told Richter that I'd be in his office at 1:00 p.m. tomorrow. I have no excuse or reason to postpone the interview."

"It seems to me that arranging counsel is a pretty good reason."

"I thought of that," she replied. "But I'm afraid it will just make the sheriff more suspicious."

"Why? He was the one who suggested you bring a lawyer, wasn't he?"

"You don't understand. When he said that, I told him I didn't need a lawyer and would come to his office tomorrow. When I got off the phone and thought about it, I realized I would be stupid not to bring a lawyer even if the interview is routine, as you say, and I didn't think I needed one. I thought you might be willing to go with me just to give me a little support."

He didn't say anything and soon he heard another sniffle. "Okay," she finally said. "I won't keep you any longer." The phone went silent.

Crap, he muttered. He leaned against his Range Rover, thinking about the conversation. He could have handled that better. But he was right. It was plain as day from the engagement letter; he'd agreed to look into Les Brimley's financial affairs and nothing more. Still, it concerned him that Susan seemed to be a basket case.

Susan had also become his client the minute he agreed to represent her, and he felt some obligation to her, however limited his undertaking had been. He knew it was ridiculous to believe that her appointment with law enforcement couldn't be postponed until she could get a lawyer. In fact, if Richter were aware of facts that made her a suspect, and regarded her as such, she might have to be given an opportunity to get a lawyer as part of her Miranda rights. But how could she be a suspect? She had an ironclad alibi as far as he knew. He himself had seen her at the Glen Arbor art show the night of the murder, and he'd heard that the friend who'd hosted the event had stated unequivocally that Susan had spent the night at her house.

But he also knew Richter. Susan was right; any change from what she'd already told him would be a red flag and an invitation for further inquiry. And if she wanted to delay the interview to retain legal counsel after telling him she didn't need a lawyer, he would immediately suspect she was hiding something. When the interview did occur, he'd badger her and attempt to rattle her in hopes of catching her in an inconsistency. His personal experience with Richter demonstrated that was true and he was a lawyer.

Maybe he'd over-reacted to her request and relied too much on technicalities. What could it hurt to accompany her to the interview if it made her feel better? He'd handled Richter pretty well in the past, hadn't he? As he punched in Susan's number, he knew he was talking himself into something and felt conflicted. He waited for her to answer. When she did, he said, "Look, I'm sorry if I was a little short during our earlier conversation. I'm free tomorrow afternoon and can go with you if you want."

Susan didn't respond for a long moment and then said haltingly, "Are you sure?"

"Yes, I'm sure. But I have to ask you a question — is there anything I should know before we meet with Richter?"

"What do you mean?"

"I don't want to be surprised tomorrow. Is there anything Richter might know that he could use to trip you up and punch holes in your story?"

"You mean about where I was that night and things like that?"

"Yes."

The phone went silent for a moment. Finally she said, "No, nothing I can think of. The art show was scheduled weeks in advance, and I never left Effie's house until the next morning after I got a call from the sheriff's office."

"What did you do for dinner? Did you go out?"

"No, we ate in. There was some food left over from the show and we made a salad."

That sounded like as routine an evening as he could imagine. "What time did you go to bed?" he asked.

"I don't know. It was late. Maybe 1:00 a.m. Effie and I had a lot of catching up to do — girl stuff, mainly."

"Did you talk about Les?"

"Briefly. Les and I were planning a trip to Tuscany in the fall and I told Effie about that."

Pete thought about her answers. There didn't seem to be anything Richter could jump on. "Okay," he said. "Let's meet in the parking lot of the County Government Center just before 1:00 p.m. We can go in together. But let's be clear about one thing — we'll consider this a one-time exception to our original agreement, but after the meeting with Richter, if you want a lawyer to represent you further in the criminal case, you'll get someone else, okay? I can recommend someone if you like."

"Yes, of course," she said. "I'm sorry to impose on you for tomorrow, but this all came up so suddenly. I didn't know where else to turn."

Later, when he was driving north again, he was alone with his thoughts once more. He thought about Julie and her request for a car. And he wondered how Richter would react when he showed up with Susan Brimley.

ELEVEN

He walked into the sheriff's office with Susan Brimley five minutes early. It was like old home week. The same receptionist was seated behind the counter working on a crossword puzzle and cracking her gum. She greeted Pete by name, and after he explained why they were there, led them down the hall to an interview room that looked suspiciously like the one in which he'd spent over two hours with then-Deputy Richter and his sidekick.

Susan acted fidgety. That wasn't surprising. Civilians were often nervous in anticipation of being questioned by law enforcement officials even if they had nothing to hide. Moreover, he could tell that Richter had rattled her just by the way he'd handled the conversation. He would never be accused of being disarming.

Pete tried to put Susan at ease while they waited for Richter and, he presumed, Detective Joe Tessler, to appear. "What are you working on these days?" he asked.

Her face brightened. "A series of paintings of old shipwrecks on the Great Lakes. I've spent a lot of time at nautical museums, including the one near Sleeping Bear. I'm very excited about the project."

"How about the Edmond Fitzgerald?" he asked, thinking about the wreck memorialized in one of his favorite Gordon Lightfoot songs. "Are you going to work that in?"

"No, the ships I'm concentrating on go back to an earlier era. Sailing ships, mainly."

"What's your approach? Are you painting them going down?"

"That's the challenge," she answered. "Just painting the ships going down would be too cookie-cutter. I'm trying to capture the essence of the tragedy in each case. That's where creativity comes in."

Pete glanced at his watch. The acting sheriff was up to his old tricks. They talked some more about art. Then Richter and Tessler walked in, a half-hour late.

Richter obviously had been told that Pete was there and didn't seem surprised by his presence. He remained standing and fixed Pete with his usual practiced stare. "Mr. Thorsen," he said, "can I see you in the hall for a few minutes before we get started?"

Pete glanced at Susan, then back at Richter. He said, "Anything you have to say, you can say in front of my client, Sheriff."

"This doesn't relate to Mrs. Brimley. I think it would be better if we talked about it in private," Richter replied. The color in his cheeks was rising, a sure sign that his temper was as well.

"It's okay," Susan interjected. "I don't mind."

Pete took his time following Richter out of the room. When they were down the hall and out of earshot, Richter stepped closer to him and did little to conceal his annoyance. He said in a low, throaty voice, "You trying to yank my chain, Thorsen?"

"I don't know what you mean, Sheriff."

Richter's expression didn't soften. "Sure you don't," he said. "First I see you sniffing around the crime scene like some cadaver dog, and now you show up with the vic's widow when we ask her to come in for a routine interview. You see what I'm getting at?"

"No, I don't see what you're getting at. There's no such thing as a routine interview in a murder case. Mrs. Brimley is my client. She asked me to come along and that's why I'm here."

"When I talked to Mrs. Brimley yesterday, she didn't say anything about you representing her. As a matter of fact, she said she was coming alone. She said she didn't need a lawyer."

"She changed her mind. From what she tells me, you're the one who said she should bring a lawyer."

"I didn't tell her that," Richter said petulantly.

"Susan says that you told her that she might want to bring a lawyer. She took that to mean she probably would need one. She brought me."

Richter narrowed his eyes and stared at Pete. "You intending to turn this interview into a circus?"

"Not unless you try to railroad my client like you did with me last year," Pete replied. "Shall we go back in?"

Richter didn't move and said defensively, "We didn't try to railroad you."

"That's not how I remember it. You treated me as an axe murderer just because I happened to have had dinner with the woman and then took a walk along the lake. Trumped up some so-called eyewitness testimony that the woman was in my car, things like that. You weren't even sure Cara Lane was murdered and you still went after me."

He clearly had Richter on the defensive because he said, "I thought it was murder all along."

"Uh, huh," Pete said dryly.

"Don't get in the way of law enforcement in this case," Richter said. "Things have changed since last year when you civilians could run around and muck up things for us professionals."

"I don't see how I mucked up anything. As I remember, I'm the one who found the killer."

"You and I both know you stumbled onto it. We had to come bail your butt out. When we got there, you looked like you'd crapped your pants."

"At least I got the right man. Can we go back in now? We've kept the others waiting long enough."

Richter stared at him for a moment, then turned and walked back into the interview room and took a chair opposite Susan Brimley. Pete followed and tried not to grin. Sparring with Richter again brought out his old combative instincts.

Richter asked Susan to state her full name and address and took her through the other preliminaries. Then he got into the meat of the interview. "Now on the night Mr. Brimley was killed, where were you?"

"I was in Glen Arbor. I had an art show at a friend's house."

"And you claim you stayed in Glen Arbor overnight, right?"

"I don't just *claim* I stayed there overnight. I *did* stay in Glen Arbor overnight. With my friend, Effie Miller."

Pete liked the way Susan answered that question. Maybe she wasn't as nervous as he thought. Richter then asked her a series of other routine questions. Susan's answers were consistent with what she'd told Pete the night before.

Richter studied his notes. "Now, how long were you married to Lester Brimley?" he asked.

"Nineteen years."

"Would you say you had a good marriage?"

"Yes, I would."

"Any fights?"

"Sure, what married couple doesn't have fights?"

"What did you fight about?" Richter asked.

She shrugged. "The usual things."

Richter leaned forward and seemed to be wrestling with how to phrase his next question. Pete had seen that crafty mind at work before. He wasn't surprised when Richter came out with his follow-up, half question and half accusation. "People we talked to said you and Les used to argue about money."

Pete rolled his eyes. It was the same sort of innuendo and alleged statements from undisclosed sources that Richter had used when he grilled him about Cara Lane. He'd kept quiet before, but now said, "Excuse me, Sheriff. Why don't you tell us the names of the people who made those statements?"

Richter fixed him with that baleful stare again. "That will all come out in due course. Now, Mrs. Brimley, would you answer the question, please?"

Pete wasn't going to let him off the hook that easily. He said, "Like it came out from the unnamed people who allegedly saw Cara Lane get in my car?"

Richter's face reddened again. "That's what witnesses told us," Richter said defensively.

"Uh, huh."

Richter gave Pete another icy stare. The bad blood between them was never far from the surface, and now it boiled over again. Pete knew he shouldn't interject personal feelings into the interview, but Richter's questions followed such a predictable pattern, it was hard not to.

"That was another case at a different point in time, counselor...."

Susan cut him short by saying, "It's okay, Pete. I don't mind answering." She turned back to Richter and said, "We did argue about money once in a while, but no more so than other married couples."

Richter glanced at Pete with a look of triumph on his face, and seemed eager to get his follow-up question in. "Why don't you give us an example of how the money issue came up?" he asked.

Susan appeared to think for a few moments. "Mainly it was over our two houses."

"You want to explain?" Richter asked.

"We have two rather large homes, one here and one in the Chicago area. Les thought we should sell one to reduce expenses. I thought we should keep both and ride out the bad economy."

Richter was busy writing in his notebook. He looked up and asked, "No arguments over shopping sprees, things like that?"

"No, I have my own resources for personal expenses. There was nothing to argue about."

Tessler interrupted and asked, "Are you independently wealthy?"

Susan smiled. "No, but I do have income of my own. I'm an artist, and my paintings command a good price."

"Getting back to your arguments over finances," Richter said, "was Mr. Brimley having financial problems with Mystic Bluffs?"

"Yes, I think so."

"Tell us about them."

"I would if I could. I don't know myself. That's why I hired Mr. Thorsen."

Richter and Tessler looked at Pete at the same time. "What can you tell us about Les Brimley's financial problems?" Richter asked.

Pete looked at Susan. "It's okay," she said. "Tell them what you told me."

"I looked over some of Brimley's financial records," Pete said. "I can't tell you much at this point other than Brimley, or more properly his development company, has over $23 million in debt on the project. Maybe more," he added, thinking of the last two numbers on the handwritten sheet. "I have no idea what the project is worth as a going concern, so I can't give you a net number. I also don't know the value of his other assets in the Chicago area."

Richter stared at Pete with a suspicious expression. "And where did you find the records you examined?"

Pete knew that Richter would give him a hard time when he found out he'd been in LB Development's office, but also knew he had little choice except to answer. "Brimley has an office near Elberta. The records are there."

Richter looked at Tessler, then back at Pete. From the smile on his face, he clearly felt he had Pete's tail in a wringer. "Now let me understand this," he said slowly, continuing to smile. "You broke into a crime scene without our permission and pawed through records that may be evidence in a murder case?"

Pete stared back at him and said evenly, "Let me correct you, Sheriff. Brimley's office was not, to my knowledge, the scene of any crime. I believe that was the seventeenth green of the Mystic Bluffs Golf Club. And I didn't break into any place. There was no crime scene tape or other signage indicating the premises were under your control, and my client," he said, pointing at Susan, "is an officer of the development company. She gave me a key and authorized me to enter the premises and look through the records on her behalf."

"You can split hairs all you want," Richter said, "but as far as I'm concerned, you entered premises material to this case without our permission."

Pete shrugged. "My answer stands."

They just stared at each other. Tessler broke the silence and said to Susan, "Going back to the night of the murder, you said you stayed overnight at your friend's house in Glen Arbor, is that right?"

"Yes."

"And your friend will testify to that?"

"Yes. I mean I haven't asked her, but I'm sure she will."

"Did you make any telephone calls? Either on your cell phone or on one of Ms. Miller's phones?"

Susan appeared to think for a few moments, then she said, "Not that I remember."

"You never called your husband?"

"No."

"Or anyone else?"

"No, as I just told you, I don't remember calling anyone."

Richter assumed control of the questioning again. "Now Mrs. Brimley, you said you went to bed about 1:00 a.m. that night, correct?"

"Yes."

"I assume you slept in separate rooms?"

"Yes."

"What time did you get up?"

Susan thought for a few moments. "I think it was about 7:30 a.m."

"Did your friend get up at the same time?"

"Maybe ten minutes later. I remember because I made the coffee and it was ready when Effie came down."

"How long does it take to drive from Glen Arbor to the Mystic Bluffs Golf Club?"

"Oh for God's sake, Sheriff," Pete said. "Are you suggesting that Mrs. Brimley, while her friend was sleeping, hopped in her car, went home and killed her husband, then drove back to Glen Arbor, all in time to make coffee?"

"I'm just trying to establish a timeline," Richter protested. "It's only a hypothetical."

"Well, work this into your hypothetical. How does a woman Susan's size drag a grown man out of his home, transport him to the golf course, and then beat his brains in with a golf club?"

Out of the corner of his eye, Pete could see that Susan was crying.

"She could have had an accomplice," Richter said. "Just hypothetically. Besides, we think the killer used a stun gun. A person doesn't have to be big or strong to fire a stun gun."

Pete shook his head and said, "Listen, we've been here more than two hours and gone over every detail of Mrs. Brimley's relationship with her husband, the timeline, and every hypothetical imaginable. I'm going to ask you straight out. Is Mrs. Brimley a suspect in this case?"

Richter and Tessler looked at each other.

"Well, is she?"

"Not at this time anyway," Tessler replied. "You agree, Frank?"

Richter nodded as he continued to shuffle his papers.

"Before you go," Tessler said, "I have a few final questions. Mrs. Brimley, do you have any idea of who might have had a motive to kill your husband? I mean, based on anything you heard or witnessed?"

"No," Susan said.

"Did he have any enemies you can think of?"

"In business, you always have enemies."

"Any names come to mind?"

"Just the people who opposed the Mystic Bluffs project."

"Did you ever hear anyone threaten Mr. Brimley?"

"No."

Richter interjected, "Are you aware that John Hicks threatened your husband?"

"No."

"He made threats at a public meeting in front of a hundred people," Richter said.

"I wasn't at the meeting."

"Anything else you'd like to tell us?"

"Not that I can think of."

TWELVE

"You two don't like each other, do you?" Susan asked.

"Let me put it this way, we're not mutual fans."

"That was easy to see," Susan said. "I've got nothing to hide, but when he sits across from you in that little room with his badge and that tight shirt with all those muscles ... I was just glad you were with me. Thank you."

"You're welcome," Pete said. "I couldn't believe it when he started to conjecture about some of that stuff."

"Do you think I'm in the clear?" Susan asked.

"Should be. For some reason, they always feel they have to focus on the spouse first in these cases. It seems to be police procedure 101."

She nodded and took a deep breath and expelled the air but didn't say anything.

Pete said, "If there's no police tape up, I'm going back to LB Development's office in the morning and make a final sweep to confirm I didn't miss anything the first go-around. Have you thought any more about whether 'Nautical' means anything to you?"

Susan shook her head. "No, I've never heard that name." Then she added, "Are you going to try to see Radke again?"

"Yes," Pete answered. "I have a feeling he was trying to dodge me, too, which I don't understand. But I am going to keep trying to see him."

Pete was pleasantly surprised when he drove up the street and saw no police tape or signs on the LB Development building. He thought he was on safe grounds entering the premises again since he'd gone on record with his justification for doing so the first time. Still, he was anxious to get in and out as soon as possible. No use needlessly courting trouble with Richter.

He used his key to gain entry, and this time went directly to Brimley's office. He pulled out the file drawers, one-by-one, looking for something with "Nautical's" name on it or documents that might shed light on the reference to "Z." An hour later, he'd satisfied himself that he'd missed nothing during his first visit.

He moved to Brimley's desk and pulled out the center drawer to look at the sheet with numbers on it again. It was gone. That's strange, he thought. He was sure he'd put the sheet back on top of the mess in the center drawer. He methodically worked his way through the other drawers in Brimley's desk, but found nothing there either. He leaned back in the chair, puzzled by the paper's disappearance. Then, through the window, he saw a sheriff's department vehicle pull up to the curb. Two men in uniforms got out; one of them was Richter. The officers walked to his Range Rover and peered in.

Damn, Pete muttered. He stuffed his legal pad into the file folder and started for the exit. He took a deep breath and stepped into the sunlight. Richter and his deputy were coming up the front walk two abreast. They saw him and stopped. With their sunglasses and thumbs hooked in their belts, they looked like cops in an old movie set in the South.

"Good morning, gentlemen," Pete said casually.

Richter and his deputy stood in front of him, effectively blocking his path. Richter had a smirk on his face. "Mr. Thorsen," he said. "You do get around. You have a nice morning rooting around in evidentiary documents again?"

"Actually," Pete replied, "it was pretty boring. Looking through financial records my client, an officer of LB Development LLC, has every right to see. If that had been up," he said, pointing toward the roll of yellow tape under the deputy's arm, "I would have checked with your office before going in. But just like before, there were no signs or tape, so I used the key my client gave me and went in and finished my work."

"For a guy who prides himself on his memory, you've been awfully forgetful lately. Didn't we just have a conversation yesterday in which I told you that those records potentially are important evidence in a murder case? You still don't see anything wrong with what you've been doing?"

"I do remember our conversation. And that conversation included me telling you that I was authorized to be on LB's premises and look through records as part of my duties for a client. As I recall, you dropped the issue and went on with your questioning of my client."

"The implication was, Mr. Thorsen, that the premises are off limits."

Pete shrugged and said, "You should have taped the premises if you wanted people to stay out."

Richter shook his head and eyed the file folder under Pete's arm. "So what did you take?" he asked.

"Nothing. These are my notes."

"Can I see?"

Pete knew he probably could require Richter to get a search warrant to look through the contents of the folder. He also knew no purpose would be served by further exacerbating the relationship with Richter by being unnecessarily combative. Besides, the file folder contained only his notes, as he'd just said.

He shrugged again and said, "Suit yourself." He handed the file folder to Richter.

Richter removed the legal pad and, page by page, looked at Pete's notes. Pete watched him. Five minutes later, Richter handed the file back to him,

"You take any documents the first time you were here?"

Pete shook his head. "Not a thing." He was thankful he hadn't taken the handwritten sheet or made a copy of it. He wished he had the sheet, but it would only cause him problems now if he did. And, in a stroke of good luck, his notes summarizing the debt with the references to "Nautical" and "Z" were still by his home phone. He'd referred to them during his conversation with Susan Brimley and hadn't put the notes back in the file.

"I'm going to tell you once more in front of a witness — don't enter these premises again without my authorization. You do and I'll throw the book at you. I'm also going to talk to the county attorney and see what he wants to do about the way you disregarded my previous instructions."

"I'm always happy to talk to Ralph."

Richter gave Pete the same old stare and jerked a thumb towards his Range Rover in the universal sign to "get out of here."

Pete was about to put on one of his oldies when Angie called.

"You really should come back to Chicago and start practicing real law again," she said. "You'd make more money, and I could keep an eye on you. The worst that could happen is you might have an affair with a married woman."

"Can't I do that long distance?" he asked innocently. "They say that an affair is sweeter if the encounters are only occasional. But you were calling to give me a report on 'Nautical,' right?"

"Who told you that?"

"You mean my supposition you were calling to report on 'Nautical?'"

"No, the part about an affair being sweeter."

"Oh that. I read it in the *National Enquirer* when I was standing in the checkout line at the food store the other day. But you were calling about 'Nautical,' right?"

"Jeez, and you call yourself the Stud of the North. Okay, here's what we found. I had our best new associate check, and she found fifty-two companies in Illinois alone with 'Nautical' in their names. As you might expect, most of them are in some aspect of the marine business. But a few seemed to favor the name for other reasons. Thought it sounded cool or something. One seemed particularly interesting. Are you ready?"

"I'm all ears."

"The company's in the commercial finance business and — get this — we found out the president is one Vincent Zahn."

"I'll be damned," Pete said. "The sheet of paper I saw in LB Development's office the first time I was there referred to both 'Nautical' and 'Z.' 'Z' must refer to Zahn."

The line was quiet for a few moments. Then Angie said, "First time. Does that imply what I think it implies? That there was a second time?"

"Well, sure," Pete said defensively. "I wanted to make sure I hadn't missed anything the first go-around."

"You didn't ignore any police tape or posted signs the second time, did you?"

"No, mother." Then he chuckled. "I did run into Richter on the way out, though. He was coming to put up tape. He wasn't too happy to see me."

"Oh, Lord," Angie said. "What happened?"

"Not much. He blustered, but then backed off when I repeated my position that I had every right to be there as long as the premises weren't closed by police tape."

"At least you're not in jail. How did you leave it with him?"

"He told me if he ever caught me in the building again without his permission, he'd throw the book at me. Oh, and he said he was going to refer my 'transgressions' to the county attorney for possible action."

"Are you worried?"

"Nah. I know Ralph Medling. He's a decent guy. He'll listen to Richter, tell him he'll look into it, and that'll be the end of the story. Now getting back to Zahn, do you know anything about him?"

The line was silent again. Finally Angie said, "You don't know?"

"If I did, I wouldn't have asked."

"Zahn is one of the crime bosses here in Chicago. What they call the Outfit now that we can't say Mafia anymore."

Pete whistled. "You think the Outfit, as you call it, or the mob as the rest of us say, was providing some of the financing for Brimley's project?"

"Your guess is as good as mine, but from everything you tell me, it's a reasonable bet. My friends in the State's Attorney's office tell me Nautical is a front for Zahn's criminal activities."

Pete thought for a few moments. "And that additional $1 million with Zahn's initial by it — you think that could be what they call juice?"

"Again, a reasonable bet, Sherlock. By the way, you know what Zahn's mob nickname is? The Fisherman. You know, swims with the fishes?"

Pete just grunted.

"You fool around with those guys and you'll be dead."

"I'm not fooling around with them, Angie. I just want the information to report to my client. Thanks. I'm indebted to you."

"You are. Now, can we talk about compensation?"

THIRTEEN

On their way to Beulah, Pete filled Harry McTigue in on Angie's report regarding Nautical and Zahn.

"I've heard of Vinnie Zahn," Harry said. "My old paper used to do a story on those mob guys every now and again. Zahn was a mid-level made guy, as I recall."

"He must have moved up. According to Angie, he's one of the kingpins now."

"You think he was financing Brimley, huh?"

"It looks that way," Pete said. "It's too much of a coincidence based on that sheet I saw in Brimley's office with 'Nautical' and 'Z' on it."

"You said that sheet disappeared, right?"

"This is all off the record, as I told you before, but someone took that sheet between my first visit to LB Development's offices and when I came back to double-check my work. I know I put that sheet back in the center drawer of Brimley's desk, just where I found it, and now it's gone."

"Do you think one of Richter's guys took it?"

"Not likely. I got the impression that neither Richter nor any of his men had been in Brimley's office until I bumped into them as I was leaving the second time. Zahn's people would be a better bet. They probably didn't want anything lying around that would tip off law enforcement that Brimley had dealings with the mob. I don't know who else would have a motive to take the paper."

Harry parked in front of Crystal Crate & Cargo with the distinctive red-framed door. Rona Martin's birthday was the next day, and Harry was feeling pressure to come up with a nice gift. "This is Rona's favorite store, you know," Harry said in a low voice, as though he were disclosing a closely-guarded secret. "They've got everything. Rona suggested I might want to look in the glass case near the cash register, but I'm going to take a spin through the store first. I want to see for myself what's available."

Pete watched patiently as Harry inspected a stack of silver trays and admired a collection of fancy glass bowls. He spent an inordinate amount of time examining cherry pitters and watched with fascination as a sales clerk demonstrated how they worked. He moved on to the fine cutlery in wood block holders and held up designer tote bags to view them in better light. He checked out flatware in elegant cases and admired an impressive array of aprons with catchy sayings.

As Pete followed him through the store, Harry whispered over his shoulder, "A lot of nice stuff, huh?" A short time later, he turned again and winked at Pete. "Well, I guess we can go to the counter now."

"If Rona told you to go there, why did you waste time touring the store?"

"Hey, I'm my own man. I don't like to be told where to go, especially when it comes to getting a gift for my girl."

Harry peered in the glass case at the array of jewelry. Two sales ladies came over to help him. He explained his mission and they started pulling out items and laying them on the counter. Pearl earrings and necklaces and bracelets and pins. For a man who professed to dislike shopping, Harry seemed to be thoroughly enjoying himself. He discussed individual pieces with the sales ladies and compared prices.

He spotted three women examining the same silver trays he'd just looked at and called them over. "What do you think, ladies?" They crowded around and admired the pieces laid out on the counter. One member of the group — a tall woman with reddish hair and a body shape remarkably similar to Rona's — became Harry's personal model. He held earrings up to her ears, fumbled with the clasps on bracelets as he fit them around her wrist, and admired the necklaces he draped around her neck. She giggled like a school girl as he tried to pin a fancy brooch on her tee shirt just above her left breast. Harry backed off after his first try. "I don't want to stick you," he said with an impish grin, then tried again. Pete had the feeling that if Rona were here, she would have dragged him out of the store by his ear.

Pete nudged Harry and said, "That's nice." He pointed to a bracelet that was still in the case. One of the sales ladies pulled it out and laid it on the counter. It was silver with a double row of blue stones.

"That *is* nice," Harry agreed. He picked it up and peered at the tag over his half-glasses. "Blue topaz," he read. "From Peru. Let me have your wrist, darling," he said to his model. She giggled again while he fumbled with the clasp. Finally she took over and hooked the bracelet. She held out her arm. Harry took her hand and looked at the bracelet adoringly.

"Ooooh," the other women cooed in unison. "That's the one!"

Harry continued to hold his model's hand and stared at the bracelet for a long time. He looked up at her, and as if he hadn't heard the other women. "Nice, huh?"

"Oh, yes," the model gushed.

"Do you have gift wrapping?" Harry asked a sales lady. They did, and Harry chatted with his new female friends while one sales lady rang up the sale and the other wrapped the bracelet.

They said their goodbyes and left. "Rona is going to love this," Harry said, holding up the gift-wrapped package. He looked at Pete and said in an earnest voice, "You know, I was looking at that bracelet all along.

That was the first thing that caught my eye when we went up to the counter."

Pete rolled his eyes and said, "You're a man of taste."

Rona's Bay Grille was closed for a private party so they stopped at a restaurant down the street. They were seated outside at a table looking out at the bay. Pete ordered iced tea; he needed a day without Thor's Hammer.

Harry looked at his tall glass and frowned. "I think I'll have the same," he said. "Rona and I have a big night planned for tomorrow, and I want to be in good shape." He got a faraway look in his eyes. "Boy," he repeated, "Rona's going to love that bracelet."

Pete smiled. "Okay, lover boy. Tell me what you hear from the sheriff's office."

Harry frowned again. "Richter has issued strict orders to his deputies not to talk to the media. He's frozen out Cap completely. Cap has to get all of his information from another deputy who can't stand Richter either. He still feeds me stuff, but I have to meet him over by Thompsonville or some other out-of-the-way place because he's scared to death of being seen with me."

Pete waited for him to continue.

"Anyway, I found out Richter is questioning everyone in town, but I guess he's focusing on the two obvious suspects."

"John Hicks and Leonard Wolf?"

"Right."

"Does that mean Susan Brimley is off his list?"

"I'm not sure she was really on it. Richter's a by-the-book guy, as you know, and the common wisdom is that family members are automatically suspects in these kinds of cases. I'm sure that's why he interviewed her."

"That's the way I saw it," Pete said.

"I'm surprised you went with her to the interview. It sucks you more into the case, doesn't it?"

"Maybe I shouldn't have gone, but she called me in a tizzy so I relented. It worked out okay. Anyway, it shouldn't involve me further because we agreed it would be a one-time exception to what's in our engagement letter, and if she's not under suspicion, I can't be involved."

"Mmm," Harry murmured.

"What's Richter doing with Hicks and Wolf?" Pete asked.

"According to Cap, he's searched both of their vehicles. I guess he's using some of the state forensic guys. He thinks throwing them a bone and using them for technical stuff will keep them out of his hair." Harry added, "He doesn't have a choice anyway. He doesn't have the resources to do things like that himself."

"I take it they're looking for evidence Brimley's body was in one of their vehicles."

"That's obvious."

"I assume the search results haven't come back yet?"

"Not that I've heard."

"Both of those guys seem too obvious," Pete said.

"I agree. As I told you before, I know John Hicks. I interviewed him many times when the controversy over the golf course was going hot and heavy. He never struck me as a murderer. Passionate as hell about the environment and animal rights, granted, but not a murderer."

"Richter knows about his threats against Brimley," Pete said. "That came out the day I was in with Susan."

"Hell, half the town heard their exchange at the meeting that night. That doesn't mean he killed Brimley. He's just a bit of a hothead."

"What about the charges against him out West?"

"I don't know the details, but I've heard it was stuff like arson and spiking trees to deter loggers."

"That's typical of those people," Pete said, "but a guy like Richter doesn't split hairs. I'm sure violence is violence to him."

"You're probably right."

"I assume Hicks and Wolf don't have alibis," Pete said.

"Nothing they can substantiate, I understand. Both guys claim they were home all night the night Brimley was killed. Both of them live alone so I guess neither has anyone to vouch for him."

"How about Wolf? What do you know about him?"

"Just what we've talked about. Lived around here all of his life. Took his Indian name some years back. Quiet man. Was opposed to Brimley's project because, to him, it desecrated land that had cultural meaning for him and his followers. Not as overtly strident as Hicks, but I think he felt just as strongly about his position."

"Do you think he was capable of killing Brimley?"

Harry's eyes took on a faraway look. "Who knows," he said slowly. "Those quiet types often can be the most dangerous. Oh, here's something I forgot to tell you and it involves Wolf. Apparently someone saw him sitting on top of that big rock overlooking the seventeenth hole at Mystic Bluffs. I think it was the week after Brimley was killed. I guess he was just sitting there for hours on end. Richter found out about that and I guess grilled him royally. A guy I know compared Wolf to a grizzly going back to the scene of a kill. That's a little unfair, but it shows the way people are thinking."

"Is Richter close to arresting someone?" Pete asked.

"No idea. I only get information from Cap and he doesn't know everything."

They called it a night. Harry's parting words were, "Rona is going to love that bracelet."

FOURTEEN

Pete kept his eyes riveted on the drawstring of Bud's shorts. He was in the classic athletic stance with knees flexed and feet apart, ready to slide in either direction. With his peripheral vision, he saw Bud fake with the ball, then fake again. Pete held his position and didn't go for the fakes. "Stay down," he told himself, "stay down." Bud did a quarter pivot and started dribbling. Pete slid over to stay between him and the basket. Suddenly Bud rose to execute a jump hook. Pete came out of his stance and jumped straight up in an effort to block the shot, but fell short. He spun around to face the basket, arms outstretched to block out Bud. The ball rattled off the rim and Pete grabbed it as it came down.

"Foul!" Pete called as Bud reached over his back for the ball.

"Bull!" Bud said with a snarl. "That was no foul! I barely touched you!"

"You were laying on my back, for crissakes!"

Bud waved a hand disgustedly, and Pete took the ball into the backcourt and started dribbling toward the basket. Bud cut him off at the fifteen-foot mark and swiped at the ball. Pete picked up his dribble to retain possession and jab-stepped with his left foot. When Bud didn't go for it, he jab-stepped again and then stepped back and let his jumper go. Bud swatted the ball back at him and it whizzed past his head.

Pete turned and saw the ball lying on the grass, off the court. He looked at Bud and said, "Jesus, you mad or something?"

"You called that ticky-tack foul on me."

Pete scowled at him. He'd witnessed that competitive streak many times before. It was one of the reasons the Boston Celtics made him a number one draft pick. Then he tore up his knee in his rookie season and went into investment banking with the firm of Harrison Stryker. Pete wasn't remotely in Bud's class as a basketball player, but enjoyed playing with him. He, too, had a competitive streak and Bud brought out the best in him.

"Let's call it a draw," Bud said. "My knees are killing me."

Two high school-age boys were standing nearby, waiting for the court. One kept dribbling his ball between his legs, periodically making a hard dribble and letting the ball roll over his shoulder and down his back. Then he would repeat the routine. Pete watched him and knew he couldn't do that even in his high school playing days.

"You guys want a game?" the boy asked, smacking his gum and still going through his Harlem Globetrotters routine.

"Not today, boys."

"We'll spot you ten points," the ball hotshot said.

Ten points was a lot. Pete and Bud looked at each other. "Sorry," Pete said.

"We're out here just about every day. You want to play sometime, let us know."

Bud waved goodbye as they left the court.

When they were out of earshot, Bud said to Pete in a low voice, "Cocky little brats. We should play them sometime and stuff their butts."

Pete watched Bud turn the steaks and press his tongs against one to test it. As he watched, Pete asked, "Did you know Les Brimley?"

"Oh sure. He used to join my group for pick-up games all the time. A constant whiner on the court. Always complaining about fouls if you got within six feet of him." He looked up from his cooking chores and grinned slyly and said, "Not at all like you. You only complain if I get within three feet of you. But Brimley, he had his own rules for everything. He'd pick up his dribble and take five or six steps before he went up for a shot. Same way with golf. He's the only guy I knew who could hit his slice into the trees, then magically find his ball on the edge of the fairway. Do you know how he'd explain that? Said the ball must have hit a tree and bounced out." Bud grunted and shook his head.

Pete laughed. "I guess he was a savvy businessman, though. And a real benefactor around town."

Bud tested the steaks again and gave Pete "that look." The one that said Pete must be the dumbest guy to come down the pike in a long time.

"You must have been listening to those eulogies in church that day. Christ, when I heard some of that stuff, I wanted to puke. Benefactor. You know when he started to get involved with projects in town? When he bought Jim Underhill's property. He knew the project he had planned would be controversial and wanted to play good guy and get the town behind him."

"That's standard for developers, isn't it?"

"Maybe. I guess my views were colored by the fact I just didn't like the guy." He gave Pete another sly look. "Maybe he had too much Chicago in him."

"Hey, you're not offending me. I'm a country boy from the wilds of Wisconsin, remember?"

They sat down to eat. Bud had prepared a salad earlier, and it would have been a meal in itself.

"Getting back to Brimley for just a minute," Pete said between bites of his steak, "have you ever heard of a commercial finance company named Nautical?"

Bud appeared to be thinking. "No," he said after a while, "I don't think so. Why do you ask?"

"In case you haven't heard, Brimley's widow hired me as her personal attorney to look into the estate's financial matters. I'm trying to piece things together. Brimley's company up here was LB Development. His lenders included a bunch of Chicago banks plus a commercial finance company named Nautical. I'm doing my due diligence. Brimley had a lot of debt on Mystic Bluffs and the story is the project was in trouble financially."

"In a small town like this, how could I not hear about Susan Brimley hiring you? But no, I never heard of Nautical. No one should be surprised that Brimley's project was having problems, though. He didn't know crap about building a golf complex. That place was just going to be an edifice to his ego."

"What makes you say that? He was a developer, and a fairly successful one I understand."

"There are developers," Bud replied, "and there are developers of golf course properties. The two aren't the same. When I was with Harrison Stryker, we had a couple of clients who were in the golf course development business. Brimley couldn't have gotten a job as a hod carrier for one of them."

Pete smiled at the reference. A hod carrier was a guy who did the grunt work for a bricklayer. Well, there clearly was at least one guy in town who wasn't a Brimley fan.

"I'm not involved in the case," Pete said, "but I guess there are all kinds of rumors around town about who might have killed Brimley. Any favorites on your list?"

Bud grunted again. "Line people up and take your pick. He made more than his share of enemies up here. I assume the same was true in Chicago. Matter of fact, I heard he got his start by screwing his old partner out of their real estate company down there. Then there are the obvious suspects. That Hicks guy and that Indian — what's his name, Wolf? I hear that genius of a sheriff of ours is looking their way, but I bet it was someone else."

"What makes you say that?"

"Just a hunch. One of them would have to be pretty dumb to kill Brimley in his back yard. Better to do it in Chicago where crime doesn't attract so much attention."

Pete had thought of the same thing several times. He thanked Bud for dinner and then drove home. The light was fading fast and the sky over the lake was rosy. The stars were faintly visible in the sky. In Chicago, the haze from pollution would have obscured everything. It was one of the compensating advantages of moving north. Kind of getting back to his roots now that he'd made his mark in the world.

When he walked in, his phone was ringing. He picked up the receiver. An unknown number according to his Caller ID. He was tempted to ignore the call, but decided to answer.

"Mr. Thorsen?" a deep, throaty voice asked.

He didn't recognize the voice. "Yes," he said, "this is Pete Thorsen. Who's calling, please?"

"A friend, Mr. Thorsen. I hear you've been giving a certain person some bad advice."

FIFTEEN

Pete was puzzled, but the call was so strange, he decided to play along. "And to whom am I supposed to have given this bad advice, *friend?*"

"Now, now, don't be touchy, Mr. Thorsen. I'm calling friendly-like, as I said."

Pete was beginning to get annoyed, but held his temper and said, "Okay, let me ask this another way. Does this person who allegedly got this bad advice from me have a name?"

He heard a throaty chuckle. Like a gargle. "I love that word. Allegedly. I'll have to start using it more myself. Allegedly. That has a nice sound to it. Allegedly."

"So you're not going to tell me who this person is?"

"This person don't want to be identified. It's *confidential.* That's another word I like. You attorney-at-laws guys think you're the only ones who can claim confidentiality?"

Pete let the bad grammar go. For the past few minutes, he had the feeling he was talking to Vincent Zahn and Zahn was referring to advice he'd given Susan Brimley. Well, maybe not Zahn personally;

but one of his henchmen. A guy like Zahn was savvy enough to leave his dirty work to underlings.

"Okay, Mr. Zahn," Pete said, taking a stab at it. "Let's stop playing games. What do you want?"

"Mr. Zahn. Is that what you said?" The voice sounded quizzical.

"That's what this all about, isn't it? Mr. Zahn and my client, Susan Brimley?"

"Zahn. Susan Brimley. You keep saying these names I never heard before, Mr. Thorsen. I was just calling about this advice you allegedly gave to a person that this person allegedly don't owe her legitimate debts. You notice how that word *allegedly* has already become part of my regular vocabulary?" His chuckled again with a gargling sound.

Pete was getting tired of the games. "Sure, you've never heard the names Zahn or Susan Brimley before. Alright, Mr. Zahn, I'm going to hang up now. This conversation is going nowhere."

"I'm sorry you feel this conversation ain't going nowhere, Mr. Thorsen. Do you mind if I call you Pete, by the way? As I said, I wish you'd think about your advice that this person don't owe his — or her — legitimate debts. You have such a nice life up there on that lake. A nice little cabin. I've seen it, by the way. Small, but really nice. And that pretty dark haired daughter at that tony — that's another word I just love, tony — private school near Detroit."

His gut felt icy at the reference to Julie. *What the hell was going on?*

"Sort of the all-American family," the voice continued. "Oh, I almost forgot," the voice said. "Just a minute, please." There was a brief silence and then he heard the Lady Gaga tune Julie had programmed into her cell phone as the ring tone.

Pete froze for a moment, then screamed, "Where did you get my daughter's cell phone?" There was no reply and no sound. He hit redial. Nothing.

He stared at the phone. Then he hastily dialed Julie's dorm room. The phone rang and rang. Come on, Julie, *answer! Answer the damn phone!* He ended the call and quickly dialed Julie's cell. All he got was a recording that Julie couldn't come to the phone and the caller should leave a message after the beep. He just stood there a while, then he flung the phone across the room. "You sonofabitch!!" he screamed. "You sonofabitch!!"

He debated what to do, feeling helpless. Then he grabbed his keys from the counter and ran outside and jumped into his car. He spun wood chips all the way out the driveway and swerved onto the highway without pausing to look for traffic.

Pete ignored the no-parking signs and braked to a stop in front of Julie's dorm. He bounded up the steps three at a time and tried the front door. Locked! He leaned on the doorbell with one hand and pounded with the other.

"Open up!" he called, "open up!" He pounded some more, harder this time. Finally, through a side-panel, he could see an inside light go on. He continued to pound. An older woman in a robe came into view. He pounded some more and continued to press the doorbell.

The outside light went on. The door didn't open, but he saw the woman peer out the side panel. Then her voice came over the intercom. "What is it, sir? You'll wake the girls."

"Let me in please! I have to see my daughter!"

"Calm down, sir. What's your daughter's name?"

"Julie! Her room is on the second floor!"

"Please, sir. You'll wake everyone up. Your daughter's not here, sir, but she's okay. Go to the campus police station and they'll explain everything."

"The police station? What happened?"

"Please, sir, go to the police station. And don't worry. Your daughter's okay."

"Where's the station?" he asked, feeling disoriented. "I don't know where it is."

"Down the street and turn left. You can't miss it."

Pete raced down the steps without thanking her, jumped in his Range Rover, accelerated down the street, and hung a left. The house-mother was right; he couldn't miss the station. It was the only building with lights on.

He headed for the door and for the first time, was conscious of the fact he still had on his athletic clothes. He tucked in his tee shirt, ran a hand through his hair, and walked in, trying to appear as calm as possible. A middle-aged officer in a tan uniform was seated behind the desk tapping on a computer keyboard. He looked up when Pete walked in.

The officer seemed surprised by Pete's appearance. After studying him for a moment, he asked, "Can I help you, sir?"

"Yes," Pete said, trying to sound calm, "I was told you have my daughter."

"What's your name, sir?"

"Pete Thorsen. My daughter's name is Julie."

"Could I see some ID, please?"

Pete fished out his driver's license and handed it to him.

The officer looked at it, glanced up at Pete, and looked at the license again. Then he handed the license back to Pete.

"This evening, your daughter and another student say they were followed by two men. They ran into their dorm and called us. Three of our officers went right over, but there was no sign of the men. Your daughter is staying with her friend for the night. I have one of our men standing guard in the dorm lobby just in case."

"Why wasn't I notified?" Pete asked.

The officer looked at him. "Do you have any idea of how many reports we get of suspicious looking characters on campus? A lot. We investigate every one of them. Most prove unfounded."

"That's no reason not to call."

"Mr. Thorsen, if we called the parents every time we get one of these reports, the place would be in a continual uproar. We investigated the report that your daughter and this other girl turned in, and determined that there were indeed two men lurking around campus. We alerted the local police, and as a precaution, Julie is staying with her friend, as I said. We were going to call you in the morning."

Pete nodded and said, "I'd like to see my daughter."

The officer glanced at the clock on the wall and said, "Sir, do you know what time it is?"

"I don't care what time it is. I want to see my daughter."

The officer gave him a disbelieving look and then reached for the telephone. He spoke in a low voice to the person at the other end of the line and then hung up.

"Okay, sir. Julie is in the dorm next door to hers." He gave Pete the number. "The man we have camped out in the lobby is expecting you. Go over and he'll arrange for you to see your daughter. I can't go with you because I'm all alone here."

As Pete walked out, he noticed the officer shake his head. Easy for him to act unconcerned, he thought, it wasn't his daughter. Pete retraced his route and pulled up in front of the neighboring dorm. It was a clone of the one Julie lived in. The outside lights were on; the lights in Julie's dorm were now off.

The officer in the lobby opened the door as Pete approached. He introduced himself and led Pete into a small waiting room off the dorm lobby. Judging from the stack of magazines, open Coke cans, and half-empty bags of chips, the officer had been hunkered down for the night when his colleague called.

"Just a minute," he said, "I'll call the girls' room." He dialed, then waited a minute or two and finally said, "Julie's dad is here. Can I bring him up?" After a pause, he said, "I know." He listened some more and then said, "I know" again. He hung up and said to Pete, "They told me it's okay. C'mon, I'll take you down."

Pete followed the officer down the hall and waited as he knocked on a door. When it opened, Julie rushed out and gave Pete a hug. "Dad, I didn't know you were coming." She clutched the robe around her and stared at him, just as surprised by his appearance as others had been. "But do you know what time it is?" she asked.

He feigned a sheepish grin. "I do now. But not when I came over. I had a workout at the motel," he lied. "I know you're a night owl so I tried to call you. There was no answer at either number. I got concerned and came over."

She looked at him again. "I'm glad it was something like that." She wrinkled her nose. "You should burn those clothes."

The young officer interrupted them. "Could we all step into your room so we don't wake the others?"

When they were out of the hall, Julie said, "Dad, you know Mikki." She looked at her sleepy-eyed friend huddled under a blanket. "He doesn't always show up unannounced at 3:00 a.m."

Mikki giggled.

"Dad, you never did tell me why you're here. You could have called."

"This just came up," he lied again. "I have a meeting in Detroit tomorrow morning and had to do some work. I was late leaving the lake."

She looked at him sympathetically. "For an old retired guy, you're awfully busy. Well, let me tell you why I had to stay with Mikki tonight."

He waited for her explanation.

"Mikki and I were walking back from the library. We were walking along talking and we noticed these two strange men behind us. Real creepy looking guys. We thought they could be stalkers, or maybe even rapists. They always tell us if we see anyone like that, don't stop to talk. Just get out of there and call the police.

"We started walking faster and they started walking faster, too. One of the men — the creepiest one — said something to us. I thought he called my name. That really freaked us out. We started running and were lucky that Mikki's dorm was right there. Mikki grabbed me by the arm and pulled me into her dorm. We ran down to her room, locked the door, and called the police." Julie looked at Mikki and said, "You saved me."

Mikki was obviously embarrassed and said, "I didn't *save* you."

"You did too. You're a hero."

"Some hero," Mikki mumbled, growing more uncomfortable by the second. "All I did was cause you to lose your cell phone."

Julie giggled. "It dropped out of my purse when we ran. I'm going to need a new phone before I go to California, Dad."

"Did you look for your phone?" Pete asked. He suspected he knew the answer and now understood how the anonymous caller was able to play her ring tone back to him at the end of their conversation.

"Sam and those other officers who work for him came over as soon as we called and looked for my phone, but it was gone."

"The other officers don't work for me," Sam corrected her, sounding embarrassed. "One of them is my boss."

Julie looked at him with adoring eyes and said, "Well, you should be the boss of *him*." She turned to Pete and added, "Sam's a hero, too. We feel so safe with him around."

Sam blushed.

Pete suppressed a grin. Julie could be so grown up at times, and on other occasions, she exhibited all the exuberance of a typical teenager. It was one of her many endearing qualities.

"Well, I'd better let you girls get some sleep," Pete said. "I'm glad you're okay, and sorry to barge in on you in the middle of the night."

"Dad, I'm going to be staying with Mikki until we leave for California. I'll let you know my new cell phone number."

"When do you leave?"

"Saturday. We finish exams on Friday. Mikki invited me to go with her family to Disneyland. I'll be out there a few extra days. It's okay, isn't it?"

"Sure, no problem, as you like to say." She didn't know how much the thought of her getting away from campus comforted him in view of what had just happened.

He turned to Sam and said, "You're going to watch out for them until Saturday?"

Sam nodded. "You have to get the details from the duty officer. But either me or another one of our officers will be keeping an eye on them at all times."

"Isn't he wonderful, Dad?"

Sam blushed again. With the whole campus police force reporting to him, Pete had the feeling the girls would be in good hands.

He gave Julie an unusually long hug and fought back the tears that were beginning to well up in his eyes. "And get your new cell phone and let me know the number so we can stay in touch."

Sam, the force's new take-charge guy, piped up and said, "I know where the AT&T store is. I'll personally take them down tomorrow. Excuse me, today." Pete noticed his chest was sticking out a little more than when he came in.

When Pete walked into the station for the second time, the duty officer didn't look thrilled to see him again. He told Pete of the plan to keep an eye on the girls just in case the two men showed up again. Sam or one of his colleagues would also camp out in the dorm lobby every night just to be on the safe side. It was essentially the same as what Sam had told him. Pete thought about telling the duty officer about the phone call that had spooked him so badly, but thought better of it. They already had a plan in place, and his story would only complicate things.

As Pete drove to the motel he'd stayed at before, he thought about what the duty officer had told him about the reason for not calling earlier, and concluded it made sense. If he hadn't received the anonymous call, and the campus police had called saying someone was stalking his daughter, he would have been worried sick anyway. Maybe he still would have jumped in his car and headed for Bloomfield Hills. Much better to handle it professionally as the police had done.

He checked into the motel and had to endure more quizzical stares from the night clerk. He wasn't used to checking in without luggage at 3:30 a.m. looking like a street bum. He finally got his key and found his room. He locked the door and peeled off his shorts and tee shirt.

After he got out of the shower, he couldn't stand the thought of putting on his smelly athletic clothes again, so he rinsed them out and climbed into bed naked.

He lay there in the darkness, thinking about what he had to do when he got back to the lake. He dozed off, but the blood-streaked walls appeared again. He clicked on the lamp by his bed and moved it to a table in the corner. He squeezed his eyes shut against the light and tried to sleep.

SIXTEEN

When Pete called Rona Martin to wish her happy birthday, he was hoping she would know where Susan Brimley was. He'd been trying to call Susan since he returned from Bloomfield Hills and had gotten no answer either on her landline or her cell.

"Hello, Pete," Rona said, "You forgot about my birthday and now you're calling to make amends, right?"

"Something like that," Pete replied. "I had to make a quick trip to Detroit and missed the big day. Happy belated birthday, doll." As soon as he said it, he realized how appropriate his gangster dialect was.

"Thank you, dear. And no excuses required."

He wanted to blame his tardiness on the woman Rona had referred to him, but just said, "The Big Guy come through with the goods?"

She laughed. "The Big Guy came through with some very nice goods. Or should I say the Big Guys?"

"Hey, I just tagged along. Harry did the shopping."

"Uh huh," she said sarcastically. "I guess I'm finally getting him trained, huh? He actually took my suggestion."

"After a little meandering through the store," Pete said. "You like the bracelet?"

"It's beautiful. Thanks for — what's the expression? — tagging along with him."

"I can't think of a more deserving woman. Say, do you know where Susan Brimley is? I've been trying to reach her."

"I'm almost positive she's in the Upper Peninsula doing research for her shipwreck paintings. Did you try her cell number?"

"Yes," he said, "but there was no signal. Maybe she's in a dead zone or something. Well, I'll let you go. I'm glad you liked the Big Guy's offering."

"Just a minute, Pete. The Big Guy wants a word with you."

Harry got on the phone, and after chiding him for flirting with his girl, said, "I don't know whether you've heard, but Richter arrested John Hicks this morning."

"I hadn't heard."

"Yeah. I called Cap and he had to call me back when he was away from the office so he could speak freely. I guess the forensics people found evidence that Brimley's body was in the back of Hicks' vehicle. Then Hicks called me. I was his phone call. He sounded panicked and asked if I could get you to represent him."

Pete groaned. "You didn't."

"Now don't get your tail in an uproar," Harry said. "I told him you're a corporate lawyer, but you might know someone who could help him."

"I'm corporate lawyer who's already got one client mixed up in this mess."

Harry ignored his comment and said, "Anyone come to mind that we could get for Hicks?"

Pete thought for a few moments. "I'm sure there are competent criminal lawyers in Traverse City or Grand Rapids. Both places are close by. I don't have any names, though. I know a few guys in Chicago."

"This is a serious case. Maybe we should bring in one of the heavyweights from our old stomping grounds."

"Maybe, if we can get one of them," Pete said. "When's the arraignment?"

"All I know is what I just told you."

"And you said they found evidence that Brimley's body was in Hicks' vehicle? What did they find — hair, fibers, that sort of thing?" He might not be a criminal lawyer, but he knew what they were looking for when they searched his Range Rover the previous summer.

"I guess," Harry said. "I really don't know."

"What did Hicks say when you talked to him?"

"Claimed he's innocent. Said he was being set up. He denied that Les Brimley was ever *near* his vehicle."

"Set up," Pete said. "By whom?"

"You keep asking questions I have no answer for."

"Didn't you ask him?"

"Well, yeah," Harry said, "but it's kind of awkward when you're talking to a guy who's just been charged with murder. He mumbled something about that Indian guy or other people in the area who had it in for Brimley and were trying to deflect blame from themselves."

Pete thought about it for a moment. "Let me make a few calls," he said.

"Can you do it right away? Hicks was really spooked. For a guy who has a reputation as an eco-terrorist and has been arrested seven times …" His voice trailed off.

"I'll get right on it."

Pete sat there after he got off the phone and thought about the criminal lawyers he knew in Chicago. Then he dialed Ira Manning's number and waited for someone to pick up. It was not usual for one of the busiest and most successful defense lawyers in Chicago to answer his own telephone, on the second ring no less, but he'd hit upon a true anomaly.

"Ira Manning here," the voice boomed.

Someone who hadn't met Manning but heard his voice on the phone might have a mental image of a strapping six-four bundle of energy with a big gut who went around slapping people on the back and doing damage to their eardrums. They would have been right. Many of Ira's friends and colleagues preferred to communicate with him by e-mail out of concern for hearing loss. He knew loud, louder, and loudest, with one conspicuous exception. When he was in court, he purred to the judge or jury like a Cheshire with its belly full of warm cream.

"Ira," Pete said, "it's Pete Thorsen."

"Mr. Norske!" Ira boomed again after a moment's pause. "How the hell are you? You must be planning an invasion of Wilmette with your Viking friends and are calling to alert me so I can get my family out, right?"

Pete laughed. "No invasion planned," he said. "Tell your neighbors they're safe for another year."

"My friends will be relieved that they don't have to stay home to protect their women. Jeez, I wish I'd been in your office on some of those Columbus Days when you hung that Norwegian flag outside your office to torment your dago partners." He paused for a moment. "I guess I can't say dago anymore. I'm politically correct now. I meant to say those Italian-American partners." He let loose with another sonic laugh.

"If Angie heard you talk like that, she'd come over and cut your heart out."

"Aw, not Angie. She's in love with me. I ever tell you that?"

"Only fifty times. Say, I've got a case for you if you want it."

"What's the case, Mr. Norske? Someone steal a batch of Coho in that metropolitan area where you now live?"

When he was finished laughing again, Pete said, "Not exactly," He proceeded to tell Ira about Les Brimley's murder and John Hicks' arrest for the crime. Ira interrupted once or twice to ask pertinent questions, but mostly just listened quietly.

"I guess that's not just a mess of Coho," Ira said, using his courtroom voice. Then he asked pointedly, "This guy Hicks, he got any money?"

"Not much, I'm afraid. You'd have to work at — how do we say — a reduced rate."

There was a rare silence on the other end. Then Manning asked, "You suppose this case is going to get much pub?"

"I do. It's already been in most of the regional papers and all of the tabloids. I expect it to get a lot of publicity nationwide."

"Well," he boomed, "you caught me on the right day. I just got the rest of my fee from Stella Lord — a half million and change." He dialed down his voice an octave or two and brought Pete into his confidence. "You know, I got that woman off on a murder rap and then she dragged her fanny over paying the rest of my fee. I had her in the office last week, and when we were alone, you know what I said to her? I said, 'Stella, I want the rest of my fee on my desk by next Tuesday, or maybe we'll find out who really killed ol' Jake Lord.' She had to hock part of her jewelry collection, but she came up with the scratch. Shoot, she's got more rocks than the Queen of England." His booming laugh was back.

The case he was referring to was front-page material even in a city used to high profile crimes. Stella Lord was accused of killing her husband, Jake, with a pearl-handled antique letter opener. It looked like a lock case for the prosecution, but by the time Ira Manning was finished, he'd convinced the jury that Jake had been done in by his jilted homosexual lover. Stella showed up in court every day in drab, high-collared dresses with doilies around the neck. The day after she was acquitted, she went back to tops that showed more cleavage than Dolly Parton.

"Well," Pete said, "you're going to have to pull another rabbit out of the hat to get John Hicks off. It looks like a tough case. From what I can tell, sentiment is running high locally to nail someone for the crime and Hicks is in the dock right now."

"So who's the State's Attorney or whatever you call them up there?"

Pete gave him the information. "One more thing," he added. "You'll either have to drive — it's three hundred miles — or you can fly into Traverse City and someone will pick you up."

Ira was obviously digesting his choices. "You mean you're not going to send your fleet of longboats for me?" His booming laugh was still ringing in Pete's ears five minutes after he hung up the phone.

He called Harry and left a message that he'd been successful in lining up Ira Manning to represent Hicks. Then he wondered, again, what motive Susan Brimley would have to lie to him.

SEVENTEEN

When Harry called back, he urged Pete to do one more thing — tell Frank Richter about Brimley's apparent involvement with the mob. His rationale was that widening the investigation could only benefit Hicks. Pete balked, saying he didn't want to become more involved in the case and, in any event, Richter wasn't likely to listen to him given the animosity they had for each other. But when Ira Manning also indicated interest in bringing the mob connection to Richter's attention, Pete relented. He couldn't very well deny Manning a favor after talking him into defending Hicks on essentially a *pro bono* basis.

He stared at the phone a few minutes, then grimaced and dialed the sheriff's office. He asked for Richter and was told the sheriff was out of town. Pete shook his head. He was already following in the footsteps of his old boss, Bill Haskins, who was notorious for his out-of-town junkets. On a whim, he then asked for Detective Tessler. To his surprise, he was put through to him.

Pete could tell Joe Tessler was on guard at first. After all, here was the office's leading antagonist calling with important information for them. Tessler pointed out that they already had Brimley's killer. It was a lock case, he said confidently. Why would they want to go off on a wild goose chase against the Chicago mob? As they talked, though, Pete sensed that Tessler was weighing the possibility that the office could have egg on its face if the Hicks case went south and they hadn't followed up on all suspects. He agreed to meet with Pete that afternoon.

Unlike his previous visits to the County Government Center, Pete wasn't kept waiting. In fact, Tessler came to the reception area personally and escorted him back to one of the interview rooms. The reed-thin detective closed the door and took a seat across the table from Pete. His longish black hair swept across his forehead like a raven's wing and Tessler had a habit of brushing it to the side to keep it out of his eyes. As Pete looked at him more closely, he seemed older than he realized. Maybe that's what working for Richter did to a man.

"I agreed to meet with you, Mr. Thorsen, but that doesn't mean I've bought into your story."

"I didn't expect you to," Pete replied. "All I ask is that you hear me out. Then it's up to you and the sheriff what you do with the information."

Tessler steepled his hands and said, "I'm listening."

"I have a couple of preliminary comments," Pete said. "Actually, one comment and one question. My comment is to stress that I haven't been investigating this case on my own. I came across the information I'm about to tell you solely as a result of my civil work for the victim's widow. But before I get into that, I'd appreciate it if you'd tell me what you've got on Hicks."

A smile crossed Tessler's face. "Now let me understand this. You call and tell me you have important information about the Brimley murder. I agree to meet with you. Then the first thing you do is try to pump me about what we have on the suspect we arrested. You're a lawyer, so you must know what 'fishing expedition' means."

Pete had a reason for starting the meeting the way he had. By getting Tessler to summarize the case against Hicks, he hoped that he would see the weaknesses and be more receptive to checking out the allegations he was about to make about the mob.

"Alright," Pete said, "let me take five minutes and tell you what the scuttlebutt is around town and you can tell me whether it's true or not. Deal?"

Tessler just shrugged and didn't comment.

"First off," Pete continued, "everybody knows that Hick was the most vocal opponent of the Mystic Bluffs project. At meetings, he often had words with Brimley."

Tessler's only response was to say, "Not only words. Hicks was heard to threaten him, too. We said that at the interview with Mrs. Brimley, remember?"

"Okay, he threatened Brimley before witnesses. Hicks has no alibi for the night Brimley was murdered."

Tessler continued to sit there and look at him.

"You claim to have trace evidence that Brimley's body was in Hicks' vehicle."

Still no reaction from Tessler.

"After that," Pete continued, "things becomes a lot less clear. I understand you found no fingerprints on the golf club."

Now Tessler interrupted and said, "What kind of idiot would leave his prints all over that golf club? Plus, in case you don't know it, Hicks was an eco-terrorist out West for two decades. Don't you think he would have learned how to cover his tracks?"

"Maybe. But you have no prints on the murder weapon. No DNA evidence, either, I understand. In fact, Hicks claims that the few hairs you did find in his vehicle were planted."

Tessler smiled. "What would you expect him to say?"

"Maybe nothing, but Ira Manning is going to rip your case to pieces on all of these points. If you don't have trace evidence, you don't have anything. No witnesses. No prints. Everything is circumstantial."

"Who's Ira Manning?"

"He's one of the best criminal lawyers in Chicago. I understand Hicks has hired him to represent him. Manning just got a woman off on charges of killing her husband in a case the prosecution thought was a lock, too."

Tessler looked uncomfortable. He said, "I thought you wanted to tell me about the mob's involvement with Brimley. So far, all you've done is rehash rumors about our case."

"Fair enough," Pete said, "First of all, you're aware of all the stories about Brimley's Mystic Bluffs project being in financial trouble, I'm sure."

Tessler waved a hand again and said, "Everyone's heard that."

"Well, what everyone has heard is true. Did you know that Brimley went to the Chicago mob because he was desperate for money to complete the project? Two million bucks, plus another million in what's commonly called 'juice?'"

Tessler's eyes narrowed and he leaned forward in his chair. "You discovered that from Brimley's records?"

"Brimley's records and other sources. I can't tell you more because I'm bound by a duty of confidentiality, but you can count on it. It's true."

Tessler looked at him suspiciously. "You have any specifics to back up your charge?"

"Yes, I do. I have reason to believe that the lender, if you want to call it that, was a commercial finance company in Chicago named Nautical Finance. Nautical is run by a guy named Vincent Zahn. Do you know who he is?"

Tessler looked like he was back in control again. "Sure I know who Zahn is. I spent four years with Chicago PD before I moved back up here."

"Zahn's a high-ranking member of the Chicago mob. Right?"

Tessler said nothing, but it was obvious he knew about Zahn.

"You starting to get the picture?" Pete asked. "So, Brimley had a lot of people who might have had a motive to kill him, including the mob. I don't know exactly what happened. That's up to you and the sheriff to figure out. But maybe — just maybe — Brimley welshed on his obligations to Zahn or was late with his payments or committed some other transgression the mob wouldn't tolerate. Maybe Zahn had him killed and set up a convenient and obvious target — John Hicks — to take the fall."

"Your whole story is speculative. Anyway, what do you expect us to do with this so-called 'information?'"

"Check it out," Pete said. "I know you've got the state guys and maybe even the FBI crawling around and just itching for a bigger role in a high-profile case like this." He played his trump card again. "Think of what might happen if something goes sour with your case against Hicks and this information falls into their hands."

Tessler stared at Pete again. "I'll take it up with the sheriff when he returns and see what he wants to do. In the meantime, I'd appreciate it if you'd keep all of this quiet. That includes this meeting."

Pete walked out feeling pretty good. He'd done a favor for a couple of friends and Tessler had given him a better hearing than he expected. Now the wheels of justice could grind. He turned his cell phone back on and checked his messages. Susan Brimley had finally answered his calls. One final ugly confrontation, he thought. He put in calls to Harry and to Ira Manning to tell them about his meeting with Tessler. Both wanted to know whether Tessler seemed receptive to what he'd said and each time Pete said he had no idea. Then he called Susan Brimley and arranged to meet her at her house that evening.

EIGHTEEN

Pete went directly to his office and spent two hours finishing his written report to Susan Brimley. Armed with copies of the report, and with his inner anger re-stoked, he climbed into his Range Rover and headed for Susan Brimley's house. It was 7:00 p.m. when he pulled in and parked behind the silver Lexus LX he assumed was hers.

He'd never been to the Brimley house before. Three chimneys towered over the slate roof, and the house had more leaded glass windows than he cared to count. The stone and timber structure only looked old; he knew it had been built less than ten years earlier. He walked to the side of the building and was greeted by a landscaped lawn with trees. A wood-rail fence separated the lawn from the bluff that dropped off to the water below. In the distance, he could see two long ore boats, and up the coast, massive sand dunes that created a striking contrast with the blue-green lake. It was easy to see why Susan didn't want to part with this particular property.

She met him at the door and gave him a hug, like she was greeting an old friend. Her clothes weren't the attire of a working artist. She wore form-fitting white Capri pants with a French blue silk blouse. The top buttons were undone.

He followed her down the hall over hardwood floors partly covered by newish Oriental rugs. The study was about what he'd expected. More wood floors and Orientals. The walls had pecan paneling with built-in bookcases along one side. Susan's paintings covered the other walls. A large desk occupied one corner, but this was not a working room; it was a room for show and entertaining.

"I'm sorry I didn't get back to you sooner," Susan said, tossing her hair. "I was in the UP doing research for my shipwreck collection. And trying to get my thoughts together after everything that's happened in the past couple of weeks."

"I know," he said. "Rona told me."

"Would you like to see my sketches?"

He really wanted to get on with his mission, but said, "Sure."

She led him down the hall to a spacious studio with stark white walls and the same panoramic view of Lake Michigan he could see from the study. Susan busied herself arranging six easels into a semi-circle. On each was a charcoal sketch of an old-time sailing ship in some stage of distress. Each sketch was different. She stepped back and waited for his reaction. He studied the drawings. There was no question the woman had talent, something he already knew from the two pieces of hers that hung in his cottage. He said, "Very nice," and asked some polite questions about the drawings. She gave him a mini-tutorial on light and color and perspective.

When they returned to the study, he declined an offer of a drink even though he was tempted, and took a seat in one of the green leather chairs by the tall bay window looking out at the lake. He wanted his mind to be clear for what he had to do. This was not a social occasion.

Susan settled into a facing chair and set her glass of wine on the end table. "Is that your report?" Susan asked, pointing to the file next to him.

He nodded and pulled out the papers and handed one set to her. Then he summarized the numbers for her. He covered the acquisition of the Underhill property; the mortgage on the land; the two appraisals; and the construction loans. He included details like the names of lenders, amounts of the loans, and due dates. He told her of the applications for permanent financing. She studied the numbers intently, then looked up at him.

"There's nothing here about Nautical. Or about that person 'Z.' Does that mean you've concluded those aren't real loans?"

He just looked at her for a long time.

She seemed uncomfortable with the silence. "What's wrong?" she finally asked.

He continued to look at her and then said in a quiet voice, "Why did you lie to me, Susan?"

Her eyes suddenly looked wary and she seemed uncertain of what to say. "What do you mean?" she asked. There was a slight tremor in her voice.

"You knew all about that loan from Nautical Finance, didn't you? And that amount next to 'Z' on that handwritten sheet? 'Z' is a reference to Vincent Zahn, isn't it?"

She frowned and asked weakly, "Who's Vincent Zahn?"

"Oh, come on, Susan," he said, his voice rising. "You know who Vincent Zahn is. The Chicago mob boss your husband went crawling to because he couldn't borrow the money he needed from legitimate sources? You know what they call that extra million, Susan? Juice." He spelled the word for her. "That's what they squeeze out of people desperate enough to borrow from them. The additional consideration a guy like Zahn demands for the use of his money."

Susan nervously took another sip of her wine. Pete continued to bore in. "You knew all about this, Susan. Why didn't you tell me?"

"I didn't know," she replied. "I hired you to give me an honest report on my husband's finances."

He shook his head disgustedly. "You planned to use the advice I gave you to try to squirm out from under Les' obligations to the mob, didn't you? When those goons came to see you again, you gave them my name and said I told you the amounts were unenforceable, at least against you, isn't that right?" He was shouting now. "How many times did those goons come to see you, Susan? Or did Zahn come himself? What did you do, unbutton your blouse for them, too? Think a little sex and blaming it on your lawyer would make your problem go away?" He flung the papers in his hand across the room. "You set those goons on my daughter!"

Tears streamed down her cheeks. She got up and ran into the hall and went in a powder room. Pete sat there, seething with rage. He tried to calm himself. Maybe he'd been too hard on her, he thought. But screw it! Julie was all he had left, and that damned woman had put her in danger!

Susan returned to the room with a box of tissues. She dabbed at her eyes and between sniffles said, "I'm sorry, Pete. I didn't know what to do. Those men …" She shuddered. "Those men. They were awful. They tried to get me to agree to pay debts incurred by my husband that I knew nothing about. I thought if a lawyer told me the debts weren't enforceable, they might go away. They slapped me, Pete!"

"Not hard enough," he said.

They sat quietly for a few minutes. Pete could see that her hands were shaking. "Why didn't you tell me the truth, Susan? We might have been able to work something out." His voice was calmer now, but the anger inside still raged.

"I was confused. And scared. Those men …"

They sat there, neither speaking. Susan's eyes kept flitting between her wine glass and Pete.

"What do we do now?" she asked weakly.

Pete ignored her question and just stared at her. Finally he said. "Let me ask you a question. What did you tell them about Julie?"

"Not much," she said in a wavering voice. "They asked whether you had any family. I told them I thought you had a daughter."

"Did you tell them where she is?"

"No," Susan said defensively. "All I told them was that she's in a boarding school near Detroit."

Pete erupted again. "Did you draw them a map, too? How could you be so goddamn stupid? You want to know what we do next? I'm resigning as your lawyer, that's what *I'm* doing." He flung a sheet of paper toward her, and began to stuff other documents into his file.

Susan rushed from her chair and picked up the sheet of paper. It was his two sentence letter of resignation, effective immediately. She put a hand to her face and came over and sat on the arm of his chair. She touched his shoulder, and said in a pleading voice, "Please don't resign, Pete. I need you."

He brushed her hand away and said, "I already have. And I'm going to make sure Zahn and those goons know it, too." He rose from his chair and walked toward the door.

"Please." Susan grabbed him by the arm. "Please. Can we start over? I promise to tell you everything going forward."

"No, Susan, it's over." He took her hand away and continued walking.

She hurried to keep up and jumped in front of him. He just looked at her coldly. She stepped closer and put her hands on his shoulders and her breasts brushed his chest. "Don't you find me attractive, Pete?"

He looked at her a few moments longer, then said, "You're pathetic." He pushed her hands away again and walked out the door.

When he got home, he fell into a chair on his porch and just sat there. He hadn't eaten that evening, but he wasn't hungry. He didn't have anything to drink, either. He just sat and gazed out at the water, watching the changing patterns as the sun set in the west.

Finally, he got up and walked inside and dialed Julie's new cell number. Her bubbly voice came on and she regaled him for ten minutes with tales of her day at Disneyland. He barely had to speak. That was okay. All he could think of to say anyway was to tell her he loved her.

NINETEEN

The stretch of the Brule River — part of the "Holy Waters" as it was known — was quiet and flowing lazily before it quickened into rapids a short distance downstream. Pete was pleasantly surprised that there were only two other fisherman in sight. He relished the solitude and felt the gentle current against his waders as he ventured farther out in the stream. He tried a few casts. Nothing. Then he stood there a while, gazing at the river, absorbing his surroundings, watching the trout occasionally rise to the surface and snap up an insect.

He wasn't daydreaming; he was "matching the hatch." He tied a different artificial fly on his line. On the third cast, a trout rose from the water and took the fly. He smiled and played the fish skillfully as it burst from the surface again, then plunged deep and tried to swim away from him. After a few minutes of working the trout, he reached into the water and grabbed the fish, disengaged the hook, and released his quarry into the stream.

Pete continued to cast and land trout, losing himself in the joy of the moment and thinking only of pleasant things. He couldn't fish the Brule without thinking of Doris' father. He was an accomplished fly fisherman and had fished most of the great trout streams of the world. Pete rarely saw him these days, but remembered how his eyes would glow as he told of his angling exploits on streams in British Columbia and Iceland and Russia and New Zealand.

He smiled as he landed another brook trout. He admired the fish; at least seventeen inches he estimated, maybe longer. He visualized Harry sitting behind his desk, grinding out copy for the next edition of his paper, cursing Pete for not re-scheduling his fishing trip for a time when he could go along. Harry was his regular fishing companion these days and only his tenacious commitment to journalism kept him from joining Pete. But after what Pete had been through with his daughter and Susan Brimley, he had to get away and so went alone. He grinned again. When he got back, he'd taunt Harry for weeks with tales of all the big trout he'd landed, the near-perfect weather, and how he damned near had the river to himself.

It was late afternoon when he decided to call it a day. He checked into the rustic two-room cabin he'd stayed in for years. The memories swept over him as he gazed around at the log walls and stone fireplace and Native American throw rugs.

After unpacking and getting cleaned up, he hiked up the hill to the restaurant and got reacquainted with the proprietress and head cook, Millie Tate. Millie had been a fixture at the small resort since he'd been coming there. If Ebba Holm had a twin sister, it would have to be Millie. Both were warm, ample women of about the same age who loved people. When he first met Millie, she had the same flaming red tresses as Ebba. Then on a trip a couple of years earlier, he discovered that Millie had magically become a blonde. She must doctor up her hair on a regular basis, because it was beginning to show the ravages of too much peroxide.

"Pete!" Millie exclaimed when he walked in the dining room. She rushed to give him a big hug. As she drew him close, Pete was reminded of another way Milly and Ebba were alike — they must buy their undergarments from the same source. Stiff and cone-shaped. They could pierce a man's chest if she held her hug too long.

"Where's Harry?" Millie asked.

"He couldn't come this time. He sends his regrets."

Millie looked disappointed. She'd taken a shine to Harry from the first time Pete had brought him to the resort. Pete enjoyed watching them flirt with each other. Harry didn't fit the image of a typical ladies' man, but he must have something because women of a certain type and age seemed drawn to him. Like that night at Crystal Crate & Cargo when Harry had singled out a statuesque woman to be his personal model and she turned as giddy as a teen on her first date. Around Rona, though, Harry was the original monogamous man, probably out of fear for his personal safety.

"He's working on a story about the murder we had in our neck of the woods," Pete said. "He had a lot of interviews to do and couldn't get away."

"I heard about that murder," Millie said. Her eyes grew large and she gave a little shudder. "It sounded awful. It's been all over the news."

Pete told her what he knew, omitting details of his personal involvement, and said the sheriff had arrested a well-known environmental activist for the crime.

"I hadn't heard that," Millie said. "So it's been solved already."

"Maybe," Pete said. "They claim to have a lot of evidence against the guy, but Harry knows him and thinks he may be just a convenient target."

Millie shook her head. "I trust Harry. He's a very smart man. But I don't know. That woman last year. Now this man. That used to be a quiet little place to live. Just like around here."

"Now you sound like Angie DeMarco. Or my daughter. They're both worried that I'm living in a nest of crime and intrigue."

She looked at Pete lovingly. "I hope you bring your daughter the next time you come. I'd love to see her. Is that other woman you mentioned your girlfriend these days?"

Pete laughed. "No, she's my former law partner. She's already married."

"Well I think it's time you found yourself a good woman and got married again. Doris would want that, to know you're being cared for."

Pete eventually got Millie off the subject, and assured her he would be around for the next two days and would be in for breakfast and dinner and they would have time to catch up. Then he finished his venison stew and took his leave.

He'd brought along his notes and laptop, but didn't feel like working on his longboat article. He broke out his flask and poured some Thor's Hammer over ice and took a sip. As he enjoyed his drink, he read a few chapters of the latest Steve Hamilton mystery. Then he checked his watch. With the three hour time difference, he wondered if he could catch Julie between legs of her California adventures.

"Hi, Dad!" Julie said. "What's shakin', baby?"

Pete had to laugh. Julie was obviously in one of her exuberant moods. They chatted briefly and agreed that Julie would call him back. They were just leaving the theme park, she said, and would be back at their hotel in a half-hour.

When Julie called, the words poured from her mouth like water from a geyser. "Mikki and I spent the morning shopping," she said breathlessly. "They have wonderful shops out here."

"I thought you bought everything you needed when I took you shopping that day."

"Well, sure, Dad, but you can't go to California and not buy *something*. When I get back, all of my friends will want to know what I bought. I can't say, '*nothing.*' They'd think I'd totally lost it. People expect you to buy *something*."

"So what did you buy?"

"Nothing big," she replied. She went on to tell him about her new bikini and assorted other treasures. "The bikini is for the beaches out here," she added. "The suits I brought with me are, like, totally old fashioned."

He preferred old fashioned bathing suits on his daughter, but said nothing.

Julie was eager to get to the next topic anyway. "This afternoon, we went to Disneyland again and it was totally awesome!" she said. "We went on a ton of rides and it was, like, so much fun. And guess what? I totally met Mickey Mouse! Not some imposter or stand-in, but the *original rodent!* I was so, like, thrilled!"

Pete smiled again. He wondered how long it would take Julie to lose her new valley-girl dialect after she returned to the staid Midwest.

Julie continued to babble on until suddenly she said, "Yikes, I've got to get downstairs. We're all going to that Polynesian restaurant tonight. Hula girls and everything. I'll tell you about it tomorrow night."

When she was off the phone, Pete was again thankful that Mikki's family had invited her to go with them. It got her out of harm's way and gave him time to work out an armistice with Zahn.

He glanced at his watch. He didn't feel like reading anymore and didn't have any of his favorite music with him. He decided to go for a walk. He took his flask and followed the path down to the river. It was a warm evening, warmer than usual for late spring, but pleasant. He ambled along, happy to be in familiar surroundings.

He sat on a log and listened to the crickets and the gentle gurgle of the river. He sipped vodka from his flask. In retrospect, he was glad he hadn't fallen for Susan Brimley's pseudo apology. Angie DeMarco once told him that his one flaw was he was too forgiving, too good-hearted. But he wasn't that way when he was mad, and he was mad as hell at Susan Brimley. He'd had clients shade the truth before, but Susan was the first one who had blatantly lied to him. That was unpardonable, particularly when it had consequences that spilled over to his family.

But he also realized that getting rid of Susan Brimley didn't entirely solve his problem. He still had to convince Vinnie Zahn that he'd been duped in the first place and now was out of the picture. How to get in touch with Zahn, that was his main problem. He had to go to Chicago again on the Kral matter when he got back. He'd use that trip to try to contact Zahn. He doubted that a mobster would just list his number in the telephone book or make it available to directory assistance. He had to think of some way to reach him and only two options occurred to him — go through Theo Radke's law firm, which he was certain represented Zahn, or go directly to Nautical Finance. Nautical, being in the commercial finance business, had to be listed somewhere even if it was only a front for Zahn's criminal activities. He would make getting Zahn's number and demanding to see him his first priority.

Having a plan, his mind wandered off to other aspects of the Brimley case. So many things about the surface analysis of the murder didn't make sense. If Brimley owed Zahn a lot of money, and it looked like he did, why would Zahn want to kill him? Not that people like him were above that sort of thing; he'd heard enough stories from Angie to know how brutal they could be when someone welshed on them. But with Brimley dead, wouldn't Zahn find it more difficult to collect? Mobsters couldn't very well just go into probate court and prove up their dirty claims, including their right to juice. It would force Zahn to find other ways to collect, like putting the arm on his widow to pay him from the estate. Susan Brimley had as much as admitted that was what was happening. Maybe Zahn wanted it both ways — kill Brimley to send a message and then collect from his widow. Certainly, that explanation made sense when he thought about the brutal way Brimley had been murdered. But maybe Zahn didn't have anything to do with Brimley's death and was just scrambling to recover his money.

As if the case weren't murky enough, the timing of Brimley's murder bothered Pete, too. If Hicks were guilty and had killed Brimley as a way of stopping his Mystic Bluffs project, why did he wait until the complex was almost complete and ready to open? All of the damage to the natural environment had already occurred. Moreover, a third party could swoop in, buy the project and open the course even if Brimley were dead. Hicks then would have accomplished nothing as far as his environmental objections were concerned.

The place of the murder was another mysterious factor. Brimley periodically made trips back to Chicago. If Hicks knew about Brimley's involvement with the mob, it would seem to be a better play to kill him there to deflect attention from himself. A car bomb or something. Some tactic the mob favored. Not tie it directly to the golf course. But maybe Hicks didn't know about Brimley's involvement with the mob. And maybe he wasn't the one who killed him, either. If Hicks were innocent, as Harry believed, who could have planted incriminating evidence in his vehicle? Again, the logical conclusion was the mob, but that brought him right back to the circular reasoning he'd just gone through.

For all these reasons, he had begun to wonder about Leonard Wolf. There was no question that the seventeenth hole area held special meaning for him. Wolf seemed like a pleasant man, but maybe his passionate feelings for the cultural significance of the property ran deeper than anyone suspected. He didn't have an alibi for that night, either. And Pete remembered what Harry had told him about reports that Wolf was seen sitting on The Rock, just staring at the surrounding area.

Or maybe, just maybe, the killer wasn't Zahn or Hicks or Wolf. But if it wasn't one of them, who was it? And what was his motive? He took another swig from his flask and trudged up the path to his cabin.

TWENTY

Night was settling in when Pete arrived at the lake. He pulled into his driveway and felt relieved to be home. When he stepped inside, the cottage felt stuffy as a result of having been closed for three days. He opened some windows and the French doors to the screened-in porch. Then he mixed a Thor's Hammer and tonic and settled down in his favorite chair to relax.

He sipped his drink and gazed at the water. It was nearing the longest day of the year, and there was still some light. The lake was glassy with interesting patterns of shadow and color. While he didn't care if he ever saw Susan Brimley again, he remembered what she'd said that night about seeing things from an artist's perspective. He continued to stare at the lake and thought he understood her point.

It was nearly 7:00 p.m. on the West Coast. That's when he told Julie he'd call her. He'd talk to her first and then check his phone messages. The blinking red light on his answering machine had been nagging him since the moment he walked in.

Pete opened more windows and found two small fans and positioned them to blow through the French doors. He mixed another

Thor's Hammer and tonic and then dialed Julie's cell number. Their telephone conversations had become a nightly routine while she was in California. He had a difficult time sneaking in a comment or two, but he didn't mind. Hearing her voice was its own reward.

When she finished telling him, in exquisite detail, everything she and Mikki had done that day, she added, "And, you'll never guess what we're doing tonight." Without waiting for him to reply, she said, "We're going to Weldon's."

"What's that?"

"Dad, Weldon's is only the *hottest* restaurant in Hollywood."

"Well just tell me when you have to leave."

"We're not going *yet*. You know Mikki's sister? The one who's a drama major at UCLA? She made our reservation for 9:00 p.m. Out here, all the stars eat late. We figure we'll be seated at our table when the stars begin to arrive. I'm so excited. They say Brad Pitt eats there several nights a week. Mikki's sister said he wasn't there last night, so you know what *that* means."

They exchanged pleasantries and agreed to talk again the following evening. He freshened his drink and pulled a chair over to listen to his messages. Bud Stephanopoulis had called four times wondering where he was. He'd bumped into those two boys again, he said in one message, and they'd repeated their challenge to a two-on-two game. From what Pete could tell, Bud had gotten tired of the twits inferring he was an over-the-hill grandpa. He wanted to take them on and teach them a lesson. On his last call, he complained that the boys would think he was dodging them, using as an excuse that he couldn't reach his playing companion. Pete chuckled.

Harry had called and left a message that he'd talked to Ira Manning on the phone. Manning had left a message for Pete, too, and wanted to talk about his upcoming meeting with Hicks and scheduled press conference to follow. Pete dialed Harry's number.

"Damn, I thought you'd moved up there."

"Hey, I was only gone three days." Then he added, "Boy, were the trout ever hitting."

Harry was silent for a few moments and then said he'd heard that fishing on the Brule was terrible recently and that he was sure Pete was just telling him stories to gloss over the fact he'd been skunked. No, Pete replied, the fishing was actually super. He proceeded to tell him about all of the trout he'd caught and the near perfect conditions. He capped it off by tantalizing Harry with the menu each night at Millie's. When he finished, he was sure Harry was sitting there beside himself with envy.

"I don't know why you couldn't have waited a week," Harry groused. "It's not like you have a busy schedule or anything."

Pete laughed. "We'll plan another trip. Now I understand you've talked to our friend, Ira."

"Yeah, he's coming up day after tomorrow. I hope you're around because I told him you'd take him back to the airport. I have that kid who does gofer jobs around town picking him up. I don't want to do it because as a journalist, I'm afraid of looking like I'm close to Hicks and therefore not objective with my reporting."

Pete said he'd take Ira to the airport, told him some more about his fishing exploits just to needle him, and signed off. Then he tried Ira and got him at home.

"Mr. Norske! You're damned lucky you're not practicing law anymore. Three days to return you phone messages? Shoot, I'd have all your clients." He cut loose with his belly laugh.

Pete explained that he'd been on a fishing trip, but would be around the rest of the week and confirmed he would be happy to take him to the airport after the press conference.

"Good," Ira said, suddenly serious. "I've arranged to meet a guy at the Traverse City airport and I'd like you to help brief him."

Pete had a couple of calls from other people, but they were nothing urgent. He'd return them the following day. He'd had enough of the phone for the night.

He freshened his drink again and clicked the television on to catch the end of the Cubs-Tigers inter-league game he'd been listening to on the car radio. The Cubs had brought up a rookie first baseman who'd hit a three-run homer in his first at bat and followed that with a double. The Cubs were comfortably ahead when he pulled into his driveway. But things had degenerated by the time he turned on the television. The Tigers had the bases loaded, and on the very first play he watched, the Cubs' left fielder misplayed what should have been a routine third out into a three-run error. The next Tigers player hit a home run and suddenly the Cubs were down two runs.

Pete turned off the television in disgust and walked to the porch. He lit one of the candles and examined the other. It was burned down and he decided to replace it. He went to the hall closet and found the box of candles Doris kept there. He looked through it. There were candles of all colors and shapes and sizes. He selected an assortment of candles and arranged them on the fireplace mantle and on tables in the living room and on the porch. Then he methodically lit them and turned off the lights. He stood and admired his handiwork.

After a few minutes, he went inside, added more Thor's Hammer to his drink, and looked through his music collection. He selected a Linda Ronstadt CD, one of Doris' favorites, and slipped it into the player. With the candles flickering around him in the gentle breeze and Linda's lyrics softly filling the air, it was almost like old times.

Pete inserted another Linda Ronstadt CD into the player when the first ended. He freshened his drink once more and walked down the back steps to the beach. The night was quiet and he could barely hear the soft strains of the music coming from his porch. That was good in a way. The last thing he wanted was to upset Charlie Cox again. He recalled how the teenagers often screamed and hollered and partied at the beach just up the shore from his cottage. Although he might have preferred quiet, he never complained to the parents. Charlie was less tolerant. He grinned and had to admit that he might have been a little loud that night Charlie complained.

The half-moon was rising and the lights across the lake were blinking off as people retired for the night. He kicked off his shoes and waded out a few yards. The water was still cold, but once he got over the initial shock, it felt good. It cooled his entire body. He waded up and down the shore and strained to hear the music coming from his porch.

Then he got an idea: why not go for a midnight swim? He hadn't done that for a long time. He stripped down to his boxers, drained his glass, and plunged into the lake. Even though he was used to the cold water on his legs, it was still a shock when he went under. He swam with a strong overhand stroke and enjoyed the solitude. Then he began to recite the names of the old Norwegian kings as he often did when he swam. *Harald Fairhair, Eric Bloodaxe, Haakon the Good.* He treaded water for a while and looked up at the moon. After a couple of minutes, he resumed swimming. *Harald Bluetooth, Sweyn Forkbeard, Haakon Sigurdsson.*

He reversed direction, and when he looked toward the shore, he saw the flames. Not just the flickering candles; flames! His cottage was on fire!

Pete swam furiously until his feet touched bottom and then bounded through the water. His heart pounded as he raced toward his cottage and up the steps. The flames were licking at one end of the living room and he could see the fire was raging in back. He grabbed the phone, dialed 911, and told the dispatcher there was a fire and gave her the address. Then he hung up before she could pepper him with more questions and keep him on the phone.

He rushed to the kitchen, shielding his face against the heat and smoke and flames. He wrenched open a utility closet door and frantically looked for the fire extinguisher. He pulled out a vacuum cleaner and boxes and other items. Nothing! Goddamn! He stood there, feeling helpless, then grabbed a bucket and filled it with water and ran to the living room and threw it on the flames. They sputtered briefly. He hurriedly re-filled the bucket and threw the water at the flames again. The flames hissed and sputtered again when the water hit them, then resumed their climb. He repeated the process, over and over, slamming the faucet with his hand because the water didn't flow fast enough. *Goddamn it, hurry!* He listened for sounds of sirens as he worked.

The flames were higher now, the heat more intense. He threw another bucket of water on the blaze. He looked around helplessly. Then he began gathering pictures from the fireplace mantle and end tables and ran to the door and threw them into the night. When he saw no more pictures, he grabbed a stack of CDs and threw them out as well. He went back for more, dropping some on the floor in his haste to get them away from the blaze. He heard sirens, but kept working. He grabbed another batch of CDs, threw them out the door and went back for more.

He heard a voice. "You've got to get out of here, sir!" He felt hands grab him and shove him toward the door. "Get out, sir!"

Fire fighters rushed up the outside steps and past him. He stood by helplessly and watched as they sprayed the flames. Another fire truck arrived and more men poured out and joined the battle against the voracious blaze.

In a half-hour, they had the fire under control, although to him, standing there in the night, mostly naked, watching helplessly, it seemed like hours. A growing crowd of neighbors had been wakened by the commotion and came out to watch. Charlie Cox was among them. The fire fighters were soaking the area around his fire-damaged cottage and continuing to spray retardant on the hot embers. In the lights from the fire trucks, Pete could see that the porch he loved was badly damaged.

His chest had stopped heaving and his pulse had returned to normal. He began to pick up the pictures and CDs he had thrown out the door. The glass on some of the pictures had shattered and most were covered with dirt from the wood-chip path. He brushed them off and carried them to his car and put them in the front seat. Then he went back and looked for more.

As he worked, he was vaguely aware of the hushed voices of the bystanders. They speculated about what might have happened. One voice was louder than the others and said, "Thank God it didn't spread to our cottages."

"Okay," one of the fire fighters announced to the crowd, "it's under control. You can go back home now." One by one, people drifted away to their cottages. A few passed by Pete to say they were sorry or to ask if he was okay. One neighbor asked, "You want to sleep at my place tonight?"

Pete looked at him and said, "Thanks, Andy, I'll be okay." For the first time, he was conscious of his appearance. He was still in his wet boxers and his hair was matted from his swim. He was sure he had soot on his face and body as well.

He continued to look for CDs and other objects he'd flung out the door. As the firefighters were leaving, they asked him again if he needed anything. He assured them he'd be okay. After they were gone, he stood there alone in the faint moonlight and staring at the burned wreck of his cottage. Then he went down to the water and did the best he could to clean himself up. He put on the clothes he'd left on the beach and found his shoes.

He stood by his car for a long time, staring at his cottage some more and thinking. A cloud obscured the moon, darkening everything momentarily. Then it passed and the scene was dimly illuminated again.

Pete got in his Range Rover, drove to town, and checked into the first motel he came to. He had to endure more inquisitive looks from the desk clerk, but after what he'd been through the past week, he was used to that. He grabbed the duffel he'd left in his car after returning from his fishing trip and found his room. He stripped off his damp clothes and flopped into bed, exhausted.

TWENTY-ONE

The following morning, Pete drove out to the lake to assess the damage to his cottage in the daylight. It was an overcast day without any wind, and as soon as he got out of his Range Rover, the stench of burnt wood filled his nostrils. He walked slowly around the structure. As it had appeared the night before, the side of the cottage facing the road had suffered the worst damage. The fire was most intense in that area, too, and the roof had been burned through in one place. The lake side, where the living room and porch were situated, showed less exterior damage.

He went up the back steps and looked around inside. Char covered the wood paneling on one side of the living room, and the fire had ruined many of the books in the bookcase. He saw Doris' leather-bound collection of the works of Elizabethan poets and grimaced. The books were badly singed. Much of the furniture showed damage as well. The porch area was worse than he had thought.

Pete was tempted to straighten up the mess left by the firefighters, but knew from experience he shouldn't disturb anything. He saw his longbow case standing in one comer of the living room. It was charred a bit on the outside, but otherwise the case didn't appear to be damaged. *What the hell*, he thought, it couldn't hurt to take his bow. He picked up the case and clicked the latch to open it. The polished yew wood appeared untouched by the fire. Pete breathed a sigh of relief.

The bow was one of his prized possessions. It was a replica of a Viking longbow made for him in Norway by an old craftsman named Ulf. One of Pete's favorite pastimes was to practice with the bow using as targets some Army surplus silhouettes strategically placed among the trees behind his cottage. When he was dueling with Marty Kral, he often visualized Kral's likeness on one of the silhouettes and gleefully plunked him with arrow after arrow. It was satisfying, but he never mentioned Kral when he practiced with Lynn Hawke, an accomplished archer in her own right, out of concern she might think him sadistic. He closed the case and set it by the porch door.

He walked down the back hall and peered in his bedroom. There was fire damage on the far wall, but otherwise the room wasn't badly damaged. At least he'd be able to salvage some of his clothes. He retraced his steps and walked down the other hall and looked at the kitchen. The rubble told the story; he wondered how he'd managed to go in there repeatedly for more water. He looked up and saw tree branches through a hole in the roof and just shook his head.

He went outside. After briefly surveying the exterior damage again, he began to collect CDs and pictures he'd missed in the darkness the previous night. He was putting them in a cardboard box he'd found in his Range Rover when Charlie Cox walked over from next door and said, "I'm sorry about the fire. I'm glad you're okay."

Pete just nodded.

Cox gazed at the cottage for a minute. "It's not as bad as I thought it would be based on the flames last night," he said. "That fire was really going."

Pete looked at him. "You haven't been inside. It's pretty bad."

Charlie seemed to be wrestling with how to phrase his next question. He finally said, "I guess this proves the danger of leaving lighted candles unattended, huh?"

Pete's head snapped around. "What's your point?"

His reaction must have startled Charlie, because he hastily added, "That's what the fire chief said last night. He said some of the candles must have fallen over and started the blaze. You were out for a swim when it started, right?"

"Yeah, I was out for a swim," Pete said sarcastically.

Charlie seemed to sense that Pete had taken offense at his comment and was in no mood for further conversation. "Well," Charlie said, "if I can do anything, just ask. You know where to find me."

"Thanks."

Pete was picking up the last of the CDs when he had another visitor. It seemed like every vulture in the county was descending on him to gloat over his misfortune. Acting Sheriff Richter got out of his cruiser and looked at the fire-damaged cottage for a while. Then, without the usual social pleasantries, he said, "I didn't expect to see the place still standing based on what I heard from the fire chief. You know, you could have burned down all of these other places, too." He gestured with his hand toward the surrounding cottages.

Pete held his temper. He should be used to the jerk by now. "What do you mean, *I* could have burned them down?" he asked.

"The chief told me he thought the fire started when you left all those candles burning unattended. He said when his crew got here and went inside, there were candles everywhere. Some were still lit and others had fallen over. He concluded the fire was your fault since you left your cottage with all of those candles burning. He said you looked like crap, too. Like you'd been drinking."

Pete looked at him with narrowed eyes and said, "It seems to me that he made a lot of assumptions. Did he add that the place would have burned to the ground before he got here if I hadn't busted my butt to control the flames?"

"You just did what any homeowner would have done in the circumstances," Richter said. "I'm going to talk to the chief again and see what his department's costs were. Don't be surprised if he sends you a bill."

Pete just stared at Richter. "Are we finished?" he asked. "I have things to do."

After Richter was gone, Pete finished picking up the CDs and went into his cottage for others that were undamaged. Then he went to his bedroom and threw some of his clothes into a plastic basket. They reeked of smoke, but a good washing or two should get the smell out.

Before he left, he looked at his cottage again and wondered how so much damage could have occurred in such a short time. And he thought about the anonymous caller's comment about his "nice little cabin."

When Pete got to his office, he immediately got on telephone. His first call was to Elmer Kovac, an arson expert from Chicago who was now living in New Buffalo. He hadn't talked to Kovac in years, but had been sufficiently impressed with him during an insurance case to file away his contact information for future reference. Kovac was semi-retired, and must have been bored because he promised to drive up the next morning.

His next call was to Susan Brimley.

"Before you get the wrong impression," he said when she answered, "I'm not calling to say I've reconsidered our conversation the other night. What I told you stands. But I have a question and this time I want a straight answer."

Susan Brimley said nothing.

Pete asked, "Did you have any contact with Zahn or his henchmen after that night? Either by phone or in person?"

She was slow to answer, but finally said, "No, why do you ask?"

"I want the truth, Susan. Did you have any contact with Zahn or his men?"

"I just told you. They didn't contact me, and I wouldn't even know where to reach them even if I wanted to." Her voice sounded whiney and she paused for a few moments. "Do you think they've dropped the whole thing?"

"I have no idea whether they've dropped the whole thing. I'm not your lawyer anymore, and it's none of my business. But you're absolutely sure you had no contact with them?"

"Pete, I've already told you twice. I didn't. I'm sorry for not telling you everything before, but ..."

"I've got to go, Susan."

If Susan was telling the truth, that left only one other possibility. He dialed the sheriff's office and asked for Joe Tessler.

"Whom shall I say is calling, sir?"

"Pete Thorsen."

The woman put him on hold. When she returned to the line, she said, "Detective Tessler can't take your call right now. He'll call you back in an hour. What's the best number to reach you?"

Pete gave her his office and cell phone numbers and hung up. He sat staring at the phone, anxious to speak with Tessler. To kill time, he looked over the partial draft of his article and made a few edits. Then he scanned the latest issue of *The Northern Sentinel.* Joe Tessler eventually called back. His expression of regret over the fire seemed genuine. He asked Pete what he intended to do until the cottage was rebuilt. Pete politely answered his questions and then got to the reason for his call.

"Have you had a chance to follow up on our conversation the other day?"

"You mean your story about the Chicago mob? Yes, I have, and I think you're barking up the wrong tree. I called my old boss at Chicago PD. He's a top mucky-muck now. I told him what you told me and how you believe that Vinnie Zahn might be mixed up in Les Brimley's murder. He was interested because the office is working on a case involving Zahn, but I guess it's going nowhere. If they could tag him with Brimley's killing …

"Anyway, he saw it as a chance to hassle Zahn, and I guess he sent some of his men to Zahn's finance place to question him. Zahn denied everything and said they had to talk to his lawyer. But then — I guess he's a cocky sonofabitch — he told them he was at an event for his niece's wedding the night Brimley was killed. Claims he has seventy-five witnesses. I guess he couldn't resist sticking the knife in and told Emmett's guys they should stop wasting taxpayer money harassing citizens like him and do something about the crime wave in Chicago."

"The Chicago PD guys didn't identify me as the tipster, did they?"

Tessler was silent for a few moments, as though he were thinking. "No," he finally said, "I'm sure they didn't. They might have said that the information they had came from our department, but I'm sure they didn't mention you. Those are real pros in Emmett's unit."

"Can you think of any way to check out Zahn's story?"

"About the wedding party? I'm sure Emmett's people could, but Zahn would have no reason to lie about something like that. It would be too easy to check out."

"Did you tell the sheriff what you were doing to check out Zahn?"

"I'd prefer not to get into internal office matters, Pete."

For some reason, Pete had a feeling he might not have. As he thought about the conversation with Tessler, it occurred to him that Zahn could have been responsible for torching his cottage — assuming, as he suspected, it was arson — under either of two scenarios. If he didn't know Pete had fingered him as a possible murder suspect, he could have started the fire as part of his continuing efforts to intimidate him, and if he did know, it could have been in retaliation.

Harry was more or less on time for once. Rona joined them. Pete had to go through a half-hour of conversation with them about the fire and what his plans were going forward. From the delicate way they phrased their questions, he could tell they'd heard about the candles and his midnight swim when the fire started. And probably about his drinking, too. They didn't raise any of those points directly, though, and he didn't volunteer anything.

When Rona had left their table, Harry asked, "Did you ever touch base with Ira?"

"I did."

"Do you plan to go to the press conference?"

Pete nodded. "I suppose I have to," he said. "I might be a little late." He hadn't told Harry about his appointment with Kovac and didn't intend to until he knew the results of his inspection.

"What kind of a defense do you think Manning's going to put up?" Harry asked.

Pete shrugged. "I'm not a criminal lawyer."

"With no alibi and a motive, he has to attack that trace evidence, doesn't he?"

Pete shrugged again. "You'd think so." He ordered another Thor's Hammer and tonic. Harry looked at the glass when the bartender set it on their table. He seemed about to ask a question, but didn't speak. Pete took a long sip of his new drink and stared out the window. It was still overcast and the water looked gray and dreary.

"How many is that?" Harry finally asked. "Four?"

Pete looked at him and realized he was referring to his drink. "It might be," he said. "But what's your point?"

"I don't know. Rona and I were talking about this a few nights ago. You seem to be drinking a lot more than you used to."

"Oh, that's a stretch, don't you think? Don't you two have anything better to do that sit around clucking about how many drinks I have?"

"Sure we do, but we're your friends and are concerned. Last night ..."

"Last night what? You been listening to those stories that are being circulated by a few people who have it in for me?"

"I heard …"

"You heard what, Harry? That I lit fifty candles and they were responsible for the blaze? What else did they tell you? That they found that fifth of vodka I had on the beach? Or was it a quart?"

"Pete …"

"Don't Pete me. Do I lecture you about eating too much? Maybe I should start counting your calories every meal we have together and preach to you about what you're doing to your body."

Harry just sat there looking chastened.

"What's my share of the tab?" Pete asked. "I've got to get some sleep." He fumbled around in his wallet. "Here," he said as he threw two fifty dollar bills on the table. "That should cover it." He got up and started out, then came back and added another bill to the pile. "I almost forgot about all the booze I had. If that's not enough, send me a bill." He walked out.

TWENTY-TWO

Pete waited at his cottage for Elmer Kovac. Before coming out, he'd stopped at *The Northern Sentinel's* offices and apologized to Harry. He only had a few true friends these days, and Harry was at the top of his short list. Harry tried to brush off the spat with a wave of the hand and a self-deprecating comment that he was the one who was out of line.

But they both knew the truth; Pete had been drinking too much. Except for his college years, when he could drink pitchers of beer without using the john, he'd been firmly entrenched in the two-drink category. And light on the booze, at that. Now four drinks and he was just getting started. And forget that light crap. He'd come to like his drinks the normal way, with a full slug of liquor. He knew when it started, too; not long after the nightmares began.

Subliminally, he knew all of that, but there was solace in liquor. When he was around Julie, he moderated his drinking. After all, wasn't he the biggest critic of Wayne Sable and all his boozing and carousing? He didn't want Julie to think of him the way she thought of Sable. But even on the occasions he was with her, he often wanted a drink. His whole life had been built on self-discipline, and he knew he had to get back on track.

Kovac pulled in just before 11:00 a.m. Pete hadn't seen him in years, but he didn't look a day older than he remembered. He was also one of the best arson experts around. While he was conflicted about it, Pete hoped that Kovac would confirm what he already suspected. He chatted with Kovac a few minutes, then left him alone to do his work.

Pete had brought his longbow along to practice and had special motivation. Angie DeMarco had e-mailed him that morning and said negotiations with Kral had broken down and that he'd filed his lawsuit twenty-four hours later. According to Angie, Kral had named all of the partners individually even though he could have just named the firm. Pete was at the top of the list of defendants despite the fact that he was no longer a partner.

As Pete sighted down the arrow and drew back the bow string, Kral's smirking countenance appeared on a target. *Thunk!* The arrow caught Kral in the shoulder. *Thunk!* Another arrow hit him squarely in the chest. Pete grinned. It was like old times when Kral was trying to oust him as managing partner. He ran his fingers over the yew wood, feeling the smoothness, admiring the craftsmanship. He was roused from his bloodthirsty reverie by Kovac's call.

"Well," Kovac said, "your nose was right. I'm almost positive someone torched your cabin." Like him, Kovac had his roots in rural Wisconsin where seasonal retreats were called cabins, not cottages. Old ways die hard.

"What's your analysis?" Pete asked.

"You had it nailed yourself. You didn't need me." He explained how structures burn. "With your cabin, there are two distinct areas of burn. One in front, the side facing the road, and another in back by the living room and porch. Come with me and I'll show you."

They walked around front and Kovac said, "Tell me what you see."

Pete looked at his cottage for a few moments and said, "A lot of fire damage."

"It's very visible on the exterior, right?"

"Right."

"Now before we go inside, let's go around back again and I think you'll see the difference."

They went to the lake side and looked at the cottage from that angle. "See any difference?" Kovac asked.

Pete studied the cottage. "There's almost no sign of exterior damage," he observed.

"Bingo," Kovac said. "Now let's go inside." They walked up the back steps and as they entered the cottage, Pete got depressed all over again. The interior, which he'd always kept orderly, was a mess.

"Pretty bad, huh?" Kovac said as they looked around. "Now let's go in front." When they reached the kitchen area, they were greeted by what Pete already knew they'd see — even worse fire damage. "What this pattern tells me," Kovac continued, "is that the fire started in front, probably from the outside, and spread inward. Some sort of fire accelerant likely was used to get the blaze really roaring."

"And the candles might have caused the fire inside, I suppose."

"In the living room and on the porch, possibly," Kovac said, "but there were no candles in other parts of the cabin. Plus the burn patterns on the floors tell me something. All of the rooms have hardwood floors. The floors in the kitchen and other front rooms burned evenly. But the floors in the living room and the porch are rough where they burned. What I think happened is that the arsonist used accelerant to get the fire going outside in front and then came around back, entered the cabin, threw accelerant around a few places, then knocked over some of the candles to ignite the blaze. The front door was locked, right?"

"Yes."

"The thing I don't know," Kovac said, "is the kind of accelerant the arsonist used. I took soil samples outside and scrapings from the floors. I'll know more when I get the lab results back. But I have no doubt it was a torch job and not an accident. It would have been impossible for the fire to start inside as a result of the candles and spread the way it did to the rest of the cabin in the time-frame you described."

Pete studied Kovac's face. "How long would it take an arsonist to do all of this?"

"Minutes. Flames are very visible at night, and once he got the blaze started, he'd get the hell out of there."

"Umm," Pete murmured. "So there's no question in your mind it was arson."

"I'll bet you a Coho dinner," Kovac said. "You have Coho up here, don't you?"

"A lot of them."

Pete thought about everything else he knew. It all fit.

Ira Manning was just beginning his press conference when Pete arrived. He'd always seen him in the office, not in court. In the office, he fancied bold striped shirts with white collars and red suspenders. Or "braces," as he called them. For a man of his girth, he was something of a dandy and got most of his clothes in the shops on Saville Row in London.

In court, though, the oversized peacock went bland and always wore a rumpled brown sport coat that looked like it hadn't been pressed in a year. Just a man of the people, he liked to say, reasoning with the fine upstanding folks who help make our jury system the greatest instrument of justice in the world. Today he wore brown.

There were well over a hundred people at the press conference including television crews from stations in Traverse City, Grand Rapids and Detroit and many print journalists. The remainder were locals who attended out of curiosity to get a peek at Hicks' expensive new mouthpiece from the big city.

"I just came from the jail," Manning began, "where I spent over three hours with my client, John Hicks. I looked Mr. Hicks in the eye and questioned him about every detail of his life and this case. I asked him every question you can imagine and some you'd be embarrassed to admit that you asked. I asked him about his background and his beliefs and his relationship with his family and his motivations and his passions. I asked him all about the battle he and others who think like him had waged to stop the Mystic Bluffs golf course from proceeding and to preserve the property for the enjoyment of future generations. I asked him about his reputation out West for supporting environmental causes.

"I've handled over a hundred murder cases. I've spent my entire career representing men — and some women — accused of the most heinous crimes. Many of the defendants appeared to be the scum of the earth and others looked like fine upstanding citizens. I always felt that in this great land of ours, for our adversarial system of justice to work the way it was intended, everyone accused of a crime is entitled to the best defense his counsel can muster, regardless of station in life and regardless of how badly he or she may be vilified in the press. After a while, you learn how to look into a person's soul, to gauge whether the accused is guilty or whether circumstances just make it look like he's guilty.

"I'll tell you, ladies and gentlemen, John Hicks is an innocent man. He's guilty of only one thing — trying to protect the natural environment that we all live in. The air we breathe, the water we drink and enjoy for leisure pursuits, the trees that provide us shade and so many other pleasures. For feeling passionate about those things, for his commitment to the environment for the benefit of our children and their children and generations of children to follow, he's been vilified. Made to look evil. And when something terrible happened to one of your fellow citizens, the authorities naturally looked his way, viewed him as a convenient target because of his beliefs. But I tell you, when I looked into his soul today, I saw a man who's committed to his cause, but not a murderer.

"Now, ladies and gentlemen, I'll take your questions."

Several hands shot up at once and Manning called on one woman.

"You didn't comment on all of the evidence the sheriff's office says it has against Mr. Hicks." The reporter who asked the question stood with pencil poised over her note pad, ready to take down Manning's response.

Manning looked at her over his glasses for a few moments, then said, "Madam, do you mean the evidence the sheriff's office *has* or the evidence it *doesn't* have? They have no witnesses. They have no fingerprints. They have no DNA evidence. Now, in this era of sophisticated crime detection, don't you think it odd that there was no DNA evidence — absolutely none — that the murder victim's body was ever in my client's vehicle? That seems impossible, doesn't it?" He shook his head. "No DNA evidence. Only seven hairs that could have been yanked from the victim's head and planted in Mr. Hick's vehicle. So when the state says it has a lock case, I ask, what kind of lock? A lock that someone forgot to snap shut? A lock that always malfunctions and won't close at all? I tell you, if I were a prosecutor, I'd be embarrassed to bring a case like this."

The reporter asked some follow-up question and Manning patiently answered them. For the next half-hour, he did the same with questions from other reporters. Then he wrapped up the news conference by saying, "Mr. Hicks is an innocent man who's just being targeted because of his beliefs. Frankly, I don't expect this case to ever go to trial. The charges should never have been brought."

◆ ◆ ◆

On their way to Traverse City, Ira Manning turned to Pete and asked, "How did I do?"

"Masterful, as usual. Do you really think Hicks is innocent?"

Manning gazed out his side window and said, "I do. I just don't see how Brimley could have been in Hick's vehicle without leaving a ton of DNA evidence."

"Apart from the hair."

"Yeah, apart from the hair, but no other indication of Hick's presence. I'm not a DNA expert, but I know enough about the subject to know that's impossible. Brimley's body was essentially naked, remember. If there was hair, there should have been other DNA evidence. And there wasn't a danged thing."

"How did the sheriff explain that?"

"He said that they're still running tests. But I'll tell you, Pete, if they found hair, there should have been more. All over the vehicle. I think Hicks is being set up just as he claims."

"Anything else?"

"Yeah. Hicks passed the Manning smell test."

"Which is?"

Manning grinned. "When I met with Hicks, I asked him what he was doing the night Brimley was killed. He said he couldn't sleep, and watched a couple of old movies on television. One was a black and white flick with Humphrey Bogart. I love that movie myself and quizzed him about it. He nailed every detail. I checked before the news conference. That movie was playing on local cable in your area between 2:00 a.m. and 4:00 a.m."

"Come on, Ira. He could have seen that movie before and known what it was all about. Even you couldn't get a jury to buy an argument like that."

Manning grinned again. "Hey, Norske, I said he passed the Manning smell test. I didn't say it was admissible evidence." He gazed out the window again. "Shoot," he added, "I've gotten juries to buy flimsier evidence than that."

The airport was crowded, but Manning spotted Adam Rose right away. He was not a big man, maybe five-ten, and had short sandy hair and wire-rimmed glasses. Pete knew his background, though. He'd been in the Navy for eight years and his old unit was SEAL Team 6 which eventually located and took out Osama bin Laden. Several years before that, Rose had fractured his leg in three places during a training exercise. No longer able to do what was required of him, he mustered out of the Navy and hung out his shingle in Chicago as "Rose Investigations." Ira had used him on cases several times and was fond of telling about the time Rose had entered a Chicago bar frequented by members of the Latin Kings street gang, and when several of the gang members crowded him, took away their knives and busted them up pretty bad. Ira had stayed in touch with Rose after he moved to Traverse City to be near his ailing mother. Ira had mentioned in the car that the assignment he had for Rose was below his skill set, but knew he needed the work and wanted to use him.

Ira introduced Pete to Rose and the three of them found an out-of-the-way spot where they could sit and talk in private. At Ira's request, Pete gave Rose the background on Brimley's murder and John Hicks' arrest. Then Ira explained to Rose what he wanted him to do — check with every place within a hundred-mile radius of Frankfort that did automotive detailing work. Then compile a list of names of people who had detailing work done on their vehicles during the two-week period following the date of Brimley's murder.

"I know what you're doing," Pete interjected, "but there's one flaw. I mentioned that the Chicago mob may be involved. If that's right, they may have taken the vehicle back to Chicago and either scrapped it or had it detailed there."

"What you say is true," Ira said. "But I'm playing the percentages. If the guy who did Brimley in was from this area, it's logical to assume that he would want to get his vehicle cleaned up as a precaution. I'm not sure that detailing would remove DNA evidence, but a layman probably wouldn't know that. If the killer was someone from the mob, then we will have gone through a useless exercise. We can't very well check with every place in Chicago that does detailing work. There likely are hundreds."

Pete could see Manning's point and agreed his plan was worth a shot. He also agreed to look at Rose's list after he compiled it to see if anything jumped out at him.

Rose sat impassively throughout Pete's briefing and his brief exchange with Ira and then asked, "When do you need this, Ira?"

Ira grinned. "You know me," he said. "Yesterday."

TWENTY-THREE

Pete propped his feet up and gazed out at the lake. It was a completely different, unaccustomed view. He looked west now, from the Beulah end of the lake, and the patterns of light looked foreign to him. He'd have to get used to it, though; he'd be there a while.

He'd spent much of the day with a realtor looking at houses for rent. He settled on a three-bedroom house with modern architecture and a view from the spacious deck. It was nice enough, but hadn't been well maintained. Lynn Hawke's house was only a quarter mile away. It was also for rent, but he'd passed on that option. It was nicer than the house he chose, but he didn't feel comfortable renting it. If he had and Lynn found out, he was concerned she might take it the wrong way. View him as a stalker or something. He knew that was silly, but it was the way he felt. Besides, he was hoping she'd return some day and they could rekindle their relationship. He didn't want to do anything to interfere with that possibility.

He'd retrieved more of his clothes from his fire-damaged cottage and gone shopping to replace essential items. Topping the list was a

CD player. It didn't have the same sound quality as his old unit, but it would have to do until he could upgrade.

But no Thor's Hammer. After Elmer Kovac left, he'd sat on a tree stump, gazing at his fire-damaged cottage, and made two vows. One was to stop drinking so much. He needed to get back to where he used to be and reclaim his reputation. Liquor had become a crutch, anyway, as he'd previously admitted to himself. The other vow was to find out who had torched his cottage. And of course he still had to get word to Zahn that he was out of the picture as far as his money dispute with Susan Brimley was concerned.

The first test of his resolve had come the previous night when he had dinner with Harry after returning from the airport. It had been a long day, but he declined Harry's suggestion of a drink and ordered iced tea instead. He told Harry why, and came clean with his friend about everything that had happened to him recently, beginning with Susan Brimley's duplicity and the stalking incident involving Julie. He also told him what Kovac had concluded about the fire.

Suddenly he had an ally, not just a friend. They'd do the liquor thing together, Harry said. He'd help Pete become just a social drinker again, and Pete could help him cut back on his calories and get on a healthier diet. Harry suggested they join the local health club and pushed Pete for days they could work out together. When Harry finished his drink, he switched to iced tea himself in a show of solidarity with his friend. He boasted that Rona's restaurant served the best tea in town, whether hot or over ice.

Harry was less enthusiastic when it came Pete's other objectives. He urged Pete to go to the state police or even the FBI if he didn't want to deal with Richter. Arson was a crime, and stalking was an offense, too. Harry wasn't fully convinced when Pete told him his rationale for doing it himself — he wanted to defuse things with Zahn, and really didn't have anything specific to go on in the case of the fire — but agreed to do what he could to help. For his part, Pete promised to revisit the law enforcement option if he pinned down who he thought had torched his cottage.

Harry persuaded Pete to split a piece of key lime pie as sort of a swan song to fattening food. He promised it was the last dessert he'd have until he lost twenty pounds. Pete had a forkful or two of the pie while Harry attacked it like it was the only good food he'd have for the next decade. The prospect of dieting can be a daunting experience.

Back home, Pete had his nightly telephone conversation with Julie. He worked up his courage and told her about the fire in their cottage. She probed and probed about the causes of the fire, wanted to know about the damage to her bedroom. Then she quizzed him about whether he thought the fire might have been started by the same cult that was responsible for Brimley's murder. He assured her again that a cult wasn't responsible for either. The fire was most likely caused by faulty wiring, he lied, and reminded her that the sheriff had already arrested a suspect in the murder case. He emphasized that the fire wouldn't interfere with her plans to come to the lake in August since he had plenty of room in his new rental house. He also put a positive spin on the fire by pointing out that they'd intended to remodel anyway. He hated to lie to her, but knew it was best for the moment. Maybe when it was all over, he'd be able to tell her the whole story.

Tomorrow was D-day. He disliked Kral with a passion, but defending against his lawsuit had become secondary to the offensive he was about to launch. He would try to get Zahn's number from Theo Radke, or failing that, from Nautical Finance. He rehearsed his strategy. He thought about making an appointment with Radke, but quickly abandoned that idea. He'd just show up at his office, demand to talk to him, and refuse to leave until he got what he was after. He'd do the same with Nautical if necessary. Somehow, word would get back to Zahn, and he'd eventually agree to see him. He thought of ways he could turn up the heat on Zahn if necessary. Zahn had plenty of legal problems already and didn't need a crazy lawyer stirring up more.

He called Angie. She was still at the office. He was not in the mood for their usual banter, but engaged in it for five minutes anyway. Then he asked her if they could meet in the evening to discuss the Kral case. She grilled him about what he had going that would interfere with their original plans to meet in the afternoon, but ultimately agreed.

Then he plugged in his laptop and pulled up the Thompson, Barrett & Radke website. He got lucky. The site had a section profiling the firm's lawyers. And best of all, it had photographs. He found Radke's page and stared at his photograph for a long time. It had been taken without a suit coat, and it seemed that Radke favored the same sort of red suspenders that Ira Manning wore. Pete's printer was at his office, so he programmed Radke's likeness into his memory bank. Then he did the same with each of the other lawyers who listed white collar crime as his or her specialty. He made notes of their names and direct dial telephone numbers.

He had less luck with Nautical Finance. Nautical did not have a website. Juice loans, presumably, weren't the type of business that one advertised. Pete searched for sites listing commercial finance companies. He finally found one that included Nautical Finance. It had a Berwyn address. *Crap.* He was hoping the office would be downtown. He copied the address and telephone number. No e-mail address was listed and there were no photographs.

Pete sat back and thought for a few minutes. He decided to time his arrival in Chicago for about noon and try Radke first. To be on the safe side, and allowing for the time zone change, that meant being on the road by 7:00 a.m. at latest. If he didn't have any luck with Radke, he'd be able to get to Berwyn and visit Nautical before the close of normal business hours. If he was a little late getting back downtown, Angie and Steve would just have to wait.

Armed with a plan, he went to his bedroom and sorted through his business clothes. Not too bad. He unfolded three of his shirts, put them on hangers, and stood back a few paces and sprayed them with the neutral air freshener he'd purchased at the hardware store. Then he did the same with two of his suits. With airing out overnight, they should be wearable by the morning. Then he threw a bunch of his smoky underwear and socks in the washer and found a garment bag and his briefcase.

He decided to go for a short run while the washer was running; there'd be no time for exercise the next couple of days. He put on a pair of athletic shorts that still smelled of smoke, laced up his Nikes, and started down the lake road at a trot. The moon was fuller than the night of the fire and it was warm again. He could see the lake shimmer in the moonlight.

As he loped along, he kept looking up at the bluff, trying to identify Lynn's house. Finally he saw it. There were no lights on, obviously, but in the moonlight, he recognized the plate glass window and the deck. He wanted to climb the steps and look around, but thought better of it. He just stood there for a couple of minutes, looking up.

When he got back to his new house, the wash cycle was finished. He threw his wet clothes in the dryer and took a shower. He moved a small table with a lamp into the corner, left the low-wattage light on, and climbed into bed and hoped he could sleep.

TWENTY-FOUR

He beat his goal of arriving in Chicago before noon, and parked in the usual garage near his law firm's office building. He sat in his Range Rover for a while, checking his phone messages and rehearsing what he was going to do when he got to Radke's office. At 12:15 p.m., he got out of his vehicle and walked west to Radke's building on LaSalle Street.

When he exited the elevator and approached the reception desk, the young woman seated there was talking to a friend. She interrupted their conversation to ask if she could help him.

"Theo Radke, please," he said.

"Do you have an appointment, sir?"

"He's expecting me," Pete lied. "Is he back from lunch yet?"

"No sir. He should be back in a half hour."

"Fine, I'll just wait over here." He moved to the waiting area and sat down. The receptionist had already gone back to chatting with her friend. So far, so good, he thought. He knew the drill at law firm reception desks. The young woman he'd just spoken to was probably a secretary filling in for the regular receptionist so she could take her lunch break. Fill-ins could be counted on not to ask too many questions. They were usually more interested in gossiping with friends who stopped by to chat.

At 1:15 p.m., she was talking to a different friend when a man walked in with his suit jacket slung over one shoulder. He wore suspenders and a red tie. Pete was positive it was Radke. He got verification of that when the fill-in receptionist said, "Hi, Mr. Radke" but, predictably, didn't mention that Pete was waiting to see him.

Time to go. Pete rose from his chair and intercepted Radke as he passed the reception desk and was about to head down the hall to his office.

"Theo, Pete Thorsen. I'm sorry to pop in without an appointment, but I happened to be close and thought I'd see if I could catch you. You might recall that we had an appointment a while back, but you had a commitment out of the office or something." Pete moved into Radke's path so he'd have a hard time passing.

Radke looked surprised by Pete's sudden appearance. He stood there for a few moments, then said, "Yes, I'm sorry about that. I've been waiting for your call to reschedule the appointment. I'm afraid I'm busy right now, though."

"I won't take much of your time," Pete said, "but I do need to talk to you. Should we go back to your office? What I have to say is private and I don't think we should talk about it here in the hall."

Radke had recovered his composure. "Now isn't a good time," he said. "I'll have my secretary come out with her book. I'm sure we can find a time for you to come in soon."

"I'd prefer to do it now, Theo. Let's go back to your office. Ten minutes, that's all I need. You probably don't want me to talk about Susan Brimley and Vinnie Zahn and things like that where people can hear us."

Radke's eyes looked wary. "I'd really prefer …"

"Now, Theo."

Radke looked at him again. "Okay, ten minutes."

Pete followed him down the hall to a corner office. Radke closed the door behind Pete and motioned for him to take one of the side chairs. He threw his suit coat on the arm of a couch, settled in behind his desk and steepled his hands. "Okay," he said, "clock's running."

Pete handed Radke the letter Susan Brimley had signed engaging him to represent her in financial matters relating to her late husband's estate. He said nothing about his letter of resignation. Radke looked at the letter and pushed it back to him.

"Mrs. Brimley says you haven't been very forthcoming when she asked questions about her husband's estate."

Radke spoke over his steepled hands. "Nothing to tell her at this point."

"I find that hard to believe. You handled Brimley's estate planning, didn't you? It's not like he's a completely new client for you." Pete had seen a copy of Brimley's will so he knew that was true. Even if Brimley had wanted to keep his wife in the dark for some reason, he surely had given Radke a list of his assets and liabilities and similar information as part of the normal estate planning routine.

"We have some information, but we want to be sure anything we give Mrs. Brimley is accurate and up-to-date. Mr. Brimley was a businessman with assets in several states. It's a complicated estate. You're a lawyer, Mr. Thorsen. I'm sure you can appreciate these things."

Pete ignored Radke's comment and said, "I know Brimley had projects in the Chicago area in addition to the Mystic Bluffs project in Michigan. What can you tell me about the Chicago-area projects?"

Radke shrugged. "Not much, I'm afraid. We just ordered appraisals. They won't be back for a couple of weeks."

"Okay," Pete said, "maybe you can shed light on this, then. We have a pretty good handle on the bank debt burdening Mystic Bluffs, but I understand he also owes Vinnie Zahn money. I can't find any paper on that debt, though. What can you tell me about Brimley's obligations to Zahn?"

Radke frowned. "Vinnie Zahn?" he said. "Who's that?"

Pete just smiled. "Oh, come on, Theo. You know who Vinnie Zahn is. Your firm represents him. I'm sure you've also read about him in the newspapers."

"I really don't know what you're talking about." He glanced at his watch. "Time's up, Mr. Thorsen. I have some people coming in. They're probably here now." He rose from his chair and stood looking at Pete.

"Okay," Pete said, "I'm a man of my word. I won't keep you. But I have one more request — I need Vinnie Zahn's phone number."

Radke frowned again. "I told you. I don't know Zahn."

"That answer is getting old, Theo. You know him. And I bet some of your partners do, too."

"Are you leaving, Mr. Thorsen? Or do I have to get someone down here to escort you out?"

Pete smiled. "I'm leaving. But here's my card. I'd appreciate it if you or someone from your firm would e-mail me with Zahn's phone number. Tell him Pete Thorsen is looking for him. We have something to talk about."

He rose to leave, then turned and added, "One last thing, Theo — if I don't hear from you or someone in your firm in the next twenty-four hours, I'm going to start calling your office a dozen times a day until I get the number. If I can't reach you, I'm going to call your partners. If I don't get through to one of them, I'm going to talk to your secretaries. I'll go all the way down to your cleaning crew if I have to. You're going to get pretty damn tired of dealing with me, Theo."

As Pete headed for Berwyn, he was feeling good about his conversation with Radke. It had been fun in a way, and he'd stolen another page from his old Army boss in the CID. Make your adversary think you're obsessed and will stop at nothing to get the information you want. He'd see if it worked.

The traffic was heavy, but he made it to Berwyn by 3:00 p.m. He found Nautical Finance's office without much trouble and parked across the street. Nautical occupied a storefront building in a rundown neighborhood. From the signage in front, the office doubled as a pawn shop.

He shut down his engine. Then he took off his tie and made sure his billfold was in his front pants pocket. He got out and clicked the automatic door lock. As he started across the street, he noticed two street toughs in dark clothing with baggy pants eyeing him with interest. He waved at them and continued to walk toward Nautical's offices.

"Hey, man," one of the toughs called, "you got any coin? We're hungry."

"Sorry boys," he replied, shaking his head, "not today."

He opened the door and entered Nautical's office. It was a large room with low dividers separating the area into four work stations. The front stations were occupied by two young men in cheap dark shirts and matching ties that ended inches above their waists. Both wore earrings; one had gaudy studs in both ears, and the other had a dangling gold hoop. Hoop asked, "Can we help you, sir?"

Pete tried to sound casual. "I'm looking for Vinnie Zahn."

The employees exchanged glances. Hoop then asked, "Who?"

"Vinnie Zahn. The man who runs this place."

They exchanged glances again. "If you're looking for a loan, we can help you fill out an application. Or if you prefer, we can talk about it."

"No," Pete said, "I have some other business to discuss with Mr. Zahn." He handed Hoop a card. "Would you have Mr. Zahn call me? Sooner would be better."

Hoop took the card and stared at it.

"Thanks," Pete said. He walked out.

His pulse jumped when he saw the two street toughs leaning against his Range Rover. Pete decided the best thing to do was to keep walking toward them as though he were unconcerned. He crossed the street, and when he got close to his car, he stopped and stared at the tough who'd propped himself against the driver-side door with his arms crossed. Pete continued to stare at him and the tough slowly moved to one side just enough for Pete to get in his car if he tried.

Pete didn't try. Instead, he smiled at the boys and said, "I just found a bill in my pocket." He pulled out a fifty and waved it in the air. "It should be enough to buy two nice dinners." Or a few bags of weed, he thought. Then he added, "But first, I want you to tell me something. Who owns Nautical?"

The street toughs' dead eyes flicked in the direction of Nautical's office, then one said, "Why do you want to know, man?"

"Because I'm thinking about doing a deal with Nautical and I like to know who I'm dealing with."

The boys looked at him with new interest and their eyes showed signs of life. "What kind of deal, man?"

"Just a deal."

"Maybe your deal's too small for Nautical. Maybe we could help you with your deal. We got connections."

"I appreciate the offer, but I was told I should deal only with the boss." He waved the fifty dollar bill in the air again.

One boy reached for it, but Pete pulled it away. "Well?" he said.

"We could take that bill off you right now, Dude."

Pete smiled at him again. "I don't think you'd want to try. Now tell me who the boss is or I'll ask someone else."

"That's Mr. Z's place. I thought everyone knew that."

Pete handed him the bill. "Thanks, boys. That's what I thought."

Pete watched the toughs head down the street. Then he got in his car and pulled away from the curb. His tee shirt felt damp against his skin.

TWENTY-FIVE

When they pulled into the health club's parking lot, Harry muttered, "Damn, I forgot about lift-off."

Pete frowned. "What's lift-off?"

"A bunch of guys at the club lift free weights. They got together and decided to hold a contest. Today's the cut-down to decide the top five."

"Are you entered?" Pete asked.

Harry got a wistful look on his face. "No," he responded, "I didn't find out about it in time. With a little practice, I might have made it to the finals, but I doubt I would have won. Too many young bucks in the contest."

Pete looked out the side window and smiled as Harry continued to drive up and down the rows of parked vehicles, looking for an empty slot. It was remarkable what three days of workouts will do for one's confidence and self-esteem. Harry gave up and pulled onto the grass at the end of a row.

They walked in the health club's door and saw the facility was wall-to-wall with contestants and onlookers. Pete was surprised to see Bud

Stephanopoulis waiting his turn to lift. He didn't recognize any of the other contestants.

"There's your friend," Harry said, pointing at Bud. "He doesn't look like a weight lifter."

"Looks can be deceiving," Pete replied. "When he played in college, he used to lift all the time before it became popular with basketball players. That's why he was such a force inside. He's got lousy knees, but still has good upper body strength."

"Mmm," Harry murmured.

"You know any of the other guys?"

"Let's see," Harry said. "Those three big guys with Western Michigan tee shirts? They all play football there. One of them has to be the favorite. That guy in the red tee works on one of the charter boats. The one with the rag around his head looking like Willy Nelson is the guy you saw at the library. I don't recognize any of the others."

"The competition ought to be handicapped," Pete said. "It's a little unfair for someone in his fifties," thinking of Bud, "to have to compete with guys half his age."

Harry looked at him like he was a complete novice to the workout culture. "That competition is what keeps some of us going," he said.

Pete kept the smile off his face until he turned and went in search of a vacant treadmill. When he found one, he adjusted the settings and then started walking. He glanced at the young woman next to him. She wore a headset and had her cell phone tucked in a holster in her shorts. That's what he should have done; brought a headset and some of his oldies.

He adjusted the controls to quicken his stride. After ten minutes, he began to feel it, so he dialed down again. He was about to get off the treadmill when he heard cheers erupt across the room. The first finalist had just been announced. He spotted Harry in the middle of the action jawing with friends like a politician. Even though they'd been there a half-hour, he had yet to engage in any athletic activity.

Pete turned the machine off and wiped his sweaty face. Then he headed for the shower room. He was just getting out of the stall when the weight lifting contestants started coming in. Harry was in their midst, this time talking animatedly with one of the football players. He stripped down and entered the shower, continuing to talk the whole time.

Pete spotted Bud Stephanopoulis and went over to him. "How'd you do, old timer?" he asked.

"Just missed," Bud said. "I'm out of shape."

"I was cheering for you to teach those young guys a lesson. Thought for sure you'd rise to the occasion."

Bud just gave him a look and shook his head.

Harry got out of the shower and came to their side of the locker room. The charter boat guy and Willie Nelson look-alike were at the end of the bench. "You guys did okay, huh?" Harry asked.

"We're both lifting in the finals," Charter Boat answered.

Harry nodded. "Good work. We need some representatives of the mature age group."

"They ought to have a bigger shower room in here," Charter Boat grumbled to his fellow contestant as he stripped off his gym clothes.

Willie nodded and peeled off his shirt, ran a towel over his upper body, and donned a fresh long-sleeved shirt. He stuffed the dirty shirt in his duffel, ran the towel over his face again, and said, "Too many people," as he passed Harry on his way out.

Pete prodded Harry to get dressed and then followed him out the door. He looked at the center without the hordes and noted how well equipped it was for a small-town facility.

"I didn't get in as much work as I would have liked," Harry said on their way to his Explorer. "I imagine next week will be a packed house again for the finals. Two old geezers against three young bucks. That'll be something."

"Hungry?" Pete asked.

"I could eat a raw goose. All I've had is a bowl of Cheerios this morning. This workout stuff is going to be a problem. I hope I burn more calories from working out than I gain from eating more as a result of my bigger appetite. Athletic activity really affects how much you eat, you know."

They found a place that was open for lunch. Harry made a show of ordering a cobb salad and then slathered it with dressing. Pete ordered a plain chicken breast sandwich without mayonnaise. They both had iced tea.

"We were in such a rush to get to the center that you never did tell me how your visit to Chicago went."

Pete told him about lurking around Thomson, Barrett & Radke's reception area and confronting Radke when he returned from lunch. He also told him about his visit to Nautical Finance.

"Aren't you nervous about putting out the word that you want to talk to Zahn?"

"A little. But realistically, I don't think there's much risk. The mob doesn't knock people off like they used to, and the people they do knock off are either their own guys or people who owe them money. Zahn should have nothing to fear from me. All I want to do is impress on him that I'm out of the situation that got me tangled up in this mess in the first place."

"Zahn won't know that."

"I'm banking on the fact that he'll have some idea why I want to talk to him. And that he'll also realize what my interests are. If you were he, wouldn't you rather have me out of your hair instead of stirring things up and causing you more legal trouble when you've got plenty already?"

"I see your point, but …"

"It's too late for second thoughts now. I've made my draw. I want to have the Zahn thing settled before Julie comes back from California."

"Umm," Harry murmured. Then he shifted gears and said, "I guess Richter and his people are holding firm on their position that Hicks is their man. They can't help but be worried after that show your guy Manning put on, though. People are still buzzing about it."

"I told you he was good. What did you think of that suit he had on?"

"Jeez, I'd be embarrassed to go out of the house looking like that. I thought he'd be a snappy dresser and read Blackstone or whoever that old English guy was."

Pete laughed. "You can't go in front of a Chicago jury looking like a dandy. Many of the people in the jury pools down there are poor and without much education. If you appear in court in a three-piece Brooks Brothers suit, you'll have a hard time developing a rapport with the folks. Ira understands that. In the courtroom, or when he's trying to get public opinion on his side, he's as old shoe as they come. One time — and I swear this is true — Ira was in court and another lawyer asked him where he got those pre-stained neckties."

"Pre-stained," Harry repeated, chuckling. "That's good."

"There was a story about Ira in the Sunday *New York Times* a few years back that said he has one of the largest collections of hand-tailored suits in the U.S. and over a hundred hand-made silk ties."

Harry just shook his head. "Do you suppose he'd sit for an interview after this case is over?"

"Maybe if I ask him. Or if you can assure him the subscription base of your paper is at least a million readers. And spring for dinner at the Manitou, of course."

Harry grunted and said, "Well, I've got to get going. Damn paper schedule. You coming to the finals?"

"When are they?"

"I'll get the exact date and time and call you."

"I'll go unless something comes up. You're going to be pulling for the old guys, I presume."

Harry got the faraway look in his eyes that always foretold that the wheels in his mind were grinding. "I think I will." He paused and then added, "You know, I wish I'd gotten organized and entered that competition myself. It would have been something to be going against those jocks."

"I would have been there cheering you on. You know that song from 'Rocky?' I would have had that blaring the whole time. You would have been so pumped that you would have been able to bench five hundred pounds."

Harry looked thoughtful again. "I wonder how much I could lift."

"Hey, you're a beast. We all know that."

On the way to the car, Harry said, "Maybe that Redd guy will take a shower before the finals."

Pete looked at him.

"You notice that he didn't shower today?" Harry asked.

"I think he just wanted to get out of the crowd," Pete replied. "I'm hoping he wears a short-sleeve shirt next time so we can compare his tattoos with the tats of that one college guy."

"He'd have no chance against that one," Harry said, snorting. "The college guy has two-color roses, a snake, a naked woman, everything."

Pete heard him, but already had his mind on the phone calls he was about to make.

◆ ◆ ◆

His routine for the next two days followed an identical pattern. Two or three times each day, he'd call Radke's direct line and each time he'd get his secretary. He would identify himself, ask for Radke, be told he was in a meeting, and leave a message that he expected Vinnie Zahn to call him. He'd meticulously spell out Zahn's name. Then he'd do the same with each of the lawyers in Radke's firm who listed white-collar work as their specialty. Most of the time he would get their secretaries, but once one of the lawyers picked up his own phone. After listening briefly, the lawyer told Pete to stop harassing them and slammed down the receiver. In some of his telephone conversations, Pete would identify Zahn as "the reputed mob boss and a client of your firm."

Pete's calls to Nautical Finance were more direct. He'd ask for Zahn, be told he wasn't there at the moment, and be asked by the person answering the phone if he could help him. He always responded by asking the person to have Zahn call him.

Late in the day, he was sitting at his desk and staring at the bay. He'd almost given up hope that his strategy of making a pest of himself would work, so when the phone rang this time, he wasn't optimistic.

"Mr. Thorsen?" a voice asked.

Pete's pulse quickened. The caller sounded like the man who'd called him the night Julie was stalked. He couldn't be sure, though. The voice didn't sound as throaty.

"Yes, this is Pete Thorsen."

"Rumor has it you're looking for Mr. Zahn."

TWENTY-SIX

"They're not just rumors. I *am* looking for Mr. Zahn."

"Maybe I can help you. Mr. Zahn is away just now."

"I appreciate your offer," Pete said, "but I need to talk to him personally."

"What about?"

"It's personal, as I said. But I have a feeling he knows."

"That sounds awfully mysterious, Mr. Thorsen."

"Nothing mysterious about it. Now when can I see Vinnie Zahn?"

"Well, if you're going to be around that little town of yours tomorrow afternoon, you may be in luck. Mr. Zahn's on a cruise up your way. He's a gracious man and said he could pick you up and take you for a ride on his boat."

"Tomorrow afternoon would be fine. Where should I meet him?"

"Be down at the harbor in town at 5:00 p.m."

"And how will I recognize Mr. Zahn?"

"Look for his boat."

"Does the boat have a name?"

"Don't worry, you can't miss it. Oh, and Mr. Zahn suggested you come alone."

◆ ◆ ◆

When Pete arrived at the harbor, Zahn's boat was already there, moored just outside the last slip at the far end of the dock. The area reserved for over-sized visiting craft. The caller was right; he couldn't miss it. Except for naval vessels or the oil sheik's yacht he'd observed cruising the Thames when he was in London on business, he couldn't remember seeing a larger watercraft.

He walked to the pier where two men were standing near the stern of the boat. Both wore white pants and polo shirts that looked a size too small for their upper bodies. One had slicked-back hair tied in a ponytail and stood with his arms folded, as if to show off his muscles. The other had closely-cropped hair that looked like it had been dyed dirty blond and held a sign that read, "Isabella II." Both men had dark complexions.

Pete felt a little apprehensive about what he was getting into. As he approached, the man with the ponytail stepped forward and asked, "Mr. Thorsen?"

"Yes," he replied. No hands were offered by either side.

"Mr. Zahn is waiting for you," the man said. Pete said nothing, but followed the two men aboard the boat.

A man came up the steps from the lower deck. He was maybe five-ten, a little overweight, with a prominent Roman nose and a deep tan. He wore white pants like his men, and a bright pink polo with an anchor emblem. The shirt was open at the neck to expose chest hair and a heavy gold chain. A pinky ring with a stone the size of a golf ball graced the third finger of his left hand.

"Welcome aboard the Isabella, Mr. Thorsen. Nice day for a cruise." His voice was thin, and his smile didn't extend to his eyes. Unlike his men, he extended his hand and Pete took it. It was a firm handshake, but not a warm one.

"Is it okay with you if we cruise up the coast while we talk? I'd like to see the sights. I've never been to this area before."

Pete thought of Les Brimley stretched out on the seventeenth green of his golf course, but said only, "That's fine, Mr. Zahn. Maybe I can point out a few things."

"That would be nice. Do you mind if I call you Pete, by the way? Everyone calls me Vinnie. We should be on a first-name basis if we're going to spend the evening together."

Pete nodded. Or maybe he should call him the Fisherman, he thought. He met Zahn's lingering gaze.

Zahn's two henchmen began to untie the Isabella II from its moorings. Pete glanced at them and said to Zahn, "I don't want to be rude, Vinnie, but I think your men should stay on shore. The conversation we're going to have doesn't concern them."

Zahn smiled again and said, "I'll send them below. I agree that they don't have to hear anything we talk about."

"No, Vinnie. I think they should stay on shore."

Zahn looked at him again and said, "Sure, Pete, no problem. I'll have them stay on shore. I can pick them up later when I drop you off. But, first, do you mind if we check you out? You don't look like a terrorist or a pirate, but you never know these days."

"I'm not carrying a weapon or wired, if that's what you're concerned about."

"I'm sure you're not, Pete," Zahn replied, "but it's just for my peace of mind. I want to be sure we can have a nice friendly conversation that stays between us. Do you mind?"

Pete shrugged and stood there feeling awkward as one of Zahn's men patted him down and looked under his shirt collar and in the cuffs of his pants. He asked Pete to take off his shoes, belt and watch. When he was finished, the man looked at Zahn and said, "He's clean, Vinnie."

Zahn turned his back to Pete and whispered something to his men. They glared at Pete for a moment and then left the boat. They stood on the pier and continued to stare at him. The boatman started the engines and slowly backed away from the dock. Pete felt relieved that he'd at least eliminated two of Zahn's men from the equation. When they'd cleared the dock, the boat moved at idle speed for a hundred yards, then accelerated as it neared the harbor's outlet and headed for open water.

Zahn was scanning the shoreline with a pair of binoculars. He lowered them and said, "Pretty town. It reminds me of some of the seaside villages in Sicily. No tile roofs, of course, but the hills and the way everything nestles close to the water. You do any fishing on Lake Michigan, Pete?"

"Occasionally," Pete replied.

Zahn laid the binoculars on a small table and said, "Could I fix you something to drink?"

"No thanks."

"Do you mind if I have something?"

"As you please," Pete replied.

Vinnie Zahn mixed a drink and took a seat in a deck chair opposite Pete. He put on a pair of small, stylish sunglasses and picked up his binoculars again. They were just passing Point Betsie and he studied the lighthouse intently. He lowered the binoculars and said, "That's the famous lighthouse they use as a guide in the Mac race, isn't it?"

"It is," Pete said. He was eager to get to the subject, but continued to act nonchalant and let Vinnie play tourist.

Vinnie looked through his binoculars again. "I have some friends who sail in that race every year. They always rave about what a beautiful lighthouse it is."

Pete nodded once more.

After looking through his binoculars yet again, Zahn lowered them and put them on the table. "I apologize, Pete. You came out here to talk and all I'm doing is looking at the sights. Rude of me. I'll try to be more attentive. Please, Pete, tell me what's on your mind."

Pete fixed Zahn with a steady gaze and said, "You may already be aware of some of this, but I'll tell you the background anyway since it ties in to my main point. We had a murder up here recently. The victim was a real estate developer named Les Brimley. Maybe you've heard of Brimley because he's from Chicago. Even though he was up here much of the time, he had a home in the Chicago suburbs and several real estate projects in the metropolitan area. Anyway, he was killed on his own golf course a few days before it was to open. It shocked our community." Pete said nothing about the fact he knew the Chicago PD had already asked Zahn about Brimley's murder. Zahn also volunteered nothing.

"I didn't know Brimley," Pete continued, "so while it was a tragic event, it didn't affect me personally. Like most citizens, I was content to follow the reports coming out of the sheriff's office. Then I was in my office a week or so after the murder, working on something, when this woman walks in. Turns out it was Susan Brimley, the murder victim's widow."

Zahn had been listening impassively, but now asked, "Did you know this woman?"

"I knew *of* her, but didn't know her personally. She's an artist and I have a couple of her paintings. I saw her once or twice at art shows, but that's it. She came to me because she knew I had practiced law in Chicago for more than twenty years, and I guess I'm the only lawyer in the area with experience in matters other than house closings or simple wills. We talked for a while and then she said she wanted to hire me to look into her late husband's financial affairs. She was wondering what she'd inherit and I guess she wasn't getting much information from the lawyer for the estate. The lawyer's name is Theo Radke and his firm is Thompson, Barrett & Radke. They're in Chicago. Ever hear of them?"

Zahn looked amused and said, "No offense, Pete, but I don't spend much time keeping track of lawyers or law firms."

Pete continued to stare at him and said slowly, "Okay. In any case, I agreed to represent Mrs. Brimley for the limited purpose of looking at Brimley's financial records and talking to Radke. When I was at LB Development's offices — in case you don't know, that was Brimley's real estate development company up here — I was struck by all of the debt the company had. He owed over $20 million to a group of Chicago banks and several million more to a couple of other parties. I asked Mrs. Brimley about those parties because I wasn't familiar with them; she told me she wasn't either. Then she asked me a lot of questions about her personal liability. I didn't have all the facts at the time, but told her she wouldn't be responsible for LB's obligations personally unless she'd signed a guarantee or something, but that the estate might be liable depending on the facts. First year law school stuff, you know?"

Zahn continued to sit impassively. Occasionally he would take a sip of his drink.

"Not long after that, I received a call from a man who wouldn't identify himself. He suggested I might want to rethink the advice I had given to a certain unnamed client. He seemed to know a lot about me and my family. The same night, I got a panicked call from my daughter. She said two men had been stalking her. A while after that, my cottage went up in flames. I eventually put two and two together, Vinnie, and concluded that the bad things that were happening to me somehow related to my work for Susan Brimley. I confronted her and she finally confessed that she hadn't told me everything she knew about her husband's affairs. She also admitted that two men had been to see her several times and she'd quoted my comments concerning her personal liability."

"That's a tragic story, Pete, but I don't understand what you want from me."

Pete just stared at him and said, "I want you to leave me and my family alone, Vinnie."

"Pete, Pete, are you accusing me of causing all those bad things that have been happening to you and your daughter?"

"It's occurred to me, and I want to straighten things out between us. I was used by Mrs. Brimley, and once I discovered what was going on, I resigned as her lawyer. Now that you know the background, I want your commitment that you'll leave us alone."

"People don't like to be accused of things, Pete. Bad things can continue to happen to someone who goes around saying things that aren't true."

A chill ran through his body. Zahn's demeanor seemed different all of a sudden, and Pete wondered whether he'd been too direct. He also sensed that backing off now would be a mistake. He continued to bluff his way through and said, "I know what's going on, Vinnie. Your finance company, Nautical Finance, loaned Les Brimley money and you had some sort of side deal whereby he owed you, too. Then Brimley was killed and things got more complicated. You decided to put the arm on Susan Brimley to get paid and viewed me as getting in your way. So to get me to back off, you had a couple of your men stalk my daughter. They probably torched my cottage, too."

"You were foolish to come out here and make these charges, Pete," Zahn said. "You a good swimmer, Pete?"

"Fair," Pete replied. "But look, I didn't ask for this meeting to have a confrontation with you. I came looking for a truce. In case you think I'm a complete idiot, let me tell you what I did before meeting you. Did you see that man with a dog on a leash taking pictures when we were still at the dock? He's not just a tourist. Then I told a friend where I was going and that if I'm not back by 8:00 p.m., to alert the sheriff and the Coast Guard. They'll be crawling all over this area if that happens, and you'll have an interesting time explaining how I left on your boat, but mysteriously disappeared. The last thing I did was leave three copies of a letter with my friend, one to the local sheriff, one to the FBI director for this district, and one to the unit of the Chicago PD that's been after you. If you think you have legal problems now, you can add a string of additional charges to your list."

Zahn's lips tightened, but then he seemed to regain control and said, "Pete, Pete, we've both a little edgy today. Maybe we can finish our conversation like gentlemen. It occurs to me that some of the things you raise could just be misunderstandings. Take the loans. It's possible that Nautical loaned money to Mr. Brimley, I just can't say for sure. Nautical makes a lot of loans and I can't be expected to know about all of them. Maybe one of our loan officers came to see Mrs. Brimley."

"It was Sal and Victor, Vinnie. Mrs. Brimley described them perfectly."

"It could have been them. They both work for Nautical part-time. But how do you know Susan Brimley told you the truth? You said yourself she lied to you about other things."

"I'm not concerned about Susan Brimley. I no longer represent her, remember? I am concerned about my daughter, and the stalkers she described look like Sal and Victor, too."

"I know how upsetting that incident must have been for you, Pete, because I have a young daughter of my own. But I have a feeling that incident might have been one of the misunderstandings I mentioned. Sal has a daughter, too, and I know he was thinking of enrolling her in a private school because the public schools in his area are so bad. I seem to remember him telling me he was looking at a private school near Detroit. Maybe he was walking around to, you know, get a feel for the school. He might have brought Victor along for company and your daughter might have seen them and thought they were stalking her. You don't have to worry about another misunderstanding like that because I know Sal concluded the school is too expensive for him."

Pete just looked at him and said nothing.

"I'm sure you don't know this, Pete, but my grandmother's name was Isabella. This boat is named after her. She was a remarkable woman. She could foresee the future, and I sometimes think I inherited some of her powers. I see a long, happy future for your daughter and am sure she'll bear you many healthy grandchildren. It's a good scene, Pete."

Pete felt like telling him he was full of crap, but kept his composure and said, "What do your clairvoyant powers tell you about the fire in my cottage?"

Vinnie Zahn looked at him from behind his sunglasses and said, "I can't help you there, Pete. I'm afraid I have no explanation for the fire."

ROBERT WANGARD

"Do you know if Sal and Victor happened to be in my neighborhood that night? You know, meeting with Susan Brimley or something?"

Zahn frowned. "What date was that?" he asked.

Pete told him.

Zahn appeared to think for a moment. "I'm positive they weren't up here, Pete. That was the day of my niece's wedding. We were all there. I take it you suspect someone of starting the fire in your cabin?"

"I not only suspect arson; an expert told me it *was* arson."

"If you want, I can have one of our people check it out. You know, to show my friendship. Nautical has contacts because sometimes it has debtors whose buildings mysteriously catch fire. Greek lightning they call it." A faint smile creased his face.

"I appreciate the offer, but it's in hand."

The breakwater loomed just ahead. Pete felt relieved. Vinnie had his binoculars out again. When he lowered them, Pete said, "Remember, Vinnie, I'm out of this mess as far as you and Susan Brimley are concerned. What you work out with her is your business. But if one more bad thing happens to Julie or me, I'm coming to Chicago to settle scores. The first thing I'm going to do is stir up every bit of legal trouble for you I can. Then I'm going to come after you personally, maybe with a friend who's a former Navy SEAL. I know where you live in Riverside, I've been to your office in Berwyn, and I know Burnham Harbor where you keep Isabella II like the back of my hand. I know your favorite restaurants, the street you walk your dog. I know where you buy cigars. You won't be able to twitch for fear of us being behind you."

"I thought we were finished with threats, Pete. You don't sound very lawyer-like when you talk like that."

"I ceased being a lawyer when my daughter was harassed and my house was torched. I'm a hunter now."

TWENTY-SEVEN

Harry looked up when Pete walked in and rushed to clasp his right hand. Then he put a hand on Pete's shoulder and squeezed it and expelled air from his lungs. "You had me worried," he said. "I was about to call Richter."

"You still have a half-hour," Pete replied.

"I know, but I don't think you realize what it's like sitting here waiting, not knowing what's going on. I wasn't sure I'd ever see you again,"

"I'm sure it was much tougher than facing down a mob kingpin," Pete said, forcing a grin and suddenly feeling drained.

Harry returned to his desk and sat there as though unsure of what to say. Then he pushed a Styrofoam box across the desk to Pete. "I got us a couple of sandwiches since I didn't know if you'd be up for dinner when you got back. If it's cold, I can zap it in the microwave."

Pete opened the box; it was a pulled-pork sandwich and bag of chips from the place next door. Harry's idea of diet food. Pete took a bite of the sandwich. It was barely warm, but he didn't care. He wasn't that hungry anyway. He took another bite and let more of the tension drain from his body.

Harry sat on the edge of his chair, seemingly waiting for Pete to report on his cruise with Vinnie Zahn. He watched intently as Pete popped a couple of chips in his mouth and finally said, "You feel up to giving me a report?"

"Sure," Pete replied. He took another bite of his sandwich and put the rest of it back in the box.

Harry was obviously relieved to see his friend still alive, but the lack of information seemed to be killing him. Finally he said, "I take it things went okay?"

Pete sensed his anxiety, so while he didn't feel like talking, he laid out his entire conversation with Zahn in detail. Harry sat wide-eyed and soaked up every nuance.

When Pete was finished, Harry said, "So I gather Zahn didn't admit anything."

"No, but then I didn't expect him to. Even if he's guilty, he couldn't very well admit to killing Brimley or having my daughter stalked or torching my cottage. As a matter of fact, we didn't even talk about Brimley's murder. It's tough to face someone like Zahn and accuse him of murder. The other stuff was hard enough."

"I guess you're right," Harry said thoughtfully.

"The closest he came to admitting anything was when he told me that Nautical *might* have loaned money to Brimley and that two of his men *might* have been on Julie's campus the day Julie and Mikki were stalked. He told me this cock-and-bull story about how his guy Sal was looking at the school for his own daughter and how he'd inherited his grandmother's clairvoyant powers and just knew that Julie was going to be okay. I took that as a signal he wasn't going to have Julie harassed anymore."

"That's a relief, huh?"

"It is if I can believe him. But as long as I'm out of the picture, he has no reason to court further trouble by continuing to go after Julie. He knows he won't have to worry about me as long as he keeps his word."

"He said all of that stuff after you told him you were no longer representing Susan Brimley and just wanted out of the middle, right?"

"More or less," Pete said.

"How about the fire?"

"I don't know. He was hard to read on that one and he had those damn sunglasses on so I couldn't see his eyes. But when I mentioned the fire, it almost seemed to come as a surprise to him. At the same time, I kept thinking about the comment the anonymous caller made about my 'nice little cabin.' But on balance, Zahn's reaction seemed different when I mentioned the fire."

"A mess, huh? I know you didn't talk about it, but what's your take on whether Zahn's the one who killed Brimley?"

Pete polished a spot on Harry's desk with his napkin, and said, "I honestly don't know, Harry. As we've conjectured many times, it seems that Zahn would just be complicating his prospects for getting repaid if he rubbed out his debtor. The common wisdom is that the mob breaks a guy's fingers or something to put pressure on him. Unless, obviously, something happened to make him change course."

They sat quietly for a few minutes, neither speaking. Then Harry added, "You must have been really pissed to say that stuff to Zahn at the end."

Pete looked up. "You mean about me coming to Chicago to hunt him down?"

"Yeah."

"I was thinking about that walking over here. The fact is, I was scared as hell the whole time, but knew I couldn't show it. It was funny, but once we got inside the breakwater again, I got pumped up. I have two people in my family that I have any contact with. Julie and my father who's in that facility in Wisconsin with Alzheimer's. My father isn't expected to live for more than a year, but Julie … if something happened to her, there wouldn't be any risk to me because the only thing that would matter would be to get the person who harmed her." After a few moments he forced a grin and added, "Maybe it's not such a bad thing to make a guy like Zahn believe he's dealing with a fellow madman."

Harry shook his head and said, "That was a stroke of genius making up that story about the Navy SEAL."

"I didn't make it up. That was a reference to Ira's guy, Adam Rose. I guess he's one tough hombre. I thought that throwing out a reference to someone like that might get Zahn's attention even if he wasn't worried about me."

Harry looked at him and said, "You know, the more I learn about this case, the more convinced I become that John Hicks is getting screwed."

"Well, he's got one of the best defense lawyers in the country. If anyone can get him off, it's Ira."

"You're still going to look over that automotive detailing information for him, right?"

"I promised Ira I would," Pete replied. He rose to leave. "Thanks for being my back-up, Harry, I really appreciate it."

"Glad to do it. We're a team, remember?"

As Harry showed him out, Pete noticed that his health club visits either were having an effect or he was holding his gut in out of pride in his role in helping Pete face down one of Chicago's most notorious gangsters. He put a hand on Pete's shoulder as they walked out and said, "I took a half-hour off and ran over to the health club to catch the finals of the weightlifting contest. You'd just left so I figured it was safe to go."

"Who won?"

"One of those college guys. You know what his name is? Jimbo Rock. That's a helluva name for a linebacker, huh? I guess he's supposed to be NFL material."

"The old guys didn't do that well I gather."

"They finished fourth and fifth. But both benched over two hundred pounds. They were just no match for those college guys."

Harry's parting words to Pete were, "If they have the contest again next year, I'm going to enter. I should be in top shape by then."

It was still light when Pete pulled into the driveway of his rental house. There was a box at the front door with a UPS delivery slip. The slip indicated the package had been sent by Adam Rose. He carried the box inside and set it on the kitchen table.

He rummaged around the refrigerator for something to drink. He really wanted a Thor's Hammer and tonic, but was reminded again of his vow to curb his drinking. And of the fact he kept no vodka around the house to avoid temptation. He settled for a bottle of spring water.

He used a kitchen knife to open the box from Rose. Inside he saw a jumble of documents. He groaned. He had hoped for a nice, neat list he could peruse in minutes. This was going to be a more tedious and time-consuming exercise than he'd anticipated. He flipped through a few of the documents and saw there were copies of invoices and other paperwork from various automotive establishments. *Crap,* he muttered under his breath.

He took his water outside and sat in one of the deck chairs and gazed out at the lake. The sun was just settling in the west. The water was choppy from the breeze and his end of the lake was empty except for a couple of power boats that periodically buzzed past. When they were close, the sound of engines filled the air and then faded as the boats headed west again.

The day had gone about as well as could be expected and he'd accomplished his primary mission. Now he'd just have to wait and see how everything played out. He didn't necessarily think that Susan Brimley was a bad person, but she'd certainly acted badly and caused him a lot of problems. By lying to him, she'd not only set him up, but had put Julie and him in the path of a very bad man. Hopefully, he'd now neutralized the threat.

His remaining goal was to find out who set fire to his cottage and he had no idea how to approach that. He glanced at his watch. He had almost an hour before he was scheduled to call Julie. He decided to go for a short run to relieve the remaining tension in his body. He donned his running gear and set out on what was becoming a familiar route.

When he got to Lynn's house, he paused and looked up. Then he started running again and tried not to think of anything except the beauty of the lake. The breeze felt good against his sweaty forehead.

After a quick shower, he called Julie. It was comforting to hear her bubbly voice even though he wished she would abandon that irritating valley-girl talk. He was still smiling when he told her he loved her and hung up.

He surfed through the television channels, but found nothing he was interested in watching. He clicked the red button on the remote and downed the last swallow of his water. His gaze shifted to the box on the kitchen table. Oh, well, he thought, he might as well get started on it before he turned in for the night.

The documents were even more difficult to decipher than he'd initially assumed. The forms were printed, but that's where legibility ended. Mechanics might know engines and tires and exhaust systems, but all of them must have finished dead last in school when it came to penmanship. Each set of documents was a bewildering mass of cryptic abbreviations, multiple orders on many forms with no logical separation, and extra charges for things like a gallon of washer fluid or a replacement wiper blade. Looking at the documents, he could understand why Adam Rose had opted to send the whole mess rather than try to compile a list.

As he laboriously sorted through the documents, he thought about what he should charge Ira Manning for doing his grunt work. Then he remembered; Manning was representing John Hicks for next to nothing. Next to nothing and all of the free publicity he'd garner by getting Hicks off from a high profile murder rap.

Pete continued to sort through the documents, trying to figure out what had been done for each invoice and identifying the vehicle's owner. Rose had at least stapled together the documents that related to a particular job, which was moderately helpful. So far, not one name or address jumped out at him. Then he saw the documents from Mike's

Body Works in Gaylord. They listed Birchwood Press as the owner of the vehicle in question. He frowned. He knew Birchwood. In fact, it was one of his clients and its facilities were located nearby in the small town of Benzonia. Why would someone from Birchwood take a vehicle all the way to Gaylord, half way across the state, for repair?

He looked at the documents more closely. He couldn't tell what kind of vehicle it was; all he could make out was the license plate number and cryptic notes that looked like "Bod wk" and "clean." A back-up invoice confirmed that body work indeed had been done on the vehicle. Specifically, the front fender had been replaced if he interpreted the invoice correctly. He wondered if "clean" referred to detailing of the interior of the vehicle or something less like running the vehicle through the car wash. He sat back in his chair, puzzled.

TWENTY-EIGHT

The next morning, Pete finished looking through the documents, but found nothing else that caught his eye. He returned to the documents from Mike's Body Works. Then he called Adam Rose and asked if he remembered more details from his visit to Mike's. He didn't have any specifics, but promised to check with the owner and call back. Pete asked him to find out whether the owner of the repair shop remembered who brought the vehicle in as well as what kind of vehicle it was and what "clean" meant. He gave Rose the dates on which the work had been done.

When Rose called back later that morning, he reported that the owner of Mike's didn't have the name of the man who had brought the vehicle in, but described him as tall and middle-aged with a cropped gray beard. The vehicle was an older Chevy Suburban that had been modified in back to remove seats and make it into something akin to a van. The other thing the owner remembered was that the vehicle had been detailed, not just washed. The man who brought the vehicle in explained that the accident was his fault and he wanted the vehicle spiffed up so the woman who ran Birchwood Press wouldn't be mad at him.

Pete stared at the phone and thought about how he could approach Ida Doell and get the information he wanted without raising all sorts of questions about his inquiry. He'd represented Ida, the owner of Birchwood Press, for the past year as a favor to Lynn Hawke. He hadn't been keen on taking on a mom and pop printing operation as a client, but Lynn had persisted and he didn't want to do anything to upset their relationship. As it turned out, he enjoyed getting to know Ida. She was in her eighties, and while she had her idiosyncrasies, still had most of her faculties about her. He knew from past experience, however, that she couldn't always be counted on to be discreet about their conversations. She had a way of blurting out things in an overly forthright manner at the most inopportune times. It was a charming trait that many people in the community had experienced, but not one he wanted or needed when he was trying to find out about the Chevy Suburban.

Then he had an idea. Shortly after he began to represent Ida, he'd reorganized her sole proprietorship into a limited liability company. The annual report forms had just arrived from the state, and while they weren't due for two months, maybe he could use them as an excuse to see her and probe for information.

He picked up the phone and dialed Ida's number. While he waited, he prepared himself for the same adventure he experienced whenever he tried to reach her by phone. A young woman cheerfully answered, "Birchwood Press," then asked him to hold while she attended to a customer. When she finally came back on the line, she asked who he was holding for. He repeated his request to speak to Ida Doell. She promised to transfer him. Then the line went silent and he heard a dial tone. He sighed and dialed Birchwood Press' number again. The woman with whom he'd spoken only a couple of minutes earlier seemed not to remember his call. He gave his name a second time and again asked to speak to Ida. The woman embarked on the same high tech exercise of transferring his call. To his surprise, Ida's halting voice came on the line. "Ida, this is Pete Thorsen," he said.

Ida seemed to digest the information and then said, "Well Peter, how nice of you to call. How's that darling daughter of yours?"

He assured her that Julie was fine and that she'd just turned sixteen and had gotten her driver's license.

"Sixteen," Ida said. He could just see her sitting there shaking her head. "That's such a nice age."

They exchanged a few more pleasantries and then Pete said, "I have some things for you to sign. Could I come by this afternoon?"

"Oh Peter, I feel like such a conglomerate these days with you as my lawyer. You come by any time you'd like. If you have time, I'll show you our new designs for the summer season."

Pete said he'd be there at 2:00 p.m. and finally was able to end the conversation. He glanced at his watch, took a deep breath, and decided he had plenty of time to run into town, get a bite to eat, and spend a half-hour getting the documents ready for his meeting with Ida Doell and her "conglomerate." He smiled when he thought of how the conversation would go. She'd tell him to be sure to send her a bill for his services. She always said that. He hadn't billed her for the minor work he'd done and she never seemed to remember to follow up on her request. It was compensation enough that she treated him as some kind of god. And he hoped it would keep his standing high in Lynn Hawke's eyes.

The Birchwood Press parking lot was mostly empty when Pete pulled in. He grabbed his file folder and walked to the Chevy Suburban parked at the end of the lot, next to the building. It was about the same vintage as his Range Rover and looked like it had been freshly washed and waxed that morning. He peered in the window. The interior looked as spotless as the outside. There was no logo or other signage on the outside announcing that it was a Birchwood Press vehicle. Pete had raised that with Ida before and suggested she put the company identification on the door to gain exposure for her business. She'd waved a hand weakly and dismissed the idea as too "commercial."

He walked into the building and down a hall separated from the production area by glass panels. One of the three old Heidelberg printing presses was in operation. As best he could tell, it was pumping out cards with some sort of animal design. Pete waved at the pressman and walked back to Ida's office. The office was at the rear of the workspace and had a glass wall so Ida could keep an eye on the entire operation. Pete saw her hunched over her desk punching the keys of a clunky black adding machine that looked older than the printing presses. He rapped on the door and waited for her to look up from her work.

"Peter," she said, "come in, come in." She struggled to rise from her chair.

Pete rushed to her side and said, "Stay seated, please." He put a hand gently on one of her shoulders and kissed the top of her head.

"So good to see you, Peter." She clasped his hand in hers and studied him. "You should see my friend Sydney in Beulah. He's a very good barber."

Pete smiled. He'd gotten his hair cut by the barber at the University Club in Chicago for fifteen years, but since moving north, he no longer had a regular barber and tended to go too long between haircuts. Harry McTigue, who didn't have to worry about those things, frequently kidded him that he must be trying to get back to his Viking roots.

"I'll stop by to see Sydney tomorrow." He grinned at her. "I'll tell him Ida sent me. Maybe he'll give me a break on the price."

She appeared not to hear him because she was asking about his daughter as though they'd never had their telephone conversation a few hours earlier. She wanted to know every detail of Julie's life. Pete told her about her progress in school, her exploits on the soccer field, and her many adventures in California. Ida appeared to soak up every detail. When Pete was finished, Ida said, "Well, when that girl comes up this summer, you tell her to come see me. When you get to be an old woman like me, you want to hear all the details so you remember what it was like."

Pete promised he would, and then said, "Your Chevy Suburban looks great. You know, Ida, you and I must have the two oldest vehicles in the county."

"After Howard got it fixed," she said, "it's better than ever. I think it'll last longer than these old bones."

"Got it fixed," he said, feigning surprise, "what happened?"

"Howard hit a deer one night. It wasn't his fault. You know how dark some of the roads around here can be. The deer jumped right out in front of him and he hit it with one fender. He felt terrible." She shook her head and looked distraught. "I thought about that poor deer for two days. I was so sad."

"Was the deer killed?"

"We don't know," Ida said. "Howard said it ran into the woods. He looked, but couldn't find it. Poor thing. He's probably laying out there someplace not able to feed himself."

Pete shook his head. "Where did you get the Suburban fixed? That place in Frankfort?"

"Oh no, Howard said that would take two weeks. He took it some other place that could do the work in a few days. Howard is such a responsible man. He felt terrible about the accident. I guess he took the Suburban to his house one night because he had to haul a couch or something. He has one of those little foreign cars that you can't get much in. You know what he did, Peter? He insisted on paying for the repairs because he said the accident was his fault and our insurance premiums would go way up if we submitted a claim. I told him he shouldn't pay because it was an accident, but he insisted."

"How long has Howard worked for you?"

"I don't remember exactly. I think it's been a year. I don't know what I'd do without him. He picks me up every morning and takes me home at night. He cleans out the gutters at my house and everything.

And can that man ever sing. He entertains the children down at the library, you know."

"Mmm," Pete murmured. He pointed at the adding machine. "What are you working on with all of the numbers?"

"Our payroll," she said. She lowered her voice. "Lynn used to do this for me, but then she had to go away. She left this girl in charge until she got back. I have to check everything she does. I don't want the checks to go out wrong. Our employees need everything to be right."

The "girl" Ida was referring to was a woman nearly Lynn's age who had big accounting firm experience. But she wasn't Lynn and hadn't earned Ida's trust yet.

"You find any mistakes?"

"Not yet, but I feel I have to check her work every time just to be sure."

Just then, the pressman stuck his head in the office door and said, "Sorry to disturb you, Ida, but there's a problem with one of the presses. Could you to come out on the floor for a few minutes?"

"Peter, do you mind?" Ida asked. "I'm the only one who seems to be able to coax these old machines of ours back to life. If you need something to keep you occupied for a few minutes, you can check over the rest of these figures. I trust you."

The pressman helped Ida out of her desk chair and she used a walker to shuffle to the production area. Pete turned around the ledgers on her desk and studied the figures. Beside the names of each employee, Lynn's successor had listed several columns of numbers, starting with the gross salary amounts and proceeding to show percentages for personal deductions and payroll taxes, yielding a net number for each employee. Under a column headed "Special," an extra hundred dollars was deducted from Howard Redd's net compensation. Obviously, that was the deduction for the cost of the repairs to the Suburban. Ida had placed a small red check by the name of each employee she'd double-checked. Pete started to tap the keys of the old adding machine and then stopped and looked at the list of names. He wrote down Redd's Social Security number on the back of his file folder and was about to continue verifying the columns of numbers when Ida came shuffling back in.

"Did you find any mistakes?" Ida asked.

"Not yet. But I was just getting started. I wanted to understand the spreadsheet so I didn't make any mistakes myself."

"Well, I'll finish up. We've got to be careful, you know. Nothing hurts an employee's confidence in the company more than a mistake in her paycheck. That's why I'm always so careful."

Pete pulled out the annual report form and the annual company resolutions and showed Ida where to sign. She stared at the documents intently, then opened her desk drawer and rummaged around until she found a fat Mount Blanc fountain pen. She removed the top with great fanfare, tested the pen on a note pad, and looked at Pete with an impish smile. "I feel like a real executive at times like this," she said as she began signing the documents where Pete had indicated. "Lynn told me you were the best lawyer in Chicago and seeing your work, I can tell why she said that. The best lawyer and the best accountant. I'm so blessed."

When she was finished signing, she took Pete out to the display area and showed him all the new cards and notepads and placemats and paper napkins they had for the new summer season. When she came to something with a fawn on it, her expression would turn sad and she would murmur something sympathetic about the deer Howard had struck with the company vehicle.

Ida was getting visibly tired so Pete graciously bowed out and let her get back to checking the payroll numbers. Then, presumably, Howard Redd would drive her home as he always did. On the way to his car, he took another look at the gleaming Chevy Suburban.

When Pete got home, he decided to do another favor for Ira Manning. And satisfy his own curiosity. He dialed the human resources manager at one of his former clients. After bantering with him for a few minutes, he asked if he would run Howard Redd's name and Social Security number through the government's E-Verify system. When the manager got back on the phone, he confirmed Pete's hunch; the name and number didn't match.

TWENTY-NINE

"**W**hat do you know about Howard Redd?"

"The weightlifter?" Harry asked.

"Yes."

Harry shrugged, "Just what we've talked about before. Why?"

"Because," Pete said, "he popped up in those materials Adam Rose sent me. From what I can piece together, Redd took one of Birchwood Press' vehicles to a place near Gaylord for fender repairs."

Harry frowned. "Why way over there?"

"I don't know. I had to be a little devious with Ida Roell to get the information I wanted, but everything she told me is consistent with what Adam Rose dug up. She said Redd borrowed the company's Chevy Suburban one night to pick up a piece of furniture. He claims he hit a deer on one of the back roads and damaged the front fender. He then had the vehicle repaired at the place in Gaylord because, according to him, they could do the work right away. He insisted on paying for the repairs because the accident occurred while he was using the vehicle for personal business."

"The part about the deer rings true," Harry said. "That happens to a lot of people."

"The work was done shortly after Brimley was killed," Pete said.

"So? Maybe it was just a coincidence."

"Maybe," Pete said. "Redd had the vehicle detailed at the same time as the repair work was done. According to the owner of the body shop, he wanted the vehicle detailed because he felt bad about the accident and wanted it to be spick-and-span when he brought it back to the company."

"Ida's such a nice lady, I can understand why he'd want to do that."

"She loves the guy," Pete agreed. "I guess he picks her up in the morning and drives her home at night. Does odd jobs for her. She can't say enough good things about him."

"That's the reputation he has around town," Harry said. "Low key, minds his own business, helps people out."

"I had his name and Social Security number run through the government's computer. They don't match. Either Howard Redd isn't his real name or he's using someone else's Social Security number."

"That's strange. He doesn't look like an identity thief."

"No, he doesn't."

"Maybe there's an explanation," Harry said.

"What would it be? Everybody says he showed up here a year ago. No one knows anything about him. He's not from this area, and as far as we know, he has no ties to anyone up here. Now we discover there's a legal identity issue."

"Are you suggesting he might have had something to do with Brimley's murder?'

"I don't know, but you put all of this together — the detailing, the timing, the fact he took the Suburban out of the area to have the work done, the apparent false identity — and it certainly raises questions, doesn't it?"

"I see your point."

"I think we should find out more about Redd if you want to have the best shot at getting your friend Hicks off."

"Hey, Hicks isn't my friend. I just don't want to see the guy screwed if he didn't kill Brimley."

"Just journalistic interest, right?" Pete said with a touch of sarcasm.

Harry paused. "Yeah, something like that. Did you tell Manning all this stuff about Redd?"

"No," Pete said, "I tried to call him, but he was in court and wasn't expected back until late and then would be in court again all day today." Pete smiled when he thought about the conversation with Manning's secretary. Knowing Ira, he probably stopped at O'Sullivan's Bar to join his criminal defense buddies for a few drinks after a hard day in court.

"I guess Ira's planning to come up here again anyway."

"I hadn't heard that," Pete said.

"You're not media. There was an e-mail from Manning's office to all of the stations and newspapers in Michigan alerting them to another press conference. According to the e-mail, he's bringing a DNA expert with him."

"Mmm," Pete murmured. That sounded like Ira. Trying the case in the court of public opinion. Then he asked, "What time does Redd usually go to the health club for his workouts?"

Harry thought for a moment. "I've always seen him there around noon. That's a good time to go. You can skip the temptation to have a big lunch and the machines are usually not as crowded at that time of day."

"Want to go?"

"You mean today?"

"Yeah."

"I thought you were driving to Chicago."

"I am. I can leave after we work out."

Harry looked at Pete with a knowing grin and said, "You're hoping to run into Redd, aren't you?"

"That would be convenient," Pete replied.

Harry paused again. "I thought you were out of this thing once you fired Susan Brimley and got the word to Vinnie Zahn."

"I drove past my cottage this morning. I still have a score to settle with whoever started the fire."

"I thought that was Zahn."

"As I told you, I don't know for sure that it was."

Harry paused yet again. "Who do you suspect if not Zahn?"

"I suspect whoever might have had anything to do with this mess."

"Why would the killer torch your cottage if it wasn't Zahn?"

"I don't know."

"It couldn't have been Hicks."

"Not unless they let him out for the night and he had a gasoline can."

Harry studied him for a long time. "You don't quit, do you?"

"Not when I'm mad, Harry. And among the lessons I learned from my old Army boss is to gather all the facts and eventually they'll lead you to the truth."

"What will you do if it turns out to have been Zahn?"

"I don't know."

"He's the only one who makes sense."

"Based on what we presently know."

Harry shook his head. "Do you realize how maddening it is to talk to someone who won't share his thoughts?"

Pete laughed. "Right now, the only thoughts I have are to work out — and maybe accidentally bump into Redd — and then to drive to Chicago."

Harry shook his head and said, "Well, if we're going to the health club, we better get going."

"I'll meet you there in a half-hour," Pete replied.

Harry was right. Judging from the parking lot, the health club usage was light during the lunch hour. He was right about Howard Redd, too. When Pete walked past the front desk, he saw Redd working on one of the weight machines. He had on shorts and his usual long-sleeved sweatshirt. The Willie Nelson bandana was knotted around his forehead.

Pete walked past Redd without saying anything. He put his bag in a locker and got on one of the treadmills, adjusted the settings, and started running. He'd been on the machine for almost a half-hour when Harry came puffing in. He waved at Pete and climbed on a stationary bike and started to peddle.

Pete kept running and watched Redd out of the corner of his eye. Redd mopped his face with a towel and started on the weight machine again. About 1:15 p.m., he draped the towel around his neck and headed for the shower room. Pete ran for another few minutes and then headed for the showers himself. He signaled Harry to follow him in ten minutes.

Redd was already getting out of the shower when Pete walked in. He loosened the towel knotted around his waist, finished drying off, and quickly slipped into a pair of jeans and a clean long-sleeved shirt. During the few minutes this process took, Pete again noticed the tattoos covering his forearms. He didn't want to stare, but couldn't help but see that they were all blue and gray. Not multi-colored roses and other adornments like the college kid who'd won the lift contest sported. Redd nodded to Pete as he passed, flipped his water bottle into a metal-mesh receptacle, and walked out.

Pete walked over to the receptacle and retrieved the water bottle with two fingers on the screw top. He was slipping the bottle into a plastic bag when Harry came in looking like he'd just gone through a two-hour workout under the supervision of a demonic personal trainer. He saw the plastic bag as Pete was storing it in his duffel with his dirty clothes and said, "You collecting bottles now for the refund money?"

Pete grinned at him and replied, "Only one bottle."

Harry looked perplexed for a moment, then a broad grin spread over his chunky face and he said, "That's Redd's bottle, isn't it?" He shook his head and added, "You're something, you know that? Richter would never have thought to do something like that. What are you going to do with the bottle?"

"I'm taking it to Chicago to see if I can talk my friend Angie DeMarco into doing another favor for me."

THIRTY

Pete got to Chicago too late to have dinner with Angie and Steve Johnson as they'd tentatively planned. He checked into the Fairmont Hotel, and after getting a sandwich in the restaurant downstairs, went to bed. It was one of those blessed nights when his sleep wasn't interrupted by images of bloody walls or eardrum-shattering blasts.

The next morning, he had a light breakfast and headed for his old law firm's offices. He went directly to the firm's mailroom. He knew Geraldo Menendez got in early. He needed a tutorial.

Geraldo saw him as soon as he walked in the mailroom and dropped the stack of letters he was sorting and rushed to greet him. He wrapped his arms around Pete in a bear-hug embrace and said, "Good to see you, man. You been avoiding the common folk?"

Pete laughed and assured him he hadn't been, then asked about Geraldo's wife and children. It took some time to get current because Geraldo had eight children. His wife, Maria, was a no-nonsense woman with a sensuous side that helped explain the size of their family. She also had an iron streak and kept Geraldo and the rest of her brood in line. She tolerated no deviation from the way she thought they should live their lives. She attended church daily and her children were always well-mannered and neatly dressed. They weren't allowed to hang around the streets where the Latin gangs ruled or to wear baggy jeans or other symbols of that culture. Each child over the age of six had assigned chores and performed them on time and to Maria's satisfaction under the veiled threat of immediate punishment. Those of school age did their homework religiously and weren't permitted to horse around even when three or four of them occupied the kitchen table at the same time.

Geraldo toed the line just as strictly as his children. He worked two jobs. During the day, he ran the mailroom at Sears & Whitney, and in the evenings, he parked cars at a near north restaurant. His earnings from both jobs went into the family coffers and Maria controlled the purse strings. Geraldo kept a small allowance that he almost always used for tattoos, or as he called them, body art. His forearms were a tangle of exquisite roses and twisted vines and religious symbols and, in one case, a serpent. Even that bore Maria's influence, however, because the serpent was part of a Garden of Eden scene.

After Geraldo finished the family saga, he told Pete about the comings and goings in the mailroom. Pete then got down to business and told Geraldo he wanted to know the basics of body art. Why, he asked, did some men have multicolored images on their bodies and others have only drab blue or gray? Was there some special significance attached to particular images? He described the tattoos he'd seen on Redd's forearms.

Geraldo listened intently and then said, "That sounds like prison art, man."

"Explain," Pete said.

"In the joint, man, you can't just go down to the corner parlor for your art. New stuff isn't permitted in most prisons because of all the gang symbols and things like that. But there are guys inside who know how to improvise and will do art on the side for cigarettes or other items of trade. Ballpoint pens are the easiest to use because you can take the ink out, but if you can't get pens, guys know how to make dye out of stuff like melted plastic or even soot mixed with shampoo."

"Are prison tattoos always blue or gray?" Pete asked, thinking of Redd's forearms again.

"Usually, man, or black. You almost never see art done in prison that has nice designs like I have." He held out his arm so Pete could see the tattoos better. Pete never had a desire to get a tattoo, but looking at Geraldo's arms, he could almost understand the reason that many men, and some women, did.

"Do inmates get tattoos, or art as you say, for the decorative element?"

"No, man, not usually. A lot of gang members get art to tell other people who they are and who they're connected with. The skinheads are big on art. They have all sorts of symbols like KKK signs and Nazi signs and numbers that convey racial messages and stuff like that. Other guys just get art to say something about their prison experience."

"What would be an example of that?" Pete asked.

"All kinds of stuff, man. Some guys have clocks with no hands to show how time has become meaningless to them. Others may have a teardrop to show their feelings or to tell everyone that they were wrongly convicted and, you know, sad. Others have spider webs and things like that. In some prisons, guys have art that's just a big slab to show the prison walls and how any thought of escape is hopeless."

"Interesting," Pete said.

"Why do you want to know this stuff, boss? You got a friend inside or something?"

"No, there's just a guy I saw with crude tattoos and I was trying to confirm my suspicions. He always wears long sleeves, but I saw him at the health club without his shirt a few times and was wondering."

Geraldo said, "Some guys, when they get out, are embarrassed about the art they got inside. Not fancy enough or they're afraid everyone will know they've been in the joint. You can have the art removed, but it costs you, man, and it hurts like hell. What did this dude have on his arms?"

"I wasn't close enough to see the designs, but they all were blue or gray."

"Sounds like the guy has been inside, boss. If the art was just blue or gray as you said, it's probably from prison."

Pete looked at his watch. He was late for his meeting with Angie and Steve. Geraldo had told him what he needed to know. He wrapped up their conversation, asked Geraldo to say hello to Maria and his children, and promised to take them all out for dinner the next time he was in Chicago. Then he took the stairwell up a floor and walked down the hall to Angie's office.

The door was open and Angie and Steve were sitting around a small conference table looking at documents. They glanced up when he walked in and Angie fixed him with a feigned disapproving stare and said, "We heard you were in the office. If you don't have a good excuse for keeping senior management waiting, we might have to dock your next check."

"I was just checking with your boss, Geraldo. He tells me you reduced his staff. He's circulating a petition to bring me back as managing partner. Said the firm was much better run when I was here."

"You know how hard it would be to get me out of this office, counselor? Besides, we'd challenge the names on this so-called petition. I once prosecuted vote fraud cases if you'll remember."

"Save your firepower for that jerk, Kral, will you? Or have you gotten the case dismissed already?"

"We were just hatching our strategy. If you're finished fomenting insurrection in the ranks, you can join us."

Pete laughed. "I'm only a revolutionary part-time. Where do we start?"

They were joined by the outside lawyer they'd retained to represent the firm and its partners, and for the next four hours, they discussed strategy and the options for defending against Kral's claims. They talked about filing a motion for summary judgment, and while there were concerns there might be factual issues that would preclude that remedy, they thought they had a good enough position to file the motion in good faith and decided to go that route. It would show Kral that they weren't going to just lie down and that he was in for a fight.

When they were finished, Pete stayed around to talk to Angie.

"What's new up north?" she asked.

"A lot. I resigned as Susan Brimley's lawyer." For the first time, he told her the full story ending with his meeting with Vinnie Zahn aboard the Isabella II. Angie listened intently.

"Why do you think Susan Brimley lied to you?" Angie asked. "She had to know that quoting advice from some lawyer wouldn't work with a guy like Zahn."

Pete shrugged. "Three million is a lot of money. She probably thought it was worth a shot. Or maybe she actually believed that legal technicalities would work because her late husband's assets were tied up in probate court."

"Screwy," Angie said. "And Zahn, you'd think he'd just put the screws on her to pay up rather than dragging you into it."

"I think his plan was and is to do just that. But somehow, I guess having me tell Susan what her legal rights were bugged him because she kept raising them to avoid paying. If you're in the juice loan business, you're not used to having your debtors raise that kind of excuse."

Angie looked at him and said, "You're out of it now, right?"

"Mostly. I hope anyway. But I'm still determined to find out who torched my cottage."

"That seems like a no-brainer. From what you tell me, it had to be Zahn's people."

"That's what Harry says, too, but I'm not convinced it was."

"Who else would it be?"

"I don't know."

"Well, if it does turn out to be Zahn, you'll be careful, right?"

"I will. And there's something I need you to do for me. Or really for Ira Manning."

"What's Ira got to do with this?"

"I arranged for him to represent John Hicks. Hicks is the guy they've charged with killing Brimley." Pete removed the plastic bag with the empty water bottle from his briefcase.

Angie took the bag and looked at it. "What do you want me to do with this?"

"I was hoping you could have one of your contacts at Chicago PD dust the bottle for fingerprints and run them through their computer."

"Is there some background I should know?"

"They found some of the victim's hairs in Hicks' vehicle, but no DNA evidence. Hicks claims he's being set up. Ira had a PI from Traverse City check all the automotive places in the area that do detailing work on the assumption the real killer would want to get his vehicle cleaned up after the murder. One guy we identified had a Chevy Suburban detailed right after the murder. We've already established that he's using an alias and want to find out more about him. He has these crude tattoos on his arms and Geraldo tells me that's the sign of a guy who's been in prison."

"My friends at the department are going to want to know more about this."

"Make up a story. Ira and I will take you to dinner at Gibsons as compensation."

"I should warn you, if I'm successful, I'm going to order one of those gooey chocolate desserts that cost more than their prime steaks."

"Ira can afford it. He just got the rest of his fee for getting Stella Lord off from a murder rap."

THIRTY-ONE

When Pete got home, he sorted through his mail. A large brown envelope with no return address caught his eye. It was postmarked from Chicago. He tore open one end of the envelope and removed the contents.

He stared at the photographs and the newspaper clippings. Everything related to a wedding. The bride was featured in all of the black and white photographs, but two other figures interested Pete the most. Zahn's henchmen, Sal and Victor, were standing in the receiving line and then congratulating the bride and groom. They were also photographed dancing with the bride and waiting in the food line with her in the background. The newspaper clippings featured the wedding which took place in Riverside, a Chicago suburb. He studied the materials more closely. There was no question the bride in the photographs was the same young lady pictured in the news clippings. Pete noted the wedding date, then thought back to the date of the fire at his cottage. The dates were the same.

Pete waited while Harry looked at the photographs and other items. He peered at Pete over his half-glasses and said, "I don't think the photos were doctored. There's no way to be sure, of course, without having an expert examine them. Those are Zahn's guys, huh?"

Pete nodded. "That's one thing I'm sure of. There's no question those are the two goons with Zahn the day I met him on his boat. They're also identical to the guys Julie and Mikki described."

"Why do you think Zahn sent this stuff to you?"

"That's obvious. He's trying to convince me that he had nothing to do with the fire at my cottage."

"Why would he care?"

Pete replied, "Zahn has a ton of legal problems already. Arson is a felony, and the last thing he needs is to have another investigation right now. If they investigate him for arson, law enforcement might look further into everything, including the fact that Brimley owed Zahn money. That implicates him in Brimley's murder, something I was unsuccessful in doing. That's why I made those statements on his boat, to make him nervous. Maybe it worked."

"Right," Harry said. "You're positive you're not interested in ..."

"Harry ..."

"Sorry, just thinking out loud."

Pete looked at him disgustedly. "I've got other news for you, too. Angie had one of her friends at Chicago PD lift Redd's prints from that bottle I took from the receptacle in the health club and run them through the computer. And — get this — his real name is Harold Romanski. He spent twenty years in the lock-up in Joliet for killing a guy during a robbery gone bad. He got out of prison a little more than a year ago."

Harry whistled through his teeth and said, "You were right again. A year ago. That's about when he showed up in this area."

"Right."

Harry leaned forward in his chair. "Do you think we should warn Ida about him?"

"Not right now, but I am going to check him out further. Do you still have friends at your old paper in Chicago?"

"Sure," Harry said, "a bunch."

"Could you have one of them search the paper's archives for news stories from around twenty or twenty-two years ago and see what he can find out about that robbery and Romanski's trial? I don't want to drive down to Chicago again if I can avoid it."

"Sure," Harry said again. "I might be able to patch into the archives myself, but if I can't, I'll contact this woman who used to work for me and have her do the search." He was silent for a few moments and then added, "It looks like this guy Romanski may be mixed up in this thing, doesn't it?"

"Maybe. Or maybe he just moved up here to start a new life. There could be an explanation."

Harry looked at his watch. "Damn," he said, "we'd better get going if we want to catch Ira's press conference."

◆ ◆ ◆

The man standing beside Ira Manning was thin and looked of Asian descent. He wore a neatly pressed dark blue suit and horn-rimmed glasses. His attire contrasted sharply with Manning's rumpled brown sport coat.

"We just came from another visit with my client, John Hicks," Ira said. "I told you a week ago he's an innocent man who's been charged with this heinous crime just because he was outspoken in his defense of our environment. This is a serious miscarriage of justice that I intend to correct just as soon as the criminal justice system will permit.

"I'd like to introduce my colleague, Dr. David Akiri. Dr. Akiri is an internationally known expert on what we commonly refer to as DNA. I said at my last press conference that the only evidence — the *only* evidence — the state has against my client is a few hairs from the deceased's head. The state has no witnesses, no fingerprints, no other evidence of any kind. Just the hairs they say they found in Mr. Hicks' vehicle. Dr. Akiri will explain to you why it would be impossible for the state not to have found other DNA evidence if, as they contend, the victim's hair was found. Recall, the state's theory is that the deceased was disabled in some way, then was transported in Mr. Hick's vehicle to the golf course where he was murdered. Dr. Akiri?"

Dr. Akiri spent the next forty-five minutes explaining what DNA is and how it can be detected even years later. He corroborated Ira Manning's statement that it would be impossible for Brimley's body to be in Hicks' vehicle without leaving some DNA evidence in addition to the hairs. He patiently answered questions from the reporters.

Ira took the microphone again and spoke in his soothing court tones. "I'm going to ask your county attorney — I have to be careful with my terminology because we call them state's attorneys where I live — to drop all charges against Mr. Hicks. If he won't do that, I intend to take this matter before the court. It would heap insult on travesty if I have to do that because it will only delay the inevitable and add to my client's expense. He's a man of modest means and the state shouldn't make him suffer more than he has already. They owe him an apology as it is.

"Now I'm sorry I can't stay around and have dinner with all of you at one of the fine restaurants in this area. I've heard nothing but praise for the wonderful food you serve up here. But Dr. Akiri and I have to drive back to Chicago tonight so I can be in court in the morning. Next time I'm up this way, however, keep your calendars open because we're going to break bread together and share some war stories."

"Boy," Harry said, "if I'm ever accused of a serious crime, I'm going to hire that guy."

Pete looked at him with a mischievous grin and said, "You worried about something?"

"No," Harry replied, looking earnest, "but with all these innocent people being charged with crimes …"

THIRTY-TWO

When Lynn Hawke called, Pete's thoughts shifted from Vinnie Zahn and Howard Redd's true identity to more pleasant memories. Lynn said she was in town for one night and asked if he could have dinner with her, Rona and Harry. He would have preferred dinner with Lynn alone, but was anxious to see her so he agreed. He sat on the deck, watching the clock, and thought back to some of the great times they'd had the previous summer.

He walked into Rona's Bay Grille five minutes early and was surprised to see Harry, who was habitually late, already engaged in earnest conversation with Lynn. Rona was huddled with three of her staff across the room. As he approached their table, Lynn looked up and saw him. She rose from her seat and gave him a firm hug.

He kissed her on the cheek and said, "Welcome home."

She sighed and said, "It's good to be back, if only briefly." She gave him the once over and added, "You're looking good. Life up north must agree with you."

Harry piped up and said, "Pete and I are working out on a regular basis these days. The next time you see us, we'll be so buff you won't even recognize us."

Pete listened to Harry babble on about their visits to the health club and how they were hardly drinking these days and also watching their calories to lose weight. Pete reconciled himself to the fact that it was going to be one of those nights.

"When did you get in?" Pete asked when there was a lull in the conversation.

"Late morning."

"Lynn had to come home to put out the fire with a couple of her old clients," Harry interjected. "That woman she left in charge of her practice hasn't worked out so well."

Pete was familiar with Ida's reservations, but he wanted to hear about the problem in Lynn's own words. "Any serious problems?" he asked.

Harry was about to answer for her again when Pete gave him a look. "Nothing major," Lynn said, "but my clients have been used to a lot of hand-holding and Barbara's not always as attentive as she could be. I'm meeting with Barbara and each of the clients who complained to see if I can patch things up. If not, I'm going to have to get someone else to look after my practice until I move back here."

"I saw Ida the other day," Pete said. "She was checking the payroll to make sure it was right. I asked her if Barbara had made any errors. She said not yet, but that didn't mean there wouldn't be some in the future."

Lynn smiled. "Ida's such a dear woman. She calls me in Seattle to tell me the same thing. Always wants to know when I'm coming back."

"A lot of us want to know that," Pete said, grinning.

Lynn smiled at him and put her hand over his for a moment.

"When I was at Birchwood the other day," Pete said, "Ida was telling me about that guy Howard Redd who works for her. Was he with her before you went to Seattle?" Harry looked like he was about to say something when Pete gave him another look.

"Yes, she'd just hired him. Why do you ask?"

"She thinks he walks on water. I guess he picks her up in the morning and takes her home at night. Does personal stuff for her."

"I met him twice. Between us, I didn't care for him. There was something about the man …"

Harry seemed to be looking for a way to insinuate himself into the conversation again and said, "By the way, Pete, my friend at the paper in Chicago is forwarding a bunch of news clippings by e-mail. I …"

Pete cut him off again and said, "Could you forward them to me when they come in? Then we can talk."

Harry promised to do that and started to say something, but before he could get the words out, Pete asked Lynn, "How are things with your daughter?"

Lynn's face grew somber and she said, "Some good days, some bad days. Sometimes I wonder why I'm out there. But I'm afraid not to be."

Pete tightened his lips and shook his head. "Is she alone now?"

"No, my son is visiting her for a few days while I'm here. As you may remember, he lives in Los Angeles."

Rona joined them. She patted Pete's hand, then said to Lynn, "These guys treating you alright?"

"Oh, it's so good to see all of you again," Lynn said. "I'm so sad that I have to be away."

"Things have been kind of exciting around here," Rona said. "Did you hear about Lester Brimley's murder?"

"I did hear," Lynn said. She widened her eyes and shook her head. "It made the news way out in Seattle. But they've arrested the guy who did it, right?"

"They've arrested *a* guy," Harry chimed in, "but we're not sure he did it."

"Oh, why's that? The papers said they have all kinds of evidence against him."

Harry said, "They claim they found some of the victim's hair in John Hicks' vehicle — he's the guy they arrested — but this high-powered lawyer Pete arranged for Hicks thinks he didn't do it."

Lynn looked at Pete without smiling. "Involved in another case?"

Harry snorted. "Involved! Pete represented the victim's widow until he had to fire her. Then someone stalked his daughter and burned down …"

"Harry, let's not be too dramatic. I got roped into the case for a brief time, but now I'm out so it's history."

Lynn was still looking at him. "How did you get roped in, to use your words?"

Harry was not about to be shut up. "Susan Brimley lied to him. She tried to weasel out of her obligations by using Pete's advice and got him in trouble as a result."

"The artist, right?" she asked Pete.

"Yes."

"I can't say I'm surprised. I knew both Susan and Les. I used to do some of the accounting work for the Brimley company. They — or at least Les — weren't always forthcoming about matters."

"Like what?" Pete asked.

"I probably said too much already," Lynn replied. "Accountants have confidentiality obligations just like lawyers."

"You're with friends," Harry said, winking. "We won't talk."

Lynn just smiled.

"Have you picked a contractor yet?" Rona asked Pete.

"Not yet."

Lynn looked at him and asked, "Are you remodeling?"

Harry, with his penchant for speaking for others, jumped in before Pete could answer and said, "Rebuilding would be a better term."

Lynn looked confused. "Why would you want to rebuild that cottage? It's a great place."

"He doesn't have a choice," Harry blurted out again. "Someone set fire to his cottage one night and damaged it pretty bad."

Lynn looked at Pete quizzically and said, "Why didn't you tell me?"

"Lynn, we talked on the phone for all of, what, three minutes? Besides, I thought my mouthpiece here," Pete said, pointing at Harry, "would have told you all about it by the time we got together for dinner."

"Was it vandalism?"

"You want to tell her, Harry?"

Harry, not picking up on Pete's sarcasm, proceeded to tell her the story in great detail. He ended on a mysterious note, saying no one knew who the arsonist was, but that they suspected that it tied in with the problem Pete had with Susan Brimley.

"Where are you staying?" Lynn asked Pete.

"I rented a house not far from your place."

"You could have rented my house," Lynn said. "Or at least you could have called me; I would have let you stay there for free."

Pete didn't want to tell Lynn the real reason he hadn't rented her house, so he said, "I wasn't sure how long reconstruction would take or when you might be coming back. The realtor told me you needed the right to give a tenant two months' notice. I didn't want to have to move again."

"You thought I might kick you out if I came back and your place wasn't finished, is that it?"

Pete just shrugged and grinned sheepishly

The women looked at each other, and Rona said in an aside, "Male pride."

The conversation changed to other subjects. Pete declined another drink, but Harry, who'd worked out just three days earlier, didn't feel so constrained. Their table was the last in the restaurant still occupied and the help was setting up for the following day. Rona offered to comp dinner and drinks for everyone, but Harry, gracious to a fault, insisted on picking up the tab. Pete saw him wince when their wait person brought the bill. Pete suppressed a grin and thought, serves you right, blabbermouth.

They said their goodbyes on the sidewalk and Pete walked Lynn to her rental car.

"Since we're neighbors," she said, "do you want to come over for a drink?"

"Love to," Pete replied.

Pete followed her through Beulah and pulled in the driveway behind her. She'd opened windows before she left to join the group for dinner and the house was cool and pleasant. He had a glass of wine even though it was his third of the evening, and they took seats on the deck. The lake shimmered in the full moon.

"You know you were really silly not to move into my house. I know the place you rented. This is much nicer, don't you think?"

"Much nicer," Pete agreed, "but I explained why I did what I did. Besides, I was mad as hell at the time, and all I could think of was getting even with whoever torched my cottage."

Lynn reached over and took his hand. "You're more involved in the Brimley case than you let on at dinner, aren't you?"

"I was. Now I'm down to finding the arsonist and helping Ira Manning a little."

"The same thing happened to you with Cara Lane. What is it?"

"I'm not sure," Pete said. "One side of me wants to stay out of things, but the other side …"

"You're playing a dangerous game, you know."

"In a way, maybe, but I've been trying to watch my back."

"That was a dirty thing Susan Brimley did to you."

He thought for a few moments, then said, "You know a lot about the Brimleys, don't you?"

"A fair amount."

"Anything you want to share with me now that we're alone?"

"I'll tell you what I know on two conditions. First, you keep it quiet. And second, you tell me what you know about Howard Redd because I know you were holding back at dinner, too."

"Deal."

Lynn took a sip of her wine. "Les Brimley was cheating on his wife big-time. He was keeping some woman in Chicago and charging everything to his company. Rent on her apartment, expensive dinners, gifts of jewelry and other items. I felt Susan Brimley had to know about it, too, but I had no evidence she did. They had a very indifferent marriage."

"When you said that Les wasn't always forthcoming, what did you mean?"

"Things material to his financial statements. Liabilities, mainly. I'm not exactly sure, but he probably understated his liabilities by millions."

"That's exactly what I concluded. As best I could piece things together, he was in hock to the Chicago mob and they wanted their money. A commercial finance company — a mob front called Nautical Finance — was involved and juice payments were due a mobster named Vinnie Zahn."

"I didn't know the details, but I thought it might be something like that. I was a forensic accountant as you might recall."

"What else do you know about Brimley?"

"That's most of it, but I always suspected that Brimley screwed his partner to take over their real estate business in the first place. Someone told me he was something of a street thug growing up, and then something happened that made him go straight. But old ways die hard. He hooked on with a real estate business, and before you knew it, he owned the company."

"Mmm," Pete murmured.

"Now it's your turn," Lynn said. "What you know about Howard Redd?"

"I'm still trying to piece it together, but I've established that he's an ex-con who spent twenty years in prison for killing a guy during a robbery."

Lynn suddenly grabbed his arm and her eyes widened. "Are you sure?"

"Positive. Someone with contacts in the Chicago PD ran his prints for me and we've confirmed that his real name is Harold Romanski."

"Do you suppose Ida is in any danger?"

"Harry asked me the same thing, and I told him I doubt it. If he was going to harm her, he'd have done it by now. But I'm trying to figure out why he's up here. I haven't found the answer yet."

Lynn continued to look shocked. "Do you suppose he had anything to do with Les Brimley's murder?"

"I honestly don't know. So far, I haven't found any connection between the two."

"Does the sheriff know about Romanski using a false name?"

"I don't think so. I'm reluctant to tell him, too, because it's possible Romanski just moved up here to start a new life. Assuming that's the case, he deserves a second chance without people dredging up his past."

"Pete being fair again."

He shrugged and said, "I'm still looking into his background. If I find something that ties him to the Brimley murder, I'll alert the sheriff. By the way, since you did work for the Brimleys, do you know anyone at his company in Chicago?"

Lynn appeared to think. "There used to be a woman — an office manager or something — named Alma Linberg. She was in Brimley's office on Foster Avenue. I don't know if she's still there."

Pete pulled out a piece of paper and wrote down the information. "How many projects did Brimley have in the Chicago area?"

"Four or five, I think. They were all in the city except for one in the western suburbs. But that was a few years ago and I don't know what changes there've been since then."

They went inside because the mosquitos were getting bad. He took a seat on the couch beside Lynn and said, "Some lady I knew last summer told me it was unfriendly for a man to sit on a facing couch when he was with a woman."

Lynn smiled at him. "Did I say that?"

"You did."

"I must have been tipsy."

"Maybe a little," Pete said.

She smiled again and turned her wine glass as if inspecting it for flaws. "You know," she said, "you should have gone into law enforcement. My dad was as good as I've ever seen, and you're a lot like him."

Pete chuckled. "That's what Harry keeps telling me. He wants me to run for sheriff."

She looked at him with an amused smile. "Are you?"

"Heavens, no. But I'm all talked out about mobsters and murderers and conniving women." He leaned over and brushed her neck with his lips. He felt the old electricity course through his body. He kissed her on the lips, tenderly at first, and then more urgently. He slid his hand up and cupped her breast and whispered, "You feel good." She moaned and snuggled closer.

He adjusted his hand to slip it inside her bra and felt her nipple harden to his touch. She moaned again and said softly, "You're getting me all worked up."

"That's not bad, is it?"

"I've got to get up early tomorrow."

"Just tell me what time you want me out of here."

She was quiet for a minute and then said, "Could I have a rain check? I care for you a lot, but …"

The disappointment surged through his body and he forced himself to say, "I understand. Will I see you before you leave?"

"Are you're going to be around late tomorrow afternoon? That's when I have to leave for the airport."

"Probably," Pete replied, "but call me on my cell phone when you're finished with your appointments."

She grabbed his hand and walked him to the door. She stood on her tip-toes and kissed him on the mouth. She looked at him a while and then said, "I'm sorry, Pete."

Pete tried to hide his disappointment. "Hey, don't be. You've got a lot on your plate for a two-day trip."

THIRTY-THREE

The next morning, Pete began to print out the attachments to the e-mail Harry had forwarded to him. He watched the cheap printer he'd picked up at the local electronics store grind away and slowly spit out pages.

As he sat there watching the machine work, he still felt disappointment from the night before. He wasn't sure what he'd expected after not seeing Lynn for almost a year. Maybe some sign beyond words that she still had feelings for him. The sight of her kindled the old fire in him, that he knew. Was he just trying to hold on to memories?

He tried to concentrate on the news stories. Harold Romanski — known as Hal according to one story — was from the north side of Chicago. He was twenty-three at the time of his arrest with no prior police record. One night, according to the stories, he forced his way into an area electronics store just as the owner was about to close. He allegedly held the owner at gunpoint while he cleaned out the cash register.

What happened next is less clear, but apparently the store owner tripped an alarm which alerted the police to a robbery in process. Then Romanski panicked, and according to the stories, shot the store owner twice and fled the scene. The police picked him up five blocks away. There was evidence he'd been running since his heart-rate was elevated and he was perspiring.

Three hundred seventy-two dollars in cash was found on Romanski's person. He claimed he was carrying a lot of currency because he'd cashed his paycheck earlier that day. His story about the check cashing turned out to be untrue.

Evidence introduced at trial included a latex glove found in the vicinity of the store. The state's expert witness testified that DNA evidence established that the glove had been worn by Romanski. The murder weapon — a cheap Smith & Wesson revolver — was found on the floor of the electronics store. There were no prints on the gun. Tests failed to show any powder residue on Romanski's hands to indicate he'd fired the weapon. However, experts testified that the latex glove might have precluded the normal powder residue from showing up on Romanski's hand. The glove the police found was a right-hand glove. Romanski was shown to be right-handed.

Romanski continued to deny the charges throughout his trial, admitting only that he had been in the store to buy a CD which he claimed he paid for in cash. The CD was not found on Romanski's person or in the vicinity of the store. Romanski claimed he was in the store alone, but the police suspected he might have had an accomplice. No accomplice was ever charged with the slaying.

The jury convicted Romanski of murder and related counts, finding he'd acted alone. Romanski continued to claim innocence at his sentencing hearing. As a result, he was sentenced to twenty-seven years in prison. He was transported to the prison in Joliet where he served his time. With credited time for pre-sentence incarceration and good behavior, he had been released from prison after serving approximately twenty years.

That was Hal Romanski's story as best he could glean it from the news stories. There were no stories, at least that had been sent to him, detailing Romanski's whereabouts after he was released from prison.

Pete studied the grainy photographs of Romanski included in some of the news clippings. They did not look like the Howard Redd he'd seen. But he reminded himself that he'd only seen him three times and the photographs were taken over twenty years earlier. He also reminded himself that fingerprints don't lie.

He sat back in his chair wondering, again, what Romanski was doing in an area where he had no apparent connection. And he wondered whether Romanski knew Brimley from their past.

Pete went for a run even though it was late morning and he preferred to run early in the day or in the evening. He glanced up the bluff when he passed Lynn Hawke's house, but didn't pause. He enjoyed the scenery and breathed deeply. He'd lost three pounds in the past week without really dieting, and felt good about that. He grinned and wondered how Harry was doing.

When he returned, he showered and then drove into town and stopped at his office. He worked on his article for a while and ran a few errands. It was 3:00 p.m. when he got back to his house. He didn't want to miss Lynn's call. He put on a Gordon Lightfoot CD and listened to the music while he gazed out at the lake. Periodically, he would check the time.

Lynn finally called and apologized for not stopping to say goodbye personally. She said she hadn't been able to see Harry and Rona before she left, either. The meetings with unhappy clients had taken more time than she'd anticipated. She said she hoped to visit the lake again later in the summer when she had more time. Then she was gone.

Strangely, the call didn't bother him that much. After last night, and as the day passed, he'd reconciled himself to reality. Maybe he was crazy to sit around and moon over a woman who was two thousand miles away and didn't seem to make him a high priority in her life. Maybe it was time to move on and not try to hold on to the past.

He got in his Range Rover and drove around the lake to his cottage. None of his neighbors were outside when he pulled into his driveway. It had only been a little more than a week since the fire, but already the place looked overgrown and deserted. He walked around the outside of his cottage and threw a few pieces of charred wood onto a pile. Then he went to the beach and sat on the sand.

As the sun sank below the trees rimming the lake, he reviewed in his mind everything he'd learned about Les and Susan Brimley and Hal Romanski, a/k/a Howard Redd. And he thought some more about who could have started the fire in his cottage and why. He came up with no answers.

While he sat there, thinking, he remembered the name of the office manager Lynn had given him. Alma Linberg, if his memory served him right. If Alma wasn't still there, someone had to have taken her place. Brimley's real estate empire was significant enough to require people to run it and it wouldn't cease operations just because the boss was dead. He thought about calling Alma to see if she was there, but thought better of it. Theo Radke, as executor of Brimley's will, probably had stepped in temporarily to guide the company's staff. If that were true, he didn't want Alma calling Radke to alert him that Pete had been snooping around. Better to just show up.

He resumed looking at the lake. Hopefully, two days in Chicago would be adequate to do what he needed to do.

THIRTY-FOUR

The only employee in sight when Pete walked into LB Realty's offices was a sturdy woman right out of a travel article about Scandinavia. In her sixties, maybe, with tight gray curls, a kind face that was free of make-up, and a plain blue dress with sensible shoes.

She stopped filing and looked at Pete over small oval glasses with rhinestone rims that were held by an elastic cord drooped around the back of her neck. After giving him the once-over, she asked, "Can I help you, sir?"

"You must be Mrs. Linberg," Pete said. He gave her his widest and most friendly smile.

She continued to peer at him suspiciously and then said, "Yes, and to whom am I speaking, please?"

"Pete Thorsen, Mrs. Linberg. Mr. Radke said you'd probably be in the office."

She continued to look suspicious. "If you're looking for the lawyer," she said, "you'll have to go downtown. His office is down there."

"Oh no," Pete said, "I'm not looking for Mr. Radke. I'm a lawyer myself and am helping coordinate things for Mr. Brimley's estate." He handed her one of his business cards.

She took the card and studied at it for a long time. Then she looked up and said, "This says Michigan."

"That's where I live now. Mr. Brimley had a project in Michigan, as I'm sure you know."

"Are you working for the Brimley family?"

"Sort of. Like I said, I'm helping coordinate things for the estate. That's what I'd like to talk to you about."

"I was about to take my lunch break."

Pete thought fast. "I'm hungry, too. How'd you like to be my guest at that Swedish restaurant down the street?"

"Tre Kronor?"

"Yes."

"That's a nice place," she said. "Are you Swedish?"

"Part," he replied. "Most of me is Norwegian."

"I thought you might be Norwegian because of the name on that card."

"The Swedish in me comes from my mother."

She peered at him over her glasses again. "The Swedes and Norwegians don't like each other very much, you know."

"Oh," Pete said, "that's way overblown. We all got along just fine where I come from."

"Where's that?

"Wisconsin."

"That's a nice state. Lot's of Scandinavian people up there."

Pete nodded his head. "Well, what do you say? Tre Kronor?"

Mrs. Linberg appeared to be contemplating her choices. "I brought my sandwich," she finally replied.

Pete waved his hand again. "Sandwiches will keep."

"I always put mine in a zip-lock bag. That keeps them nice and fresh." She appeared to think some more about his invitation. "Tre

Kronor is an awfully good restaurant," she said, telegraphing the way she was leaning.

Pete waited for her to make her decision.

She studied his face. "Are you married?"

"Widowed."

She expelled air in a sign of relief. "Me, too," she said. "I guess it's okay. But I have to be back in an hour." An impish smile creased her plump face and she said, "I can't be taking one of those three-martini lunches."

Mrs. Linberg hung a sign in the window and set the hands on the clock to tell the world she'd be back at 1:00 p.m., locked the door, and they walked the two blocks to Tre Kronor. When they were seated, they perused their menus. Pete watched Mrs. Linberg study hers for an inordinately long time. The clock was running and he finally suggested the Swedish pancakes. Her face widened into a smile she'd been doing her best to control since he first walked in the office. "You sure know your Swedish food," she said.

Pete ordered the pancakes as well, and then eased into the conversation. "How long have you worked for LB Realty, Mrs. Linberg?'

"Oh, you don't have to call me Mrs. Linberg. You can call me Alma like everyone else does. I can't be sitting here having lunch with a handsome young man and be called Mrs. Linberg. I'm a modern woman, you know."

"I'll call you Alma only if you call me Pete."

Alma smiled as if she thought they were finally getting somewhere with their relationship. She appeared to think about his question and then said, "I've worked for the company for almost thirty years. Course it wasn't called LB Realty all that time. It used to be called Friscetti Real Estate when Mr. Friscetti owned it. But then he died and Mr. Brimley took over and changed the name."

"What happened to Mr. Friscetti?"

Alma shook her head. "There was an accident when they were putting up that apartment building out in Naperville."

"Mr. Friscetti was killed?"

Tears welled up in Alma's eyes and she nodded her head. "Yes, it was a terrible thing. He wasn't all Swedish, but he was a lovely man."

"His name sounds Italian."

"Like you, his mother was part Swedish. I think that's why we got along so good."

"I see," Pete said. "And when Mr. Friscetti died, you said Mr. Brimley took over?"

She nodded again. "Mr. Friscetti made him a partner in the business after only a few years." She lowered her voice to barely more than a whisper and said, "I could never understand why. Mr. Brimley hardly knew what a four-plus-one was."

Pete had been around Chicago long enough to know that four-plus-ones were the way developers got around zoning laws that restricted the height of buildings. Four stories were entirely above ground, and the fifth was partly below ground level. Units on the lower level were euphemistically known as "garden apartments."

Alma continued to grapple mentally with what had obviously been a traumatic time in her life. "I don't know what happened," she continued. "I guess the police don't know, either."

"Did the police suspect something?"

"I guess they did," she said. "They kept coming around for a couple of years, but then they just stopped."

Pete processed what she'd told him. It was consistent with the suspicions Lynn had expressed the night they were together. He then asked some background questions even though he already knew the answers and that information really wasn't what he was after.

"How many properties does LB Realty have?"

"Oh," she said proudly, "it's a big company. We have five projects around Chicago alone. And then there's that fancy new golf course with houses around it that Mr. Brimley was building up where you live."

"Are all of the projects in the Chicago area four-plus-ones?"

"Four of them are. But the one in Naperville, that was different. I guess they don't have four-plus-ones out there. That started out to be one building, but after Mr. Friscetti died, Mr. Brimley built three more." She shook her head, and added, "They must have a lot of people out there. Mr. Friscetti would never have approved. He was so careful about everything."

"Including money?"

Alma finished chewing a bite of pancake. She leaned across the table, pointed her fork at him and said, "The Chicago buildings were all paid for, but the Naperville buildings and that golf course ... whew, I'm always writing checks for those places."

Pete then shifted gears. "How about Mrs. Brimley," he asked. "Have you gotten to know her?"

Alma lowered her voice again. "I don't think Mr. and Mrs. Brimley got along so good. Always yelling at each other and everything." She shook her head disgustedly.

Pete decided to take a stab and see what Alma's reaction would be. "Did the fact Mr. Brimley paid the rent on an apartment for his lady friend have anything to do with their quarrels?"

"Oh," she said, "you know about that?"

Pete nodded. "I do. Mr. Brimley charged the rent on the apartment to the company, I understand. Is it an expensive place?""

Color drained from Alma's face. "Mr. Brimley told me to never to talk about those things or he'd fire me," she said quietly.

"Mr. Brimley's dead, remember?"

She looked at him skeptically, as if she was afraid that Brimley would return from the grave and exact terrible revenge for violating his commandment. "I don't think I should talk about that apartment."

"I understand," Pete said. "It's not really important to the work I'm doing for the estate, anyway. I'm just a little surprised that Mr. Brimley would spend money on other women when he was so strapped for cash in his business."

Pete could see the indignation rise in Alma by the way she reacted to his observation.

"It's not only the business, you know. Mr. Brimley still owes money to the Friscetti family. It's not fair to them for him to spend all that money on some scarlet woman for jewelry and things." She leaned closer again. "You know, he missed some payments to Mrs. Friscetti and she needs the money."

"That's bad," Pete said, shaking his head sympathetically. "Where's the apartment he rents for this woman? In one of the four-plus-ones?"

Alma looked horrified. "Oh no, it's in that fancy building they call Lake Point Tower."

Pete shook his head again to show his disgust. "That's expensive," he said.

Alma leaned close again. "You know," she said, "I think the woman may be one of those exotic dancers or whatever they call them. Carmella Cain. That's her name. Course I don't know if that's her real name or just a name she uses. Some of those exotic dancers use stage names, you know."

She looked at the clock on the restaurant wall and said, "Oh my, I've got to get back. Mr. Radke or someone might be looking for me. If I'd known we were going to have such a nice time, I would have put out a different sign. I don't want people to think we're out of business or anything. Mr. Radke told me it was important that we show continuity so people would think nothing happened."

Pete paid the bill, and during their walk back to LB Realty, decided to find out if Alma could help him with some other information he needed.

"On a completely unrelated matter," he said, "there's a man I'm trying to locate who once lived in this area. I used to know him. His name is Harold Romanski. He goes by Hal. You ever hear of him?"

"Romanski. Romanski. No, I don't believe I know the gentleman."

"He grew up just a few blocks from here. But you've never heard of him?"

"No," Alma said, "that name doesn't sound familiar. But I live west of here, and don't know everyone in this neighborhood. Unless of course they rent one of our apartments or something. You should talk to Bok. He's lived in this area all his life and knows everybody."

"Bok?"

"Yes."

"That's an unusual name."

"I don't think Bok is his real first name, but that's what everyone calls him."

"Do you have Bok's phone number?"

"Oh, he doesn't have a phone. Says they're too expensive and he never uses a telephone anyway."

"How do I get in touch with him, then?"

Alma thought about it for a moment, then said, "He brings me coffee every day at 9:00 a.m. now that Mr. Brimley isn't here anymore. You could see him some morning when he comes by." Alma got a faraway look in her eyes. "Mr. Brimley didn't like Bok hanging around the office, but with him gone, we have more time to talk. You'd like Bok. He's a nice Norwegian man just like you."

After he told Alma he'd see her in the morning, she grasped his arm as he was on his way out and winked at him and said, "Don't tell anybody about our three-martini lunch, Pete." He assured her his lips were sealed. He also said he'd bring his own coffee in the morning.

As he was driving to the Fairmont Hotel, he couldn't help but smile when he thought of the day and his lunch with Alma. It was remarkable what springing for a plate of Swedish pancakes would do for one's knowledge base.

When he reached Lake Shore Drive and headed south to the Loop, he began wondering how he could get in touch with Carmella Cain. He knew he couldn't just go to her building, ring her intercom button, and be buzzed up. Buildings like Lake Shore Tower had doormen and tight security measures. He'd have to come up with something a little more creative. He smiled again and wondered if exotic dancers listed their phone numbers.

He pulled up in front of the Fairmont Hotel and left his Range Rover with the valet. After checking in, he found his room and hung up his garment bag. Then he dialed Angie DeMarco's number and left a message that he might be a little late for their dinner engagement. He looked in the telephone book for Carmella Cain's number and found a lot of Cains listed, but no Carmella. He had better luck with directory service. He was connected to a number and waited as the phone rang. No answer. He didn't leave a message when an answering machine clicked on. He'd try Carmella again in an hour.

He took a brief nap and tried the number again. Still no answer. This time he decided to leave a message. He identified himself as a lawyer in Michigan, and said he was calling about a provision in Les Brimley's will mentioning her name. He left his cell phone number and then waited.

Two hours later, his cell phone rang. He could see from the caller ID that it was Carmella Cain. He smiled. The prospect of an unexpected inheritance from a lover could be a powerful inducement to call back. Carmella said she was shopping on Michigan Avenue, and got his message. She sounded eager for the details. He said he was only going to be in the city for a short time, but if she wanted to meet him in the Fairmont Hotel bar in a half-hour, he could explain everything. She said she'd be there, and after trying to get more information, finally got off the phone.

He called Angie and left another message that he'd meet her at Gibsons a half hour later than they'd originally agreed. Then he freshened up and slipped into his suit. He headed for the elevator ten minutes early. He skipped the cocktail seating area in the lobby and staked out two stools at the small bar and ordered plain tonic water with two slices of lime.

As he sat there watching the hotel's revolving doors, he wondered what he hoped to learn from Carmella. At the same time, he remembered, again, what his old boss from the CID used to say about investigative technique. Gather as much information as you can, even if some of it seems irrelevant at the time, then sift and winnow it until the truth finally reveals itself. He was still in the gathering phase; the sifting and winnowing would come later.

He saw a woman with several shopping bags using her hips to keep the revolving door moving. She wore form-fitting black pants and a white blouse with a bold black and shocking pink design. That had to be Carmella Cain, he thought. He slid off his stool and walked toward the door. As he got closer to her, he could see the heavy eye make-up and the comb that held back her blonde hair that was coarse from too many trips to the salon. Her lipstick matched the pink accent color of her blouse. He intercepted her as she was about to approach the hotel desk.

"Ms. Cain?" he asked.

"Yes, I'm Carmella Cain. And you must be Mr. Thorsen."

"Yes. I have two stools at the bar."

When they were seated, Carmella looked at his drink and ordered a glass of white wine with ice cubes. She crossed and re-crossed her legs and tapped her finger nails on the bar as she waited for her wine.

"I'm glad I caught you," Pete said. "I'm working on the Brimley estate, as I said in my message. I assume you heard the sad news?"

Carmella continued to fidget. "Yes," she said, "it was a real shock."

"I agree," Pete said. "Have the police been to see you?"

Her body stiffened and her eyes showed alarm. "Why would they want to see me?"

"I don't know, I was just asking. You've been together with Les for a while now I understand. Many times the police want to question people who were close to the victim."

She reached in her purse and pulled out a cigarette, but didn't light it. She held it between her first two fingers and periodically would raise it to her lips.

"I hate this no-smoking law," she said, glancing at the bartender. Then she added without making eye contact with Pete, "Did they question that bitch Les was living with?'

"Susan Brimley? I think they did. In a small town like Frankfort, Michigan, you hear pretty much everything the police are doing. Susan was one of the first people they questioned, I understand."

"I bet she had something to do with it," Carmella said. She raised the unlit cigarette to her lips again.

"Why do you say that?"

"Is this conversation private?"

"Well, sure," Pete lied. "I'm a lawyer. Anything you say to me stays between us."

"Les was worried about something. I don't know what it was, but he was different recently. I wanted him to spend more time down here and less in Michigan, but he said he couldn't until he got that golf course open." She seemed to be thinking about something. Then she said, "You know, we were going to be married as soon as he divorced that bitch."

"Is that right? I didn't know that. Anyway, Les apparently wanted to provide for you. I can't tell you the exact amount you'll receive until we determine the net value of the estate, though."

She sat there with the cigarette held high in the air, as if she were enjoying a good smoke, and said, "He was a millionaire, wasn't he?" Again, her eyes didn't meet his.

"Yes, many times over," Pete replied, "but you have to net off the bank debt and other obligations. As I said, we're in the process of doing all of that."

"When will I know how much I get?"

"I can't say exactly. The probate process in Cook County is very slow."

"How about my rent? Will the company continue to pay that?"

"I assume so, but I don't know for sure. Alma Linberg would know things like that. Well, we've got to wrap this up because I have another appointment this evening. I just wanted to meet you so we'll have some connection going forward. We'll no doubt be talking again."

He slid off the bar stool and started to say goodbye when she interrupted him and said, "Let me ask you a question. Will my inheritance be jeopardized if I see other men?"

"Gee, I don't think so. Mr. Brimley is dead, so I don't see …"

"Good, I don't want the bitch to use that against me and wind up with everything just because I have a date now and then."

Pete watched her head for the door with hips swaying and men gawking. With the unlit cigarette dangling from her mouth, Pete could almost see her in tassels hugging a pole in some smoky strip club. He couldn't wait to tell Angie about his afternoon date with the exotic dancer.

THIRTY-FIVE

Pete fought the rush-hour traffic and when he exited on Foster Avenue, he saw a Starbucks and pulled off the busy street to get a large coffee to go. He doctored it up with cream and sweetener and was on his way again. After navigating through the heavy traffic for fifteen minutes, he turned right on a side street a block away from LB Realty's offices and found a parking spot. He walked back with his coffee in hand and wondered what Bok would be like.

When he walked in, Alma was busy stuffing documents into file folders. She saw Pete and rushed to greet him. "That was such a nice lunch yesterday. Those Swedish pancakes were delicious. But the next time we have a date, we'll have to plan ahead and allow more time. We have so many things to talk about." He felt relieved that it was probably a little early to look at wedding magazines to plan their big day.

Bok walked in promptly at 9:00 a.m. He wore a white shirt with a frayed collar and a narrow dark tie knotted loosely around his neck. Even though the weather was warm, he had on a rumpled brown hip-length coat and a nondescript matching felt hat. He carried two large Styrofoam cups in a wire carrier. He placed the carrier on a desk and removed his hat, revealing a shock of tangled white hair. His skin was weathered and flecks of red showed on his cheeks. When Pete saw him, he couldn't help but think of the old Norwegian men who used to gather in his family's yard every summer for their annual get-together.

"Bok," Alma said, "this is Pete Thorsen. He's Norwegian, too."

Bok looked at him, then removed the cups from the carrier, handed one to Alma and kept the other for himself. He pried off the lid and took a sip of the hot brew. Then he asked, "Does he work here?" Bok spoke as though Pete weren't in the room.

"No, he's helping with Mr. Brimley's estate."

"Another lawyer," Bok said, still not acknowledging Pete's presence.

"His mother was part Swedish," she volunteered proudly.

"I thought you said he was Norwegian."

"He is, mostly."

"That's a mongrel. You've got to be one or the other. You can't be both Norwegian and Swede."

"Lots of people intermarry these days, Bok."

Bok finally looked at Pete and said, "If you're Norwegian, how come you're a lawyer? Why don't you have a real job like a railroad engineer or a metal worker?"

"My father was a carpenter," Pete said. "He wanted me to get an education and do something with my mind, so I went to law school." Part of that was correct. His dad was a carpenter, but Pete was the one who wanted to get out of his environment and rise in life.

Bok continued to look at him and asked, "Are you a storyteller?"

Pete was surprised by the question and looked right back at him and replied, "I'm a writer, if that's what you mean."

Bok waved a hand dismissively. "Norwegians tell stories. They don't need fancy words on paper to tell about their experiences."

"I don't want to argue with you, Bok, but the Norse people were always good at putting their stories on paper. Did you ever hear of the Icelandic Sagas?"

Bok scoffed again and said, "Sure, but real Norwegians always told stories face-to-face. You're probably too young to know that."

Pete just shrugged.

"What have you written?" Bok asked.

"Lot's of things," Pete replied. "I'm currently writing an article on Viking longboats."

Bok gave a little nod. "Those were good ships," he said.

Alma expelled air and seemed to be relieved that Bok and Pete were finally bonding. For the next half-hour, the two men exchanged stories. Pete had to reach far back in his past to come up with a story when it was his turn. He noticed that Bok loved to embellish his stories with detail so he laid it on with a soup ladle when it was his turn.

When there was a lull in the storytelling, Pete seized the opportunity to shift the conversation and get into his real reason for being there. "I understand you've lived in this area for quite some time, Bok."

"Fifty-six years," he replied proudly.

"By any chance do you remember a fellow named Harold Romanski. Hal grew up in this area I believe."

Bok took his time answering. "Sure," he finally replied, "I remember Hal. He lived just down the street from me."

When Bok didn't volunteer further details, Pete asked, "He went to prison, right?"

Again Bok took his time answering. "They say he killed the owner of Foster Electronics during a robbery one night. He was sent to that prison in Joliet."

Pete had listened carefully to what Bok had just said. "What do you mean, 'they say he killed the owner?' I heard he was convicted of the crime by a jury."

"Hal wasn't a bad kid. He just had bad friends."

"But none were involved in the robbery, right?"

Bok crumpled his empty Styrofoam cup and tossed it in the wastebasket. "I never believed that. I always thought someone was with Hal that night. I knew Mrs. Romanski. No son of hers would have carried a pistol. She kept a close eye on her boys."

Now Pete was intrigued. "Who do you think might have been with Hal?"

Bok looked at Alma who was looking down and fidgeting with some papers. Like she knew something, or at least had heard Bok express his suspicions before. "I don't know for sure," Bok said. "Maybe it was Lester Brimley."

A jolt shot through Pete's body. He stared at Bok for a few moments, then asked, "Hal Romanski and Les Brimley knew each other?"

Bok looked at him like he was a complete ignoramus. "Sure," he said, "they lived a block apart. Lester hung around with a rough crowd. Mrs. Romanski tried to keep Hal away from him, but you know how young people are. Their friends can do no wrong as far as they're concerned."

Pete was still getting over his surprise when another question occurred to him. "Did the police question Les Brimley about the killing?"

"Lester had an alibi that the police couldn't break, and Hal claimed he acted alone so that was that. But I always thought Hal was covering up for Lester."

"Why would he do that?"

Bok again took time before he responded. "Young people are different, as I said. They hang together and protect each other. Seems to be an us versus them thing. It's strange."

Alma, who'd been staying out of the conversation but Pete could tell was listening intently while she filed, piped up and said disapprovingly, "You don't know that's what happened, Bok."

Bok looked at her and said, "You weren't around like I was, woman. I saw them boys growing up. It was like they had a blood oath or something. I tell you, Hal was covering up for his friend Lester."

Alma didn't say anything, but continued to sort her papers.

"It was like when Mr. Friscetti died. That was strange, too. Lester was there at the time the accident happened. I tell you, that boy was bad. I could feel it in my bones."

Alma looked up from her filing again and said, "They say a big piece of construction equipment fell on Mr. Friscetti."

"That was a construction crane, Alma," Bok said with an aura of superior knowledge. "Mr. Friscetti was an experienced real estate man. He never would have been standing that close to that crane. And how did it tip over anyway? I never saw that happen to a crane before."

"Bok thinks he's one of those detectives and knows everything," Alma said, continuing the bickering between them. "Whatever happens, he has a theory," she said with the same air of certainty Bok had just displayed.

"Then why did the police keep coming around and asking questions, Alma?" Bok asked, his voice rising. "They didn't spend their time out here for nothing." The battle of words between Alma and Bok was heating up.

Alma gave him a nasty look.

Bok wasn't done. "You told me yourself, Alma, how Lester didn't make all the payments to Mrs. Friscetti. I tell you, Lester was not a good man."

Alma came back with, "That don't mean Mr. Brimley had anything to do with Mr. Friscetti's death. Innocent until proven guilty. Isn't that what you always tell me?"

Pete tried to defuse the bickering by saying, "I understand Mr. Brimley bought the business from Mr. Friscetti's family when Mr. Friscetti died."

"Yes," Alma said, "they had an agreement."

Bok grunted and said, "He stole the business from the family. I tell you, he wasn't a good man."

Now it was Alma's turn to attack. "You don't know anything about it, Bok. You don't even know how much Mr. Brimley paid for the business."

"That's because you wouldn't show me the agreement."

"It's confidential, Bok."

Bok waved a hand dismissively. "Then why did you show the agreement to the police?"

"The police can see anything they want," Alma shot back. "That doesn't mean that every old man who thinks he knows everything can see personal documents like that."

Pete decided that he had what he needed and would get out of the bickering between old friends. He'd been able to corroborate what he already knew, which was, as Bok put it, Les Brimley was not a nice man. More important, he'd stumbled onto information that might turn out to be the key to the Brimley murder case. Les Brimley and Hal Romanski knew each other and once had been close friends. One wound up in the slammer for twenty years and the other became a wealthy real estate man who was brutally murdered on his dream golf course. Maybe there was an explanation for why Hal Romanski assumed a different name and wound up in his old friend's backyard, but Pete was beginning to wonder.

As he walked out, he heard mild-mannered Alma and crusty old Bok continuing to jaw at each other. Arms were waving and voices were rising. Pete had a feeling that not much work was going to get done at LB Realty that day.

THIRTY-SIX

Pete stayed on I-94 when he got to the branch and headed for Bloomfield Hills. He was anxious to see Julie even though they'd spoken daily when she was in California. Now that she was back, he had to be sure she was safe until he was comfortable the danger had passed.

When he got to the school, he went directly to the campus police station. He looked a lot more presentable than the last time he was there. The officer on duty that night was there in addition to the chief of campus police. He'd called earlier and said he had further information about the stalking incident and wanted to speak to them about it privately.

He spent the next half-hour giving them the background and explaining what he believed had happened. He started with Brimley's murder and the work he'd agreed to do for his widow. Then he told them how he'd gotten in the middle of a dispute between the widow and some people who claimed Brimley owed them money. He said he'd unwittingly become a pawn in the tug-of-war between them and had resigned his engagement for the widow when he found out what was happening. He sanitized his story somewhat and didn't tell them that the bad guys were Chicago mob figures because that would only complicate things. Nor did he tell them about his cottage. Again, that wasn't strictly germane to what he wanted to achieve and, like the mob connection, would only raise a lot of questions.

When he was finished, he told the officers he thought he was out of the line of fire and that he doubted the stalking incident would be repeated. Nevertheless, he said, now that Julie was back on campus, he thought prudence dictated that special procedures be put in place to ensure her safety just in case. The officers agreed and said they would assign a plain-clothes officer to shadow Julie around campus and watch her dorm at night. They agreed to keep the plan in effect until Pete felt it no longer was necessary.

Pete walked out of the station feeling good about Julie's safety. He glanced at his watch. He was an hour ahead of schedule and walked slowly around campus to kill time and think. Then he headed for Julie's dorm and climbed the stairs to her room. Her door was open as usual and she was sitting in a chair with one leg slung over the arm and gazing out the window.

"California dreaming …" he crooned.

Julie turned and saw him and said, "Hi, Dad." After giving him a hug, she looked at her watch and added, "You're early. It's not 3:00 a.m. yet." She giggled at her joke.

"Very funny," Pete said. "You adjusted from California?"

"It's kind of boring around here," she answered. "There aren't many kids on campus, and after California … You know, I could see myself going to college out there."

"There are some great schools in California. Just don't pick some leftist school and become a hippy."

"Dad, there are *no* hippies in California anymore. That's ancient history." A thoughtful look settled over her face. "But I wonder … the weather's so nice, maybe I'd flunk out if I went to school there."

"Well, you've got plenty of time to consider schools."

"Not really, Dad. I have to start looking around next year." She got the faraway look in her eyes again. "Time passes so fast. It seems like yesterday that I started here."

"Well," Pete said, "if we don't get something to eat soon, I'm going to pass out and then you'll have to work your way through college. Ready?"

They walked down the stairs and cut through the back door to the lot where his car was parked. He fished the keys from his pocket and clicked the unlock button. He felt a tug at the keys and turned to see Julie's hand on them.

"Could I drive?" she asked.

Pete looked at her and then remembered. "Well, sure," he said as he released the keys. He walked around to the passenger side and got in. It felt strange. The day that most parents dread had arrived.

Julie started the Range Rover and pulled out of the mostly-empty parking lot. She turned on her left signal light even though there were no other cars in sight and proceeded to the street bordering campus where she repeated the routine. He found himself watching her every move and was impressed with her caution.

She found a parking place a half-block from the restaurant and par-allel-parked flawlessly. They got out of the car and she put the keys in her purse. "How did I do?" she asked as they walked to the restaurant.

"Perfect," Pete said.

"Am I a safe driver?"

"Very safe," he replied, cringing at the thought of where the conver-sation was headed. But she dropped the subject. They entered the res-taurant and were shown to a booth. Both of them immediately started perusing their menus.

Julie ordered the Greek salad with dressing on the side and com-mented that she'd gained three pounds in California and had to take it off. Pete ordered a buffalo burger with fruit. Given that Angie had complimented him on his sleek body, he felt he could afford it. Besides, he was starved.

For the first half-hour of their lunch, Julie rehashed stories of her California adventures. He'd heard most of the stories during their nightly telephone conversations, but he didn't mind listening to them again. Her youthful exuberance was infectious.

"Dad, remember that conversation we had on Parents Day? The one about the car?"

"I do," Pete said, beginning to feel dread again.

"When I was in California, Mikki raised the issue with her dad. The whole family joined in because it's really a family issue, you know. Her dad was there, obviously, and her mom and her sister. I was invited to participate, too, because I was staying with them and I'm almost like Mikki's other sister. It was a really good discussion. We wrote down the pros and cons of car versus no car. It was all very scientific and very analytical. Mikki is a *very* smart girl, you know. Want to guess what we decided?"

Pete had about resigned himself to the answer and just shook his head.

"No car," Julie said triumphantly.

Pete's optimism soared. He hoped the precedent would spill over to his daughter, but tried to keep his response casual. "That was a very sensible decision," he said.

"And," Julie continued, "I'm going to do the same as Mikki. We're going to support each other. Sort of give the other kids a sign that we're above obsessing about things like cars. We've already told most of our friends, and you know what, they almost *envy* us because of our mature decision. One girl who was going to get a car changed her mind and isn't going to get one now. We're going to be like a band of sisters — helping each other out and supporting each other. So what do you think of *that*?"

Pete tried to control his elation and said, "I think you girls made the right call."

"And Dad, do you remember our other conversation?"

Pete thought for a moment and then said, "About Paris?"

"Yes," she replied. "I've definitely decided to go. Since I'm not going to buy a car now, maybe you can reward me by paying part of the cost. Then I would still have money in the bank and my summer wouldn't be too expensive for either of us."

"I don't see why not," Pete replied. "Do you have a budget?"

"Not yet, but I e-mailed several schools and asked them to send materials. And get this, Dad — Mikki might go with me. That would be so awesome. Mikki and Julie in Paris. I might even write a book about our experiences when we get back. I'd make so much money that I wouldn't even need help from the trust for my senior year. Think of how *that* would look on my college applications."

Pete smiled at her and said, "That sounds wonderful. If you have the school materials by the time you come to the lake, bring them along and we'll do some planning. Is Mikki a good artist?"

"I think she's got awesome talent, but of course she's my friend so what would you expect me to say?" Her face grew serious. "She may be a little behind me because, like, I've been drawing and stuff since I was *three*. But with a couple of courses next year, I think she'll be ready by the summer."

Pete nodded and smiled again.

"Dad, I know you don't seem too worried, but have they put the guy they arrested in prison yet?"

"He's in jail, but he's awaiting trial. If he's convicted, he'll go to prison."

Julie looked thoughtful again. "But you still think it's safe for me to come to the lake even if he's not in prison yet, don't you?"

"Absolutely. Didn't I just say the man was in jail?"

"Well, sure, he's in jail *now,* but what if he escapes or something? Maybe he has friends, too. And I know what you said, but from what friends tell me, a lot of people still believe a cult was involved."

"Julie, for the last time, no cult was involved. But I'll tell you what, we'll talk on the phone right before you come, and you can decide if you're comfortable being up there. Deal?"

"Okay," she replied skeptically.

Pete paid the bill and they walked out of the restaurant and down the street to where his car was parked. He fumbled around in his pants pockets, searching for the keys. Just when he thought he might have left the keys in the restaurant, Julie said, "Looking for these, Dad?" She jangled the key ring in front of him.

"I forgot," he said sheepishly.

Julie backed up a few feet, turned her left signal light on, and eased out of the parking slot into light traffic. Pete watched her with admiration, thinking he never put on his signal light in situations like that.

"You know another reason I decided not to get a car until I'm a senior, Dad?" Before he could answer, she continued and said, "The car would just be setting around all summer while I'm in Paris. That's not good for a car. Mikki's dad told me that."

He'd never met Mikki's dad, but he liked the man more and more based on what he'd heard from Julie. The guy obviously understood teenage girls.

Back at Julie's dorm, they said their goodbyes and Pete was in his Range Rover again and headed for the lake. It had been a short visit, but a productive one. He felt good about the security plan he'd worked out with the campus police, *and* the car conversation couldn't have gone better. As a bonus, Julie had lapsed into her valley-girl speak only once. Slowly his mind drifted back to his conversation with Bok and the friendship between Les Brimley and Hal Romanski.

THIRTY-SEVEN

Pete sat in Rona's Bay Grille nursing a glass of iced tea, impatient for Harry to arrive. He was anxious to tell him about his trip to Chicago. While he didn't always take Harry's suggestions on strategy, he valued him as a sounding board.

Harry finally rushed in, and after waving to some people he knew, sat down at Pete's table and said, "Welcome back. I haven't seen you for a week." He looked at Pete's iced tea and ordered the same.

"Three days," Pete corrected him. "I was in Chicago and then made a detour to see Julie."

"She back from California?"

"She is, and I worked out a plan with the campus police to keep an eye on her. And get this — she's dropped her request for a car."

Harry grinned. "How did you pull that off?"

"I didn't do anything. When Julie was in California with her friend, the girl's dad convinced both girls that getting cars before their senior year wasn't a good idea. I'm going to submit the guy's name for father of the year."

Harry shook his head and said, "Lucky, huh?"

They made their meal selections. Both ordered trout, butter-flied and grilled, with an extra helping of steamed asparagus in place of potatoes.

"How did Chicago go?" Harry asked.

"Well, I had drinks with an exotic dancer."

Harry grinned again and said, "I bet there's a story behind that."

"There is." He told Harry about his visit to LB Realty and his lunch with Alma Linberg and all of the dirt she'd told him about Les Brimley. He mentioned the apartment Brimley was renting for Carmella Cain and the jewelry he'd bought for her on the company's tab. He also told him of how he'd deceived Carmella into meeting with him.

Harry had an eager look on his face. "What was she like?" he asked.

"Like her name. You know what she asked me? Whether her inheritance from Les Brimley would be jeopardized if she saw other men."

Harry choked on his iced tea. He wiped his mouth with a napkin and then said, "Distraught, huh?"

"Yeah," Pete said, "real distraught." He watched a cabin cruiser power into the harbor and said, "You know, apart from merchants who had their economic fortunes tied to Brimley, I haven't heard many people say good things about him."

"I haven't either, but what's your point?" Harry asked.

"Just an observation," Pete replied. "But it sort of complicates things. If that many people disliked him, it increases the universe of potential suspects, doesn't it?

"Yeah, I guess you could look at it that way."

Pete looked out the window at the activity in the harbor again. Then he bumped his glass against Harry's and said, "But the most interesting thing I learned is that Les Brimley and Hal Romanski a/k/a Howard Redd knew each other."

Harry studied him for a while and then said, "You're kidding."

"Alma Linberg — she's the woman in Brimley's Chicago office — introduced me to an old man who's lived in the neighborhood for over fifty years. He remembered Les and Hal from their boyhood days and said they were best friends. He knew all about the incident that resulted in Romanski going to prison, and was sure Brimley was involved in some way even though he was never charged."

Harry looked earnest and said, "I read all those stories about the robbery, and I didn't notice anything about a second person being involved."

"You must have missed it. At least two stories mentioned that the police were looking into whether Romanski really acted alone. I re-read the stories when I got back, and it's evident the police had suspicions that Romanski had an accomplice. The old man — his name is Bok, by the way — confirmed that Les had been questioned, but he had an alibi and Romanski insisted he acted alone. Bok likened it to a blood oath whereby you didn't rat on a friend."

"The fact that Romanski and Brimley knew each other, that's unbelievable."

"Not only knew each other, but were best friends according to Bok. It kind of makes you think about why Romanski is up here under a phony name, doesn't it?"

"Maybe he came up here because of his old friend."

"Maybe," Pete said. "Or maybe he was up here to settle scores."

Harry stared at Pete for a while and then said, "You think?"

"I don't know, but it makes you suspicious when you know the background, doesn't it? And to complete the picture, both Alma and Bok told me that Mr. Friscetti — he's the guy who owned the predecessor to LB Realty — died in a suspicious accident. That gave Brimley a chance to buy their real estate business for a song. All of that occurred a few years after Romanski went to prison. I guess the police investigated Friscetti's death, but ultimately dropped it. But crusty old Bok kept implying that he thought Brimley was involved somehow."

Harry kept shaking his head and said, "You've got to tell Richter about all this stuff. It proves he's got the wrong man in Hicks."

"It doesn't *prove* anything, but it certainly raises a lot of possibilities they should investigate."

"Well, I still think Hicks is innocent."

"More and more, I'm inclined to agree with you."

"You know," Harry said, "Richter should have dredged up all this stuff himself and checked it out before he arrested anyone." He looked admiringly at Pete, but the look Pete gave him in return made him back off from what he was about to say.

Pete tapped his spoon lightly on the table a few times and said, "You know, all this sleuthing provides new insight into Brimley's murder, but I'm no farther ahead than I was a week ago when it comes to finding out who set fire to my cottage and why."

"There could be an explanation for that," Harry said. "Maybe there were two streams of crime. Maybe Zahn was after his money and saw you as a threat. Maybe he had his men stalk Julie, knowing it would spook you, and maybe they decided to torch your cottage to put added pressure on you. Maybe Romanski killed his old buddy Les Brimley for reasons that go back to the days of their youth." Harry sat back in his chair obviously pleased with his analysis.

"I've been thinking along the same lines, Watson. Except maybe someone wanted me to think Zahn was the arsonist because he wanted to throw me off."

Harry looked at him thoughtfully. "So what are you going to do?"

"I'm not sure. I thought you might have some brilliant ideas."

Harry appeared to think again. Then he said, "Well, the first thing you've got to do is get this information to Richter."

"I was thinking about that," Pete said. "But I've already gone to him — or at least to Joe Tessler — and tried to convince him the Chicago mob was behind the murder. How do you think he'd react if I approached him again with a different story? Forget about what I said before. Hal Romanski a/k/a Howard Redd is really the man you want. He'd laugh me out of the state."

"But don't you think you've got to give it a shot? We owe it to John Hicks, don't we?"

"Harry, I don't *owe* John Hicks anything. I don't even know Hicks, and I've already done more to help him than I probably should have from the standpoint of my personal interests. My goal is to get out of this mess, remember?" Then he added, "Right after I find the guy who burned my house down, that is."

"I know how you feel," Harry said sympathetically, "and I can't say I blame you. At the same time, you've had a strong sense of right and wrong for as long as we've been friends. It wouldn't cost anything but an hour of your time to do the right thing for Hicks."

Harry was right, of course. He did have a sense of right and wrong. He'd tried to follow that credo all his life. Sometimes it had gotten him in trouble, but he was always proud of himself for doing the right thing. When it came time to pass from this world, he wanted to be able to submit a brief in favor of being permitted to enter through the pearly gates rather than being directed the other way. Scandinavians didn't fare well in hot conditions.

"Let's shift gears for a few minutes," Pete said. "If someone torched my place, not because he was mad at me, but because he wanted to point a finger at someone else, who would it be?"

Harry went into his deep thinking mode again. After a couple of minutes, he said, "I can only think of a couple people. That Indian guy, Leonard Wolf, comes to mind, or maybe Howard Redd. But I doubt if it was either of them because neither was under serious suspicion. I still think it was Zahn's men who torched your place."

"I've thought this through a dozen times," Pete replied, "and nothing makes sense. *Unless* whoever did it realized that Zahn would be a prime suspect if all the facts were known and he thought it would be wise to point another finger in Zahn's direction."

"Who would that be besides the guys I mentioned?"

"That's the question, but it weren't Zahn, it would have to be someone who knew about my conflict with Zahn."

"Makes sense. So who do you think *that* could have been?"

I told exactly four people about my suspicions concerning Zahn. You, Rona, Joe Tessler, and Susan Brimley."

"You don't think it was one of your friends do you?"

"No, and I don't think it was Joe Tessler, either.

Harry looked at him for a long time. "That leaves Susan Brimley."

"Right."

"Do you think she's the one who killed her husband?"

"I don't necessarily think she killed her husband, but I'm beginning to wonder if she knows who did."

Harry just shook his head. "This is a real rat's nest."

"Getting back to what we were talking about earlier," Pete said, "do you really think I should take another run at Frank Richter or Joe Tessler and try to convince them to investigate Romanski?"

"I do," Harry replied. "I promise, I won't ask you to do anything else to help Hicks, but I think we should give this a try because of all of the stuff you've dug up on that guy Romanski."

"How do you think I should approach it?"

"I think you should approach it head-on. Tell them, like we discussed, that there are two lines of crime here. A juice loan, which may not be their business, and a murder, which clearly is. Tell them you began to realize this as you dug around trying to figure out who started the fire at your place. You don't have to tell them the details of everything you found out about Romanski; you can maybe make something up. But the key points are that Redd's not who he claims to be, that he's an ex-con, and that he and Brimley knew each other from way back when. Then Romanski, when he gets out of prison, just happens to show up in Brimley's backyard where Les was spending most of his time because of the golf course."

"Are you sure you don't want to run for sheriff, Harry? You seem to have some pretty good instincts for law enforcement matters."

Harry gave him a puzzled look and then burst into laughter. "Only if you'll finance my campaign and agree to serve as my first deputy." He gazed across the room with a smile on his face. "We'd make quite a team, wouldn't we?"

"Yeah," Pete said. "What were the names of the sheriff and his deputy in that old Andy Griffith show?"

"Before my time," Harry said.

"Well, I'll try Tessler again. He's easier to deal with than Richter."

"I think that's smart," Harry said.

"One more thing. Until all of this plays out, I think we should keep this conversation just between us. No pillow talk, if you get my drift."

"Now hold on. Rona's …"

"I know, I know. I love her, too. But the more people who know something, the greater the risk that something will slip out."

"Me and Rona don't have any secrets from each other." He glanced at the bar where Rona was talking to the bartender. "What if she starts to grill me? I noticed her glancing at us all night. She's probably wondering what we've been talking about."

"Make something up if she asks."

"You don't understand," Harry said. "A woman like Rona always finds out what she wants to know. She probably won't sleep with me unless I tell her."

"A little abstinence will do you good."

Harry glared at him and asked, "When are you going to try to see Tessler?"

"In the morning."

Harry nodded. "You want me to ask around about Redd or anything?"

"Not now."

THIRTY-EIGHT

When Joe Tessler didn't return his call, he tried again later in the morning. This time he was put on hold for several minutes, and Tessler finally came on the line. "Joe Tessler," he said.

"Joe, it's Pete Thorsen. Could I come in to see you sometime today?"

"Not unless you can get over here and we can finish our conversation in the next half-hour. I'm leaving shortly and won't be back until tomorrow."

"Tomorrow would be fine."

"What's this about?" Tessler asked.

"I have some new information regarding the Brimley murder."

Tessler sighed. "What kind of information?" he asked.

"There's a guy up here I think you should check out. He's an ex-con living under an alias. Name he's using is Howard Redd, but his real name is Harold Romanski. He knew Les Brimley well and moved up here not long before Brimley was murdered. He …"

"Let me stop you there, counselor. If my memory is right, you came to my office a week ago and tried to convince me the Chicago mob was behind Brimley's death."

"Yes, but …"

"And as I recall, I took your information seriously and had the Chicago PD check out the man you accused. Not only did he have an alibi, but my old boss accused me of sending his men on a wild goose chase that wound up embarrassing his unit. Now suddenly you call with information on a new guy you want us to investigate. If I were a suspicious man, Pete, I might conclude that you're working with your fat friend to divert our attention from the real killer who we have in our lock-up right now."

"You mean the man you have no evidence against other than a few hairs that obviously were planted?" Pete asked.

"We've got more than that. We're holding a press conference of our own to introduce the special prosecutor we just brought in from Lansing to handle this case and to review some of the other evidence we have against Hicks. Your pal Manning isn't the only one who knows how to stage trials in the media."

"I think you're overstating things when you call Manning my pal."

"Oh, come on, Pete. Word around town is you were the one who got that publicity hound to represent Hicks. Bringing a so-called expert up here to pontificate on DNA evidence and tout Hicks' innocence. Tomorrow you're going to find out why we view the case against Hicks as a lock."

"Did more test results come back?"

"Better than that, Pete, better than that. Check with our office this afternoon if you want the time of our press conference."

"So you're not going to check out Redd?"

"We have a small office and no time to investigate everyone in the county when we already have the real killer in jail."

Pete made a sandwich and sat on his deck to eat. He wasn't surprised at the outcome of his conversation with Tessler. In fact, he probably would have reacted the same way if someone had come to him with urgent information about a murder case and then, just days later, had approached him a second time with a completely different story.

He finished eating and called Harry to fill him in on the conversation with Tessler and tell him about the press conference. Harry was disappointed with the outcome of Pete's conversation with Tessler, and already knew about the press conference. He'd just received an e-mail the sheriff's office sent to the media.

They spent a few minutes speculating about the evidence Tessler implied they would unveil the next day. Neither had any idea of what that evidence would be. After they finished their conversation, Pete called Ira Manning and left a message telling him of the press conference and that he and Harry would attend and let him know the results.

He leaned back in his Adirondack chair and thought about Les Brimley and Hal Romanski. If Romanski's move north was motivated merely by his desire to start a new life, it's inconceivable he wouldn't have been in contact with his old friend Les Brimley at some point during the past year. And if they had been in contact, it was equally unlikely that Susan Brimley wouldn't have known about it. He wanted to see Susan's eyes when he asked her about Hal Romanski.

◆ ◆ ◆

He pulled up behind Susan's silver SUV, got out and walked to the front door. He rang the doorbell and waited. After a couple of minutes, Susan opened the door and seemed surprised to see him. She wore jeans and a loose-fitting smock covered with paint splatters.

"Pete," she said, "come in. I've been painting."

He stepped inside and said, "I'm sorry to barge in on you. I happened to be in your neighborhood and thought I'd stop rather than call. I want to ask you about a man named Howard Redd. He works for Birchwood Press. Do you know him?"

She furled her brow, and after a few moments said, "No, I don't think so. Why do you ask?"

"I know you do some design work for Ida Doell, so I thought you might have met Redd when you were at Birchwood. I have information — don't ask me the source because it's confidential — that Redd's real name is Harold Romanski. He goes by Hal. Have you ever heard of him?"

Susan didn't flinch when she heard the name. "From Chicago?" she asked.

"Yes, originally. I guess he and Les were good friends growing up. Then I heard Romanski had some problems with the law and moved up to this area after he got out of prison. Did Les ever mention him?"

"Yes, I believe he did," Susan replied. "I seem to remember that Hal Romanski was involved in a robbery or something. It was a long time ago, but I recall Les telling me about Hal and saying he'd turned bad. I haven't heard his name in years. Why are you asking about him now?"

"Just wondering," Pete said. "When I was in Chicago, I stopped at LB Realty's offices and the woman who works there — what's her name, Alma? — told me about Les and Hal. I guess they were pretty thick at one time."

"What were you doing at LB Realty?"

"I have some things I have to finish up for my old law firm and happened to be near Foster Avenue. I was curious about LB Realty and decided to stop in."

Susan Brimley nodded and didn't say anything.

"Well, I'll let you get back to your painting. "But as far as you remember, Les didn't say anything in the past year or so about Hal Romanski being up here, huh?"

"Not that I remember. If he'd known, I'm sure he would have said something."

"Well, I'd appreciate it if you'd keep our conversation quiet. Maybe Hal just moved up here after he got out of prison and is just trying to start a new life under a different name."

As Pete walked to his car, he mulled over the conversation he'd just had with Susan Brimley. She didn't give away anything when he mentioned Hal Romanski's name or Howard Redd's name. She acknowledged hearing about Romanski, though, including the fact he'd been involved in a crime. He wasn't quite sure how to interpret that. At least, she hadn't blatantly lied to him again.

THIRTY-NINE

"Ladies and gentlemen," Sheriff Franklin Richter said, "before we start this press conference, I'd like to introduce several people. This is Ralph Medling, our county attorney, whom many of you know. Next to Ralph is Connie Ryder," he said, pointing to a slight woman of middle-age with hair pulled back in a bun and a no-nonsense expression on her face. "Connie is the special prosecutor from Lansing added to the county's staff for purposes of the Hicks case. Last, this is Detective Joe Tessler, the senior detective in our department.

"To begin, I'd like to put this case in context." He hitched up his pants and slicked back his hair with the open palm of one hand the way Pete had seen him do countless times. "A few weeks ago, we had a brutal murder in our community. I've been in law enforcement in this county for sixteen years, and I've never seen anything like it. The sheer savagery was stunning.

"After a thorough investigation, we arrested John Hicks and charged him with the murder of Lester Brimley. It's not our intention to try this case in the court of public opinion, like the defense has been doing, but I'd like to summarize for you some of the facts that led us to arrest Mr.

Hicks and charge him with this crime." He looked over the crowd and squinted into the bright sunlight.

"First of all, those of you who live in our community or the surrounding area know how controversial the Mystic Bluffs project has been. As your chief law enforcement official, I've not taken sides. Instead, like many a concerned citizen, I've watched the proceedings from a neutral corner, as they say. I watched the Native American groups make their case and those concerned with the economic fortunes of this community make theirs. I've listened to the arguments of citizens concerned with the expansion of our fine airport and those concerned with the impact of the project on the natural environment of this lovely area.

"During the course of all of this, I heard the views of groups expressed in the most vociferous of ways, but none more heated or bitter than the comments made by John Hicks. At a hearing attended by well over a hundred people, he made what everyone present considered to be a death threat against Mr. Brimley. I'll digress for a minute and say while I'm informed that it may not be admissible at trial, Mr. Hicks has a long history of violence on environmental-related matters. He's been charged seven times with crimes such as arson and malicious destruction of property and spiking trees with the intent of injuring or killing loggers.

"My point is that John Hicks has a long history of serious charges against him, whether he was convicted or not, and he was heard to threaten Mr. Brimley specifically before numerous witnesses. As we investigated this brutal crime, we determined that Mr. Hicks had no alibi for the night in question. He claims he was watching television that night. Isn't that something every accused felon could claim? Next, we found trace evidence that Mr. Brimley's body had been in the back of John Hicks' vehicle. Recall that Mr. Brimley was wrenched from his home in the middle of the night and transported to the golf course where he was killed in a most savage fashion. Now, I'd like to turn it over to Detective Tessler for an explanation of other evidence we have against John Hicks."

Joe Tessler walked to the microphone carrying a plastic bag with a bulky black and yellow object in it. Tessler held up the bag and said, "We found this under the floor boards in John Hicks' house. I don't know if you can see it, but it's a TAZER M26C stun gun frequently used by police departments and other law enforcement agencies.

"For those of you not familiar with stun guns, let me briefly explain. They're used for a variety of purposes, including for self-protection against assailants or intruders and by the police when they want to disable a suspect and not use a firearm. Basically, stun guns emit 'electrical noise' that disrupts the signals that communicate messages back and forth between the brain and the rest of the body. The effect is to disable a person for some period of time. This particular model can disable a person for fifteen minutes or longer.

"We believe this stun gun was used to disable Mr. Brimley long enough for the killer, who we believe was John Hicks, to bind and gag him and get him into the vehicle. This is consistent with the Medical Examiner's findings that traces of duct tape or some other adhesive were found on the victim's skin."

A hand went up and Richter stepped forward and called on the man. The reporter, from a Grand Rapids station, asked, "You said that the stun gun could disable a man for fifteen minutes. I'm not intimately familiar with this area, but it seems to me that it would take longer than that to bind and gag the victim, transport him to the golf course, then put him in a golf cart and drive him to the seventeenth green."

"Good observation," Richter said. "We believe it's likely that Hicks shot Mr. Brimley multiple times with the stun gun. The Medical Examiner also believes that if the victim had been disabled repeatedly, he would have become weakened and thus more pliant at the end and easier to deal with."

"You said you found the stun gun under the floor boards of John Hicks' house. Can you provide details?" another reporter asked.

"Yes. We conducted a second, comprehensive search of Mr. Hicks' home," Richter explained. "One of our investigators noticed that a board on the hardwood floor appeared to be loose. We removed the board and found the stun gun hidden beneath the floor."

The media representatives asked numerous other questions. Richter or Tessler patiently answered them all. Then Richter summed up. "So, ladies and gentlemen, the next time Ira Manning or someone like him breezes into town and tries to get his client off by blowing smoke and pretending evidence doesn't exist, you remember what you heard here today. Not all wisdom lies in Chicago or Detroit or New York. We have pretty good people up north, too, and we have a sense of doing right not only for our criminal defendants, but for the hard-working men and women who have a right to be secure in their homes."

Harry said to Pete, "Maybe I was wrong about Hicks. That sounded like a pretty persuasive case."

"It's easy to make a case when no one is arguing the opposite side. When do you suppose they came up with that stun gun?"

"I don't know. Recently, it sounded like. Or maybe they've been holding it in reserve for a moment like this."

"Have you talked to Cap recently?"

"Not for several days."

"Why don't you call and ask him?"

"Now?"

"Yes."

"Maybe he won't even talk to me."

"You'll never know if you don't call. He wasn't at the press conference. Maybe he's out and about somewhere and alone."

"Okay, I'll try." They sat in Pete's car while Harry punched in Cap's cell phone number. Then Harry said, "Cap? Harry. Can you talk?" Pete couldn't hear Cap's response, but after a long moment, Harry lowered the phone and held it against his body and whispered to Pete, "Richter has him on traffic duty."

Harry listened some more and muttered "Uh, huh" a couple of times. Then he said, "I've just come from the press conference. How long have you guys known about the stun gun?" He listened again and then asked,

"How did they find out about it?" He listened again and said "Uh, huh" a couple more times and then lowered the phone.

"He said they just found out about the stun gun three days ago. Someone called with an anonymous tip and said he saw Hicks practicing with the stun gun one evening. He claims he noticed because of the bright yellow color. The caller said he didn't think much of it at the time, but with the buzz going around about Brimley's murder, concluded he should let the authorities know. According to Cap, they searched Hicks' place again and found the stun gun under a loose floorboard, which is consistent with what they said at the press conference. He said they tried to trace the anonymous call, but it was made from a public phone or something. They assumed the caller just didn't want to get involved."

FORTY

"Adam, Pete Thorsen."

They exchanged pleasantries and Pete asked about Rose's mother. Then he got down to business.

"I'd like to hire you for a couple of days." He gave Rose a detailed summary of everything that had occurred in the past week, including his suspicions about Hal Romanski a/k/a Howard Redd. He explained his plan and what he wanted Rose to do. When Pete was finished, he said, "Interested?"

"Sure," Rose replied, "but are you positive you want to do this?"

"The first stage anyway. Then we'll talk about the rest of it."

"Okay."

"One last question," Pete said. "Do you carry?"

"When I think I need to," Rose answered.

Pete didn't think he needed to tell Rose to bring his piece. There wasn't much question that the man knew his business. When they were off the phone, Pete thought about his meeting with Vinnie Zahn. In retrospect, he should have sent Adam Rose as his emissary.

◆ ◆ ◆

Pete deliberately parked between two SUVs in the Birchwood Press lot to be as inconspicuous as possible. He slid the seat back and lowered his body. He could see both Romanski's red Mazda3 and the Chevy Suburban from where he lay in the nearly horizontal seat. He punched a number into his cell phone and waited for Rose to answer.

"Yes?"

"It's all clear down here. I'm looking at Romanski's vehicle now. The Suburban's here, too."

"Let me know if either moves."

"I will." Pete ended the call and waited. As he watched the door and the two vehicles, it reminded him of the time he'd laid in wait for Kurt Romer and tailed him to his meth lab. He hoped his day would be less adventurous in the case of Hal Romanski.

As he watched customers come and go, he wondered what Rose would find in Romanski's trailer. Rose asked him what he should look for, and Pete had to admit he didn't know. He made sure to tell Rose every detail of his investigation thus far so if he did see something that might be relevant, it would cause him to look further. As he was thinking about their plan, Pete saw Romanski come out of the building and walk to his Mazda. Pete grabbed his cell phone and called Rose's number again.

"He just came out of the building and walked to his car," Pete reported.

"Let me know if he moves," Rose replied. "I'm in the process of photographing some things."

Pete was about to ask him what he'd found, but the phone went silent. Romanski opened the Mazda's trunk and looked inside. Then he closed the trunk lid and walked back toward the building carrying a cardboard box.

Pete called Rose again. "He went back inside."

"Okay."

Pete leaned back and waited some more. Two women came out of the building and headed his way. The sound of automatic doors unlocking rang in his ears. The women approached their SUV and, before getting in, the driver looked at him lying almost prone in his seat. Then she got behind the wheel and pulled out of the parking lot and headed north.

Crap, Pete thought. There went one side of his cover, the side facing the building and the two vehicles. He tried to lower the seat more, but it was back and down as far as it would go. He shifted his position to make himself less conspicuous. He felt foolish as he waited and wondered what customers would think if they saw him in that position. He consoled himself with the thought it was better to be embarrassed than for Romanski to see him sitting there, watching, and become suspicious.

Almost an hour later, Pete's cell phone rang and Rose said, "I'm out. I'll meet you at your place."

Pete adjusted his seat to an upright position, fired up the engine, and left Birchwood's parking lot. He accelerated so he was going five miles over the speed limit. He was anxious to see what Rose had found.

◆ ◆ ◆

When he got to his house, Adam Rose's pickup was already parked in the driveway. He'd told Rose to make himself at home and he apparently had. Through the sliding glass doors, he spotted him sitting on the deck with a can of beer in his hand.

Pete got a beer of his own and joined Rose. "Find anything interesting?" he asked.

"Not a lot," Rose replied, "but I found a few things that might interest you. As soon as I finish this beer, I'll load my photographs onto your computer and show you."

Pete wanted to pump Rose for more information, but was careful not to appear too anxious. After all, he was sitting next to a guy who'd been through this sort of thing countless times and he didn't want to appear to be a bumbling amateur.

"But before I show you the photographs, I thought you'd be interested in something else." He tossed Pete a small plastic bag.

Pete caught the bag and looked at its contents. There were three small brown pellets inside the bag. Pete looked at Rose and asked, "What are these?"

"I think they're fire pellets."

Pete looked at Rose and frowned.

"I had an insurance case a few years back where the arsonist used pellets and a small can of starter fluid as accelerants. The pellets look almost like dry dog food, but are highly flammable. They were originally made by a company in Ohio. They were intended for igniting charcoal grills and the like. The Consumer Product Safety Commission concluded they were unsafe because of their volatility and made the company take them off the market. But a more potent version of the pellets started showing up underground. They've become a favorite of arsonists. With a little starter fluid, they ignite a blaze as fast as a can of gasoline or kerosene or some other liquid accelerant, but are much easier to transport. Instead of carrying a large can of liquid to the scene, the arsonist can take a bag of pellets and a small can or bottle of starter fluid. Much easier to conceal and carry inconspicuously in a backpack or even a bag."

"I wonder why Kovac didn't mention that?" Pete asked.

"He would have no way of knowing. The pellets are completely consumed by the flames and the residue is more difficult to detect than liquid accelerant. I just happened to notice the pellets when I was examining the ground around the trailer. Romanski must have spilled a few when he was transferring them to a bag or something. I left most of the pellets on the ground, but took a few to show you."

Pete frowned again. "Why would Romanski want to torch my cottage?" he mused. "I didn't even know the guy."

Rose shrugged and said, "We don't know for sure that he did, but the pellets certainly raise a reasonable suspicion as you lawyers like to say. I didn't see an outdoor grill or any other use for the pellets. Let me use your computer for a few minutes and I'll show you what else I found."

Pete set him up at the kitchen table and watched as he placed a tiny camera near the computer and retrieved some electronic paraphernalia from a small duffel. Pete let him work and went back to the deck. The fire pellets had surprised him. He still couldn't imagine why Romanski would want to set fire to his cottage, but the evidence was beginning to indicate that he had. The evidence also was consistent with his hunch that Zahn wasn't responsible for the fire. Stalking Julie to intimidate him, yes, but not the fire in spite of the anonymous caller's comment that night about his "nice little cabin."

He was sorting all of this out in his mind when Rose called from the kitchen. He'd transferred the photographs to Pete's laptop and printed out copies. He handed Pete several sheets of paper. "The first few pages are the prison's inventory of Romanski's possessions at the time of incarceration. I found the inventory in a desk drawer. I'm not sure you're interested in this, but thought I should shoot it just in case. They use the inventory as a checklist when they return the stuff to the prisoner when he's released."

Pete scanned the sheets. It contained an itemization of what you'd expect to find such as a watch, a pen knife, a jacket, other items of clothing, and the like. Nothing unusual.

"One item on the list is a medallion on a heavy silver chain. I saw the chain hanging on the mirror in the bedroom and took a shot of it."

Pete squinted at the photograph. "What's it say on the medallion?"

"HR separated by a little heart, then the initials SW."

Pete grunted. "Sounds like something from an old girlfriend.

"The next three photographs were taken outside the trailer in the gravel driveway. Those are the pellets."

Pete nodded and said, "I'm surprised you even noticed them. They look just like the gravel."

"Training," Rose said. "With Team 6, attention to detail was the difference between staying alive and being blown to kingdom come."

The last photograph was of a piece of paper that obviously had been crumpled up and then smoothed out because it showed a mass of creases. A telephone number was on the sheet. Nothing else, just a telephone number. No name, no place of business, nothing.

"Romanski isn't the best housekeeper, or the most careful one," Rose said. "I found this wadded up on the floor behind a wastepaper basket. I called the number. It's a place called Aaron's Gun Shop in Gary, Indiana. I asked for the manager and inquired about stun guns. He told me they carry the largest collection in the Midwest, including just about all TAZER models. I told him that I wanted to keep my purchase confidential, and he bragged about the shop's confidentiality policy. He boasted of not turning over records unless the request came from law enforcement backed by a proper warrant."

Pete looked at him. "Do you suppose Romanski bought the stun gun, used it to help murder Brimley, then planted it in Hicks' house to incriminate him?"

"That would be my guess," Rose said.

"Harry McTigue's contact in the sheriff's office said that they got an anonymous call tipping them off to the stun gun. That could have been Romanski, too. The call was made from a pay phone or another untraceable number."

"There you go."

Pete asked, "What did you do with the piece of paper?"

"Wadded it up again and placed it behind the wastepaper basket where I found it."

Pete was now sure. There were just too many signs that Hal Romanski had killed Brimley. Thinking back to the robbery and slaying that resulted in Romanski going to prison, maybe there was an accomplice that night and maybe that accomplice was Brimley. Covering up for

Brimley might have seemed like the noble thing to do at the time, but as the long years in prison wore on, Romanski's mind-set probably changed and the hate began to fester.

Pete looked at Rose and said, "I think we should leave the note." He had typed a note on his laptop earlier and printed it out on a plain sheet of paper. He retrieved the note and read it over:

Hal–

I know who you are and what you did. I don't want money. Meet me at Mystic Bluffs, seventeenth green, tonight at 11pm and I'll explain what I do want to remain silent.

Come alone because I'll be watching.

A Friend

Adam read the note and then looked at Pete and said, "The other option is to go to the sheriff."

"I tried that," Pete said. "I didn't go to the sheriff, but I went to his lead detective on the case. He's actually more reasonable than the sheriff, and I got nowhere with him. They're so dug in that Hicks is their guy that they view someone who tries to point them in a different direction as just trying to create a diversion."

"It's risky," Rose said.

"You can cover me, right?"

Rose nodded, but said, "It's still risky."

"Romanski burned down my house."

Rose looked at him for a few moments, then said, "Why don't you stay here. I'll leave the note inside his front door. He shouldn't be home yet."

Pete watched Rose leave and then looked at his watch; seven hours and then they'd see whether his plan to serve as a guinea pig would work.

He gazed over the lake and wondered, again, what reason Romanski would have to torch his cottage unless he was pointing one more finger at Zahn. But how would he know about the conflict with Zahn?

FORTY-ONE

Adam Rose treated the hoped-for meeting with Romanski as a military exercise. He insisted on arriving at the course two hours ahead of schedule and drove his pickup just in case Romanski was familiar with Pete's car. Rose cased the area like he was about to launch a commando attack on a high-priority target.

He was dressed in black from head to toe, and the first thing he did when he got out of his truck was to smear black grease paint on his face and the backs of his hands. Pete didn't ask him if he was carrying; he already knew the answer. The strap around his neck secured a pair of night vision goggles. Pete was thankful for the goggles because, with them, Rose could see Romanski coming and be in a position to monitor him just in case he was inclined to try something.

Pete had on his usual casual clothes. The only addition was a broad-brimmed hat that Rose handed him. He clamped it on his head and felt a little silly. He wasn't a hat guy even in the winter. As the light faded, he felt he still stood out like a fat man on a beach. But that's what decoys were supposed to do.

Rose had positioned him by the green so his back was protected by one of the mounds and then slipped into the darkness. Adam assured him that he'd be close by and watching everything, he just didn't say where he'd be. He wondered how far Rose could see with the night vision goggles.

Pete concentrated on getting his visual purple, drawing on his own military training. He tried to feel his surroundings, incorporate them into his consciousness — the shapes of trees around him, the contours of The Rock looming overhead, the rise of the mounds surrounding the green. It grew darker. Soon he could see little as night settled over the course. Clouds obscured the stars and made it even darker.

He sat there, hardly moving, wondering what time it was. For some reason, Rose didn't seem to care if he wore clothes that, to him, stood out in the darkness, but made him take off his watch with the luminous dial. He felt like he'd been on the mound for hours. It must be close to 11:00 p.m. by now.

He thought he saw something move among the bushes separating the seventeenth hole from adjacent parts of the course. He sat completely still. Visions of Romanski and the vicious way he'd killed Les Brimley flashed through his mind. He could almost hear the golf club striking Brimley's skull and cutting into flesh and bone. Again and again. He wondered whether Romanski would come to the meeting armed. He also thought of the deadly skills he must have learned to survive in prison for twenty years among some of the most violent and conscienceless human beings on the planet.

He thought he saw movement in the bushes again. Then a twig snapped! Goddamn, what was it? Was it Romanski? He wished he knew where Rose was.

Then the night was quiet again and he waited some more. He tried to avoid thinking of anything that would detract from his mission. He kept his anger kindled at a high level by imagining flames licking the foundations of his cottage and snaking upward and Romanski's evil face smiling in satisfaction at his handiwork. He sat there like a hunter and not the hunted.

Another twig snapped! Pete strained see who or what was making the noise. The same sound again! It had to be Romanski! He knew it! Then the shadow of a deer appeared from the brush, barely visible in the blackness that shrouded everything around him. Even though the deer was only twenty feet away, he could barely see it as it walked silently across the green.

Then he waited some more, fighting to stay alert, imaging menacing sounds all around him. He tried to keep his senses at a high level. Tried to keep his anger stoked.

"I don't think he's going to show. It's almost midnight."

Rose's voice was soft, but still startled him. His heart jumped at the sound, then he heaved a sigh of relief. He stood and stretched his muscles, still saying nothing. Rose was just a shadowy figure even though he was standing only five feet from him.

"You okay?" Rose asked.

"Yeah, fine," Pete answered. "I wonder why he didn't show."

"Hard to know. Maybe he's trying to come up with a plan. Or maybe he's already split the area."

Pete was both relieved and disappointed. Relieved that the confrontation with Romanski didn't occur. Disappointed that his plan to lure Romanski into the open hadn't worked. "Maybe the note spooked him," Pete said.

"I don't know," Rose replied, "but I think we should find out. If he has split, we should alert the authorities so they can post an APB as soon as possible."

"What makes you think the sheriff would put out an APB? His office has already blown me off once when I approached them with information about Romanski."

"Yeah," Rose said. "But we have more on Romanski now. If we can't get any satisfaction from your local sheriff, I know the head of the FBI's local field office. We can call him. You said yourself that the feds are chomping at the bit to get into this case."

They walked back to where Rose's truck was parked off the access road behind a dense thicket of bushes. Rose spent ten minutes getting most of the grease paint off his face and hands, then they headed for the trailer park where Romanski lived. Rose turned in the park and wound through the rows of Gulfstreams and Aerostars and Monaco Knights to where Romanski's trailer was parked. They saw Romanski's red Mazda parked by his trailer. And his trailer was dark.

"It looks like he's still here," Pete said.

"So it appears."

"I don't think we should pound on his door to verify he's in the trailer," Pete said. "Or do you see things differently?"

"No, I agree. We're going to have to wait for the morning to see if his Mazda moves. We'll have to take a chance that he's not in some other vehicle hightailing it across Ohio. He has access to that Chevy Suburban, right?"

"As far as I know."

"Let's abort for the night and check on whether he's still here in the morning. Then we can decide what to do."

When morning came, Pete wanted to go fishing or play some one-on-one basketball with Bud Stephanopoulis or even just listen to his old-ies. Anything but chase killers and arsonists and face down mobsters. Rose was already up and dressed and drinking black coffee when he entered the kitchen. The sight of him helped rekindle Pete's ardor for the fight. He didn't want to show weakness in the presence of a former member of Team 6 for whom the previous night had probably been a boring training exercise.

When he was dressed and had grabbed a bite to eat, they headed to the trailer park in Rose's pickup truck. Romanski's Mazda was gone.

They drove to Birchwood Press and saw the red car in the parking lot. The Chevy Suburban was also there, parked in its customary spot along the side of the building.

They returned to Pete's house and discussed options. It came down to three. First, drop the entire thing and console themselves with the knowledge that they'd done their best. Second, talk to Richter about the new evidence they'd found and hope he'd finally expand his investigation to include Hal Romanski a/k/a Howard Redd. Or three, take another run at Romanski themselves. They concluded, again, that the sheriff was too dug in to agree to check out Romanski and that they couldn't just drop the matter. That left taking another run at Romanski. Pete felt his juices starting to flow again.

Pete sat down at his laptop and began to type. Rose looked over his shoulder and suggested a change or two. Pete printed out a copy of the message on plain paper again. It read:

Hal:

You made a mistake by not showing last night.
You have one last chance. Same place and same time tonight.

A Friend

They drove to the trailer park again. Pete climbed out of the pickup and slipped the note inside the outer door. Then they returned to Pete's house, sat on the deck, and waited for the clock to run.

"What motivated you to join the SEALS?" Pete asked.

"You don't so much join as you audition. Most guys wash out because they can't take the training. I managed to hang in there because I didn't want my brother to gloat."

"Was he a SEAL?"

"No, he was an Army Ranger. He was seven years older, always ribbing me that I wouldn't be able to do what he did. I wanted to show him."

"I didn't realize until recently," Pete said, "that the SEALS have airborne capability, too."

"Most people equate SEALS with water. Actually, the name stands for Sea, Air and Land. They're the premier special ops forces in the world today."

For the next hour, Rose told stories about the elite force for which the drop-out rate during training approached ninety percent. He told of some of the missions he'd been on.

"Most missions are covert and never see the light of day. The exceptions are the ones like the operation that took out Osama bin Laden. How about you, Pete, were you in the military?"

Pete laughed. "I was with the Beer Brigade in Germany for a couple of years."

"Beer Brigade," Rose repeated. "That's good. What did you do when you weren't tippling?"

"Drove a jeep, mainly. For most of my tour, I was assigned to a major in the CID."

"That's the detective arm, isn't it?"

"Sort of. We mainly investigated crimes by service personnel. It was actually kind of interesting. My boss handled some high profile cases while I was there. It was fun to watch him operate and I did learn a lot about investigation technique."

"So that's where you get your penchant for sleuthing, huh?"

"Some of it might have rubbed off on me, but with this case, I just got caught up in circumstances." And, he might have added, he didn't much like being pushed around or lied to.

They went into town for something to eat and came back and killed more time. Pete read the paper and fussed around with some other things. Rose must have done two hundred push-ups. He washed his black garb and cleaned his Glock twice and inspected his night vision goggles. Obviously, he was preparing himself mentally for a repeat of the night before.

As the sun settled behind the hills rimming the lake, Rose said, "Time to go."

They repeated the routine of the previous night. Pete didn't feel any less exposed as he waited at the seventeenth green. Every real or imagined movement in the brush, every noise in the night, put him on edge. The wait seemed interminable, made worse by the fact he had no watch.

At midnight, Rose appeared at his side again without making a sound and said, "We're nothing-for-two, Pete." As they walked back to the pickup, Rose, who was in the lead, said over his shoulder, "I think we should swing by the trailer park again and see if Romanski is there. It seems odd he wouldn't make some move now that he knows someone is aware of his true identity."

"Okay," Pete said. He felt deflated that their plan hadn't worked for the second straight night. Maybe they should have tried some other approach or some other venue. Second thoughts continued to run through his mind as he watched Rose clean himself up again. On the way to the trailer park, he thought of what he could say to Richter or Tessler to convince them to investigate Hal Romanski a/k/a Howard Redd.

FORTY-TWO

They drove slowly past Romanski's trailer. His Mazda was there again, only this time a faint light illuminated one of the trailer's small windows.

"Looks like he's home," Rose said. He kept driving and then pulled off the road at the edge of the trailer park.

"Do you suppose he's calling our bluff?" Pete asked.

"Could be," Rose answered. "He could be testing us to see if we'll really come after him or report him or just go away."

Pete thought about it a while, then said, "Maybe he's not really home. Maybe he just left that light on to throw us off."

"Possible," Rose said.

Pete continued, "He could have taken the Suburban."

Rose looked at him. "Want to check?"

Pete really wanted to just go home, but cranked up his resolve said, "Yes."

Rose moved his truck to a less conspicuous place and turned off the lights. They walked back toward Romanski's trailer. When they got close, Rose motioned that he was going around to the back. Pete nodded and moved closer to the trailer. He looked around for something to stand on so he could peer in the trailer's window. He found a concrete block and quietly moved it to the ground below the window. He looked around. The street was quiet and there were no people or dogs in sight. The only light came from a utility pole at the end of the street.

He stepped up on the concrete block and slowly elevated his head to the level of the window. A gauzy curtain covered the opening. He moved his head to the left so he could see in. Everything was opaque. He shifted his position slightly so he could see the area to the left. Through a crack between the edge of the curtain and the wall, he saw a figure slumped in a chair. Like he'd been watching television and dozed off. He stared for a long time, but the figure didn't move.

Rose came around the corner, moving noiselessly as usual. When he got close, he whispered, "I see him in there. From the back window, it looks like his head is at an odd angle. Maybe he's sleeping."

"That's what I see from here, too."

Rose motioned for Pete to get off the concrete block, then stepped up himself. He peered in the window for a long time. Then he stepped off the block and shook his head and said, "It's impossible to get a good look through that curtain."

Pete stepped up on the block again. After staring at the figure for a while, he scratched the outside of the trailer a few times. No reaction from the slumped figure. He scratched again, louder this time. Still no movement in the trailer. He looked at Rose and shook his head, then knocked on the exterior of the trailer. He knocked again, loud enough this time to resonate in the night air. Still no movement inside.

He stepped down from the block and whispered to Rose, "He didn't twitch that I could see."

Rose whispered back, "If he didn't hear your last knock, he must be a very sound sleeper or dead drunk. Or dead."

Pete looked at Rose and frowned. "Do you think?" he whispered.

Pete peered in the window again and knocked on the outside of the trailer even louder. Pete looked at Rose and shook his head.

"I'm going to try the door," Rose said. Before Pete could say anything, Rose had moved silently to the front door and used the bottom of his shirt to protect his hand as he turned the latch. It was open! He carefully pushed the door wider and stepped inside. Pete followed. "Don't touch anything," Rose whispered over his shoulder. He walked slowly down the trailer's hall and when he reached the area illuminated by the lamp, he stopped. Pete stepped to one side so he could see.

The figure in the chair had a purple wound on the right side of his head. A trickle of blood had dried on his face and stained his shirt. The cheap carpet that covered the floor showed dark blotches as well. A silver-plated revolver dangled from the fingers of his right hand.

Suddenly Pete was back in that study with the white walls covered with garish red streaks and the blood seeping toward him on the floor. He saw the old man point his shotgun except there were no sounds. Only hate on the man's face. Pete stepped back to get away from the blood. Rose's voice jolted him back to a conscious state.

"Let's get out of here. Be careful not to touch anything on the way out. I'll meet you back at the truck."

Pete stood there for a few moments, staring at the figure and shaking. Then he slowly backed down the hallway. When he reached the door, he nudged it open with a knee and slipped through the opening into the night. The street was still quiet. He gulped air for several seconds, breathing hard, and then started for the truck at a brisk walk. When he reached it, he climbed in and slumped back in the seat. He sat there, continuing to breathe hard. Rose arrived minutes later. Without speaking, he fired up the truck and pulled slowly out of the park. Once on the highway, he turned on his lights and proceeded toward town at a slow speed. He turned in the grocery store parking lot and pulled up near the dozen or so vehicles that were in the lot.

Pete was still reeling from the sight of the dead body. He looked at Rose. He was sitting behind the wheel with a stoic expression. Pete said, "We should report this to the sheriff."

"I agree," Rose said, "but the question is whether you want to call and identify yourself or make an anonymous call saying you heard a gunshot in the park and they might want to check it out?"

Rose didn't have to elaborate. Knowing Sheriff Richter's animosity towards him, Pete was certain he'd be courting trouble if he came clean and told Richter the entire story. Breaking and entering and explaining away a dead body would just be the beginning. It would take him six months to extricate himself from the barrage of threats and charges that would follow. He'd suffered enough as a result of the mess Susan Brimley had gotten him into through her duplicity and selfish actions.

They found a pay phone in town and Rose called out of mutual concern that the officer on duty might recognize Pete's voice. Rose followed the script they'd discussed and then hung up.

Driving back to Pete's house, Pete asked, "What did you do in the trailer when you stayed behind?"

"I made sure the piece of paper with the gun shop's number was more obvious in case the sheriff doesn't bring in a skilled forensics team. Remember, I've got two clients in this hunt. And I picked up this."

Pete looked at the piece of paper Rose handed him. It was the second note they'd left for Romanski. "You didn't find the first note I take it?"

Rose shook his head. "We'll just have to take a chance Romanski burned it or something."

Pete leaned back in his seat and tried to relax. It was finally over.

◆ ◆ ◆

After Adam Rose left for Traverse City, Pete had another mission he didn't look forward to. As he drove to Birchwood Press, he thought about what he would say to Ida Roell. She likely would be devastated by the news of the death of the man she knew as Howard Redd.

He was still wrestling with what to tell Ida when he walked into Birchwood Press' facility. He saw her sitting behind her desk looking at some papers. He rapped on the door and said, "Ida, do you have a minute?"

"Peter," she said after she looked up. "What a pleasant surprise. Do come in."

Pete entered her office and sat down in one of the side chairs. His mind was racing as he tried to think of how best to get into the reason for his visit. What he had to tell her wasn't the kind of news that he could spring on her after ten minutes of polite small talk. He had to come right out with it and express his sincere condolences. Ida made it easier.

"I have some sad news, Peter," she said. "Yesterday afternoon, Howard came to me and said he had to leave the area. He apologized and said a matter had just come up. He drove me home last night just like he always does and we said goodbye and everything. He was such a wonderful man. He arranged for another employee who lives out my way to pick me up in the mornings and take me home after work."

"So you got to say goodbye?"

"Yes," Ida said, "but that doesn't make it any easier. Good men like Howard don't come along very often. We hugged each other and both of us cried."

He knew he had to tell her the truth and said, "Ida, Howard killed himself last night."

She looked at him for a long moment, as though what Pete just told her didn't register immediately. Then she said, "Oh, my," and just sat there.

Pete tried to think of what else to say, but all he could come up with was, "I'm sorry, Ida."

"Will there be a memorial service, Peter?"

"I don't know. I'll find out and let you know."

Ida sat there a while longer and finally said, "I feel like I'm losing my entire family. Lynn moved away. Now Howard's gone."

Pete said a few more words of condolence and then left. Driving back home, he remembered Bok's words that Hal was basically a good kid. Obviously, life had dealt him a bad hand.

FORTY-THREE

Pete was in his office putting the final touches on his longboat article when Harry called and said Richter was going to hold a press conference that afternoon to announce their conclusion that Hal Romanski had killed Les Brimley. Pete agreed to join Harry because he was curious about how Richter would handle the announcement.

When they arrived, all of the usual suspects from the media were there and more than a few local citizens as well. Richter, Tessler, and a couple of other deputies were there, huddling together and awaiting the 2:00 p.m. start time. Following the recent pattern, Cap was not there. Richter glanced at his watch and stepped to the microphone.

"Good afternoon, ladies and gentlemen. This is a good day for justice in our county, but a sad day for the human condition. As many of you know, we had a suicide here two weeks ago. Some of you might have known the man. Around here, he went by the name Howard Redd. What you probably don't know is that wasn't his real name and we've had Mr. Redd under investigation as a suspect in the Les Brimley murder case.

"I'll try to summarize the facts, then I'll take your questions. About three weeks ago, it came to our attention that Howard Redd, who'd moved to our area a year ago, might not be who he claimed to be. We investigated and discovered that his real name was Harold Romanski or Hal for short. Then we found out that Mr. Romanski was also an ex-con. He'd spent twenty years in prison in Illinois for killing a shop owner in Chicago during a botched robbery attempt.

"As our investigation progressed, we discovered that Mr. Romanski also knew Les Brimley from years ago. As a matter of fact, they were boyhood friends. That made us more curious as to why Hal Romanski, who had no ties to this area, moved up here after he got out of prison.

"We made the final connection when we found Hal Romanski dead in his house trailer two weeks ago. We combed the trailer with a fine-tooth comb, as they say, and discovered some interesting things. First, we found a phone number for a gun shop in Gary, Indiana. We determined that the shop sells a wide range of stun guns in addition to other weapons. Recall, that earlier, we'd determined a stun gun was used to disable Les Brimley to get him out to Mystic Bluffs Golf Club where he was brutally murdered.

"I personally went to Gary with Detective Tessler and another of our officers. Coordinating with local authorities, we descended on the gun shop. The owner realized that he had no defense and so let us examine his records. We found that one Howard Redd, the alias used by Romanski, had purchased by mail order the exact same model TAZER stun gun we found earlier and that we've been convinced was used to disable Mr. Brimley.

"Next, during our search, we found a suicide message on Romanski's computer. I'd like to read the text to you. It says, 'It's better this way. My life is ruined anyway. At least I made that — and here I have to delete the expletive — Les pay for letting me rot in prison for a crime he committed.' Recall I said earlier that Romanski was convicted of killing a shop owner during a robbery attempt. The jury found that Romanski acted alone, but before he killed himself, Romanski pointed a finger at

Les Brimley as his accomplice and the one who really killed the shop owner. We'll never know if Romanski's accusation is true, but it certainly establishes a motive for Romanski's actions in this case.

"Finally, in examining Romanski's computer further, we determined that he'd made numerous Internet searches regarding the use of DNA evidence in criminal cases." Richter turned to Joe Tessler and asked, "What was it Joe, thirty-eight hits?" Tessler nodded and Richter continued. "Of course, we've known all along that the lack of DNA evidence against John Hicks was the weak spot in our case. Romanski apparently realized that, too, and planted the stun gun under the floorboards of Hicks' house to provide more evidence against him. Naturally, we were suspicious of the stun gun from the beginning because of the anonymous tip we received. But, as I said, we eventually saw through Romanski's sinister actions. It's just too bad that he didn't live so the public could have seen justice done at trial. Now, I'll take your questions."

"Why do you think Romanski didn't flee the area after he killed Brimley?" a reporter asked.

"We'll never know the answer to that question for sure," Richter intoned, "but our best guess is that he felt he'd be less conspicuous if he just waited it out. If he had fled, we would have put two and two together earlier and put an APB out for him so it wouldn't have been long before we had him anyway. He probably thought that he'd be better off staying put and planting incriminating evidence against Hicks who was the most logical suspect. But as I said, we'll never know for sure. Next?"

"Sheriff, why do you think Romanski took Les Brimley all the way out to the seventeenth green to kill him?"

"The perpetrator took that secret to the grave with him," Richter replied. "We just don't know what was going through his twisted mind. All I can say is that criminals sometimes do things that baffle us all. We'll just have to leave it at that."

Another reporter asked, "Will charges against John Hicks be dropped?"

"Yes, he's being processed now and will be released this afternoon."

Pete nudged Harry and whispered, "Want to stay?"

"No, I think I've heard enough."

Walking back to their car, Harry said, "You know, this case is going to seal Richter's bid for reelection. With his fine detective work and the way he descended on that gun shop with a task force like Elliott Ness …"

Pete just shook his head. "The thing I didn't know about was the suicide note Romanski left on his computer. Now it makes sense why he hated Les Brimley so much."

"Yeah," Harry replied. "Twenty years in the slammer for something you didn't do is enough to fuel a lot of rage in anyone."

Pete said, "I should have connected the dots. I remember Bok telling me that Chicago PD questioned Brimley at the time. They must have had some suspicion that Brimley was involved in the robbery, but I guess they couldn't break his alibi."

"The only thing left dangling is why Romanski torched your cottage. Assuming, of course, he did."

"I think he did based on the fire pellets Adam Rose found by his trailer," Pete said. "As for his motive, do you remember what Richter said about the DNA-related hits they found on Romanski's computer?"

"Yeah, that was something."

"That says to me that Romanski was paranoid about pointing the finger at others. Besides Hicks, he was obviously trying to incriminate Zahn as well. I just don't know how he knew enough about Zahn's involvement to do what he did."

"Mmm," Harry murmured. "This is one for the books, huh?"

"Yeah, thankfully the book is closed. You want one last piece of pure conjecture?"

"Sure."

"I think Romanski took Brimley out to the seventeenth hole and killed him there because it was symbolic for him. Romanski's life was ruined and his friend Brimley, the guy who really killed that store owner, was riding high. The crown jewel of Brimley's career was the

Mystic Bluffs project and the seventeenth hole was featured in all of his marketing material. What better place to knock Brimley from his perch than the seventeenth hole?"

Harry shook his head. He put a hand on Pete's shoulder and grinned mischievously. "Well, this keeps your batting average at a thousand percent. Listening to Richter, I realized you were wrong about everything."

FORTY-FOUR

Pete was in a good mood after he got off the phone with Angie DeMarco and Steve Johnson. News of the court victory in the Kral litigation took away some of the emptiness he felt with Julie's departure to return to school after two weeks at the lake. The judge hearing the case had granted the firm's motion for summary judgment on three of four counts of the lawsuit against Pete and the other Sears & Whitney partners.

They spent a half-hour discussing how to answer the remaining count. They also rehashed possible counterclaims against Kral and settled on three that they felt would pass muster under the court's pleading rules. The counterclaims would put Kral on the defensive and not let him just take unwarranted shots at his former partners.

Pete glanced at his watch. It was 9:00 a.m. in Chicago; he wondered if Bok had brought Alma coffee. He dialed LB Realty's number and waited. Alma's businesslike voice answered with, "Good morning. This is LB Realty, Alma speaking. How may I help you?"

"Alma, this is Pete Thorsen. We haven't talked in a while."

"Pete! Are you in the city? I was just thinking about some of those Swedish pancakes."

Pete laughed. "No," he said, "I'm in Michigan, but I promise to take you to Tre Kronor the next time I'm in Chicago."

"Can Bok come too?" she asked hopefully. "He doesn't like the pancakes as much as I do, but he said you two had a good conversation that day and would like to talk to you some more."

"I enjoyed talking to him as well. Is he there, by the way?"

"He just walked in with our coffee. Just a minute." Pete could hear her tell Bok that Pete was on the phone, that he was going to take both of them to Tre Kronor the next time he was in Chicago, and that Pete wanted to talk to him.

Pete waited and then heard Bok's gruff voice come on the line. "Hello," he said.

"Bok, Pete Thorsen. How are you?"

That innocent question prompted a ten-minute monologue by Bok concerning how he was. He described his sore knee and bad back and the results of his last visit to Dr. Epstein. By the time that segment of the conversation was over, Pete had a fairly complete knowledge of Bok's medical history and current ailments. Bok went on to tell of his favorite menu items at Tre Kronor, beginning with his *most* favorite dish and going down the list from there.

When Pete got an opening, he slipped in a question. "When we visited earlier this summer, we talked about Les Brimley and Hal Romanski. Do you remember if either of them had a steady girlfriend in those days?"

Pete listened as Bok gave him the lowdown on all of their friends, male and female. Pete waited patiently for an opening again and then asked if Bok remembered when Les and Susan Brimley were married. There followed another monologue which included everything but the names of the bridesmaids.

When he got off the phone with Bok, he couldn't help but think that the old gentleman might have his share of physical aches and pains, but still possessed a razor-sharp memory for the people in his neighborhood.

Pete wasn't surprised to see the Allied Van Lines truck in the Brimley driveway when he arrived. Rona had told him Susan was moving. He walked past the truck and asked one of the movers whether Susan Brimley was around. The mover jerked a thumb towards the house and continued to haul boxes into the van.

Pete entered the house through the open front door and spotted Susan down the hall talking to one of the movers. He walked in her direction. She saw him and stood there with a surprised look. "Pete," she said, "I wasn't expecting you."

"I heard you were leaving. I thought I'd stop and say goodbye."

"That's nice of you."

"Where are you moving to? Back to Chicago?"

"No, California. There's an artists' colony in Carmel. I need a new start."

"California. My daughter was just out there. But she was near Los Angeles."

"I don't care for Southern California. I prefer the north."

"Well, either area has better weather than the Midwest." He paused and just looked at her. "Have you made peace with Vinnie Zahn?"

Susan's lips tightened and she said, "What do you mean?"

"The juice loan, remember?"

Her face was impassive. "I can't talk about my personal affairs. You're not my lawyer anymore. Remember?"

"I do remember," Pete replied. Then he said, "I guess I can understand why you're moving to the West Coast. Everybody you knew in the old hood, to use the current vernacular, is gone. No reason to move back there, right?"

"This conversation is becoming bizarre. You've said goodbye. Now if you'll excuse me, I'm very busy as you can see."

Pete continued as though he hadn't heard her. "Your old sweetheart, Hal, is dead. Sad the way his life hit bottom and he spent half his natural life behind bars for a crime he didn't commit. And then Hal's best friend, Les, married his sweetheart. What was your maiden name in those days? Wozniak? Did you know that Hal kept that medallion throughout those long years in prison? The one with "HR + SW" inscribed on it? And while he was rotting behind bars, his so-called best friend not only had his girl, but was living high on the hog as a successful real estate man until one day his past caught up with him."

"If you …"

Pete cut her off. "You were in contact with Hal after he moved up here, weren't you? That's how he knew so much about what was going on. About Vinnie Zahn and how you tried to use my advice to squirm off the hook for the juice loan, things like that."

"If you don't leave," she screamed, "I'm going to call the police!"

He continued to ignore her threats and said, "You're rid of both of them now, aren't you Susan? The childhood sweetheart with that nasty criminal record for something he didn't do. And his guilty best friend, your husband, who developed an annoying bimbo habit. But you skated from everything, didn't you? You even wound up with the money. Less of course what you have to pay Vinnie Zahn to get him off your case."

"Get out!" she screamed and threw the vase she was holding at him. Pete put up his arm as the vase sailed past his head and shattered against the wall. The movers heard the ruckus and stopped to stare.

Pete gave Susan one last look and walked past the movers without speaking. He got in his Range Rover and drove slowly toward town, reflecting on how imperfect justice could be.

ABOUT THE AUTHOR

Robert Wangard is a crime-fiction writer who splits his time between Chicago, where he practiced law for many years, and northern Michigan. *Malice* is the second in the Pete Thorsen Mystery series. The first, *Target*, was widely-acclaimed by reviewers. Wangard is also the author of *Hard Water Blues*, an anthology of short stories. He is a member of Mystery Writers of America, the Short Mystery Fiction Society, and other writers' organizations.